ELLEN LIVES ON

For Maureen
love

Lynda

ELLEN LIVES ON

LYNDA HADDOCK

Matador
9 Priory Business Park,
Wistow Road, Kibworth Beauchamp,
Leicestershire. LE8 0RX
Tel: 0116 279 2299
Email: books@troubador.co.uk
Web: www.troubador.co.uk/matador
Twitter: @matadorbooks

ISBN 978 1789014 617

British Library Cataloguing in Publication Data.
A catalogue record for this book is available from the British Library.

Printed on FSC accredited paper
Printed and bound in Great Britain by 4edge Limited
Typeset in 11pt Minion Pro by Troubador Publishing Ltd, Leicester, UK

Matador is an imprint of Troubador Publishing Ltd

For my father

ONE

That morning, Ellen's mother had been alive and now she was dead.

After school that Friday afternoon Ellen walked home from the bus stop as usual. As she wandered through the Winslet Estate to the small, pebble-dashed council house she shared with her mother, she found herself staring at the gardens of the estate's semi-detached homes. Each one was different: some were carefully planted with roses and flowering shrubs, others were just scrap yards, places where children's out-grown bicycles and empty boxes were stored. As she passed them, Ellen remembered Pat, her best friend from primary school, and the game they had often played together of awarding marks out of ten for each garden. Pat had failed her eleven-plus exam and was at a different school now so Ellen never saw her. She missed her.

Ellen had her key in her hand as she walked down the short front path to her house. But when she tried to open the door, the key wouldn't go in. She fiddled and pushed for a minute or two; the lock seemed to be stuffed full of something hard. Something was wrong. She banged on the door, shouting, 'Mum, Mum, are you there… Mum?'

There was silence. She thumped again, with both hands this time. Still no reply. Anxiety began to grip her, a tight band around her heart. She banged again. Then she tried, uselessly, to push against the door with her shoulder. No movement. She walked round the side of the house and tried the back door, but it was locked. When she leant down she could see that the key hole there too was blocked with something. All the windows were firmly shut. The kitchen curtains were closed.

Ellen's mind whirled. What should she do? She recalled that morning at home. Her mother had been up for breakfast, looking pale and sallow in the red silk dressing gown her father, who had been a sailor, had once brought home from Singapore. Unusually, she had kissed Ellen before she left for school.

'Whatever happens now, I want you to know that I've always done the best I could for you,' she had said.

There had been something Ellen couldn't quite understand in her mother's voice. It could have been longing, or regret, or an urgency to explain something that she couldn't quite say. Ellen wasn't sure, but the moment had stayed with her all day. As she recalled it now, the panic that had been growing within her intensified; it was as if a hole had opened in her lungs and filled up with blood-red flame.

– – –

Ellen didn't know the next door neighbours very well. On one side, there were two children: the son already grown up and in the army; Joyce, his sister, was a couple of years older than Ellen but she went to the secondary modern school round the corner from the estate and so the girls had never got to know each other. As Ellen's heart thumped, Joyce pushed open the garden gate and started to walk down the path to her house. Ellen remembered that Pat and she used to award this garden five out of ten.

'Joyce...' she called, tentatively. 'Joyce – is your mum in? I seem to be locked out of the house... I don't know what to do.'

Joyce looked surprised. Ellen felt self-conscious and awkward in her High School uniform of striped tie and navy blazer with a blue trim. She was still wearing her beret with its gold badge. Joyce's school didn't have a uniform.

'Dunno – I'll go and see. Have you tried knocking? Where's your mam?'

Ellen waited while Joyce climbed the back steps and called to her mother. The wait lasted a minute, two minutes, three minutes… What should she do? Then Joyce's mother, Mrs Boyle, appeared in her overalls, peeling her hands out of rubber gloves.

'What's up, love?'

'I'm sorry to bother you, but I can't get into the house. The key seems to be stuck… I don't know what to do.'

'That's odd. I haven't seen your mam today, come to think of it… Come in and wait here. She's probably popped out somewhere. Did you forget your key?'

'I've got my key, but the locks are jammed.'

'Well, our Arthur will be home shortly – he's on leave, you know. He'll have a look at it for you. Come in, love.'

Ellen had rarely been inside the Boyles' house before. The kitchen and living room mirrored hers, but the bathroom was downstairs, by the back door. This must be where Mr Boyle washed when he got home from the pit. Ellen had often seen him tramp down the Crescent in his heavy boots, his face black with coal dust. A little later, if Ellen and her mother were in the back garden, they would hear him shouting to his wife from the bathroom.

'All right, I'm done now, Ma. Come and do me back.'

Only a few weeks ago, when she heard this, Ellen's mother had said, 'For goodness sake, it is 1971. Why does he come home all dirty like that? There are showers at the pit now!'

A few weeks. It seemed like a lifetime ago.

– – –

3

The wallpaper in the Boyles' sitting room had a pattern of flowers and stripes. There was a large plastic-covered sofa, and a television in the corner. Ellen sat stiffly on the edge of the sofa. The panic round her heart was intensifying. But Mrs Boyle asked her about school and what she had done in the summer and she somehow found herself answering, despite the insistent heavy beating of her heart. Joyce, apparently too shy or embarrassed to talk to Ellen, had gone upstairs to her bedroom. Ellen wasn't sure how long she sat there before Arthur arrived.

'Hello Ma,' he said cheerfully. 'Get t'kettle on.' And then, seeing Ellen, 'Oh, who's this? Haven't seen you for a long time, young lady. How's that posh school of yours?'

Arthur had a warm smile and gentle air, for all his height and strength. Ellen sensed sympathy in his sharp blue eyes.

'What's up, love? You look pale as a ghost.'

'It's mum… the house… I can't get in. The locks are jammed. I don't know what to do.'

'Do you want me to come and look? See what brute strength can do?'

'Yes please.'

Ellen followed Arthur next door and watched him as he examined the locks. She felt as if she were forcing herself to breathe. The look of concern on Arthur's face deepened. He leant his shoulder against the door and pushed. Nothing.

'Look, love, I don't want to frighten you, but I think we should call the police.'

Ellen could feel her shallow breath and her heart thumping. She couldn't get her words out.

'Would you like me to do it, love?' said Arthur, gently. 'I'll go t'phone box now.'

Arthur ran the few steps up the path, hopped lightly over the gate and jogged to the end of the street until he reached the red telephone box. Mrs Boyle, who was hovering in the background looking concerned, said, 'Come inside for a bit, love, while we wait. I'm sure it's nothing.'

But Ellen couldn't move. She stood looking at the steps, fixing the dark green door in her mind, trying to breathe. Afterwards, she wasn't sure how long she had waited until the police car arrived. She was dimly aware of Arthur standing next to her and exchanging worried glances with his mother. It felt as if there were no such thing as time. A single birdcall broke the silence of the early evening. Then a police siren, distant at first, grew louder and louder. Ellen found herself wishing that the sound had nothing to do with her, that it wasn't that of a police car destined for her house. At the same time she felt certain that it was. It was only seconds later that a flashing light appeared in the street and the car squealed to a halt. A policeman and policewoman jumped out, slammed the doors and ran down the path to Ellen's house. Ellen couldn't have described them afterwards, but she remembered the policeman's voice, low and urgent. He was talking to Arthur.

'You've knocked again I tck it?'

'Aye.'

'Ok, let's go in – step back everyone please.'

And the policeman lifted a long battering ram that had been hanging by a strap over his shoulder, and rushed at the door. It seemed to give way easily and Ellen thought fleetingly about the care her mother always took to double lock the door at night and how safe she had felt when this was done. No one could reach her then. How mistaken she had been. How fragile it had all been, after all.

The policeman pushed through the door. Immediately he stepped out again, just as Ellen moved forward to follow him. There was no time in those moments. Ellen saw the look of horror as the policeman's face seemed to collapse; heard him shout, 'Get out.' And entered a world that had changed for ever.

— — —

Ellen was vaguely aware of the policewoman putting her arm around her shoulders and leading her down the path to the Boyles' house and into the sitting room, where she sat straight and still on the edge of the sofa. She felt that the others in the room – Mrs Boyle, Arthur, the policewoman – were all watching her. Mrs Boyle brought her some tea in a cup with gold edging sitting on a matching saucer and Ellen wondered why she was being offered the best china. The tea was very milky and sweet. Her hand shook and the teacup rattled in its saucer as she lifted it. As she was trying to swallow a sip of the drink, the policewoman took her walkie-talkie handset from her belt and left the room, pulling the door behind her. But the door didn't close and Ellen could hear her voice.

'There's been a death – looks like suicide – 11 Fossett Crescent, Winslet Estate. Yes… hanged herself from the stairs. There's a daughter, about fifteen. An ambulance is on its way. We'll need the duty social worker and possibly an emergency bed for the night… OK, I'll stay here until the social worker arrives.'

As she listened Ellen felt a curious detachment. A calm and puzzled brain outside her body seemed to say, 'Oh, so this is what it's like when this happens. I'm the daughter of a mother who has committed suicide. This is how I react.'

Mrs Boyle and Arthur came to sit with her. One of them put an arm around her shoulders. She heard their voices but couldn't understand what they were saying. It was all just words. Best to sit here, very still. If she didn't move maybe the world would stop and she would never have to do anything ever again.

It was late and the sky was black when Andrea, the social worker, arrived. She seemed to Ellen to be not much older than she was herself. Andrea had short neatly cropped hair, round cheeks and wide eyes partly concealed behind a pair of brown-rimmed spectacles. Her eyes darted around the room nervously as she entered.

'Ellen, I'm Andrea, and I'm going to take you somewhere safe this evening. I'm so sorry about what has happened.'

Ellen looked at her and said nothing. She felt as if she wasn't really there.

'Finish your tea and we'll go.'

'I don't want it,' said Ellen, putting the cup down on the table with two trembling hands. She followed Andrea silently out of the house. Several hours had passed since she'd returned from school and in that short time her life had stopped. Everything now would be different – always.

Arthur and Mrs Boyle stood by the front door as she left.

'If there's anything you want, love…' said Arthur. Ellen watched him as his sentence trailed away. What could he do? What could any of them do?

She stepped carefully on the path's concrete slabs, noticing the weeds growing in the cracks. The door to her house was open a little and she could hear voices inside. A policeman she hadn't seen before was standing in the gateway to her garden path with a strip of police tape in his hand. It was as if the house wasn't hers anymore, had nothing to do with her. As they approached Andrea's car, an ambulance, its light flashing, pulled up behind the police car.

'Hurry,' said Andrea, with a note of alarm in her voice. 'Let's get into the car quickly.'

The thought passed through Ellen's mind that the ambulance was here to take the body – her mother's body – away.

'No, no,' she shouted. Andrea turned and put an arm around her. 'You must get in the car, Ellen. Come along.'

Ellen sat in the passenger seat and turned her face to the window, seeing nothing. All was blank. Her chest seemed to be filled with a huge granite boulder, grey and bleak like the rocks by a rainy sea. The words 'hanged herself from the stairs' seemed to repeat themselves somewhere in the air outside her head. For a moment, Ellen remembered a picture she had seen of the lynching of an American slave. The dead man hung, loose and swaying on a tree branch, his arms heavy by his sides, his head lolled forward onto his chest. The crowd below his feet seemed agitated, excited almost. A woman had looked straight at the camera and smiled as the picture was taken. Unbidden – and only for a moment – an image of a figure hanging at the dark bend in the staircase at home edged into Ellen's mind but it shifted out of her awareness as quickly as it had come. She couldn't – mustn't – let herself think about this.

When she spoke, Andrea's voice seemed distant, as if it were travelling through a murky mist. 'I need to contact your relatives, Ellen. Who is there?'

'Only grandpa. He lives in London.'

'Can you give me his telephone number?'

'He doesn't have a phone. He can't afford it. But I know where he lives: it's 24 Watley Buildings, Paster Street, London SE17.'

Ellen knew the address well. Grandpa wrote to her from time to time, letters that included drawings of what he had been doing – a stick man going to the shops or digging potatoes. The letters always made her laugh and gave her a warm, safe comfortable feeling. She wished grandpa were here now.

'OK – I'll write that down when we get there.'

'I need to see him. I want grandpa to come.'

'We'll contact him, Ellen. Don't worry. Give me a day or two. I'm sure you'll see him soon.'

A day or two. It could have been forever. Ellen lapsed into silence. She was surprisingly uninterested in where they were going. In these few hours the life she knew had been snatched away. Whatever happened to her now would just happen.

TWO

They arrived at a 1930s semi-detached bungalow in a long suburban street on the edge of Fineston. A kindly, middle-aged woman called Barbara, with greying curly hair, met her at the door and took her to a narrow room at the back. On the single bed was a small case that Ellen recognised.

'You'll find some of your things in there.'

Ellen felt outrage – who had been to her house, into her room and rifled through her possessions? How dare they? The case was made of stiff red board and she'd taken it with her on a school trip to the Lake District. Her mum had bought it specially. Ellen remembered feeling rather ashamed of it because all the other girls had carried expensive looking leather bags. She felt a wave of guilt and remorse at the memory of her ingratitude now.

Later, Ellen couldn't remember very much about her stay at Barbara's. Her room had a wall lined with bookshelves. It was obviously used as a work room or study when not in use as a bedroom. Beyond the window, a light illuminated a small square garden covered in grey paving stones. An apple tree spread its branches over one corner of the yard and a Russian vine, with grubby white flowers, straddled a leaning wooden fence at the bottom. Bleak was the word that came into Ellen's head as she stared. A voice behind her made her jump.

'Put your things in here, dear,' said Barbara, pointing to a tall cupboard squeezed into the narrow space at the bottom of the bed. 'I haven't had time to clear everything but there's a bit of room in there and you won't be here long.'

Ellen opened the cupboard and saw a long black coat, covered in a plastic bag, hanging from the rail. Wellington boots and a rucksack were stacked on the floor. On the single shelf were a pair of cotton trousers, an anorak and a plastic holder for maps that, Ellen knew, was used by hikers when they were out walking. This was someone else's room, someone else's space, someone else's life. She stared at the map holder and wondered if she would ever go walking in the countryside again. Sometimes, when grandpa had been staying with them, he had driven Ellen and her mother out to the Yorkshire moors. Ellen remembered the pleasure of putting one foot in front of another on springy turf and watching the mountains change colour as the sun moved across the sky. She had loved it when there was no one else in sight and she was alone in vast peace, reassured by the plaintive mewing of the buzzards overhead. She was alone now, but it didn't feel peaceful. It felt frightening and dark. The band about her heart felt tighter than ever and the world seemed bleached of colour. What should she do now? How was she going to live her life? A voice behind her interrupted her memory.

'You'd better have something to eat, dear, before you go to bed.'

'No, no, I couldn't, I just want to go to bed.'

Ellen felt Barbara watching her closely and wished she'd go away. She just wanted to be alone and still in the darkness. But she knew that Barbara meant well; she sensed a comfortable acceptance in her even though she said little.

'Thank you, but really I just need to sleep.'

'Very well, dear. I'll bring you some hot milk and a glass of water. Then you go to bed and try and rest. The bathroom is just next door.

I've put a clean towel in there for you. Just get some sleep and I'll see you in the morning – get up whenever you like.'

Ellen woke up the next morning feeling frightened. For a moment her mind was blank and then the fear gripped her chest and heart; it felt like a sleek, live animal that had taken possession of her body. What was it for? Then the memories – those three moments that were to stay with Ellen forever. They would hang in her memory and run, like a film, behind her eyes each evening before she went to sleep and each morning when she woke up: a policeman bashing at the door until it opened; the look on his face after he had stepped inside and seen what was there; his pushing her away as he shouted, 'Get out.'

Ellen breathed deeply. Every morning would be like this from now on.

She didn't know what to do. For a while she just lay there and then she looked at her watch: half past eight. Time to get out of bed probably. Often at home on Saturday she had stayed in bed and read until ten o'clock. On a good day, her mother would bring her a cup of tea and, later, they might go into town together and do the week's shopping at the new supermarket that had opened near the market place. What would happen here?

Just then, the insistent note of a telephone ringing startled the silence. Ellen heard Barbara pick it up.

'Fineston 3965. Can I help you? Ellen? Ah, that's her grandfather. I'll just get her.' Then, more loudly, 'Ellen – it's for you. It's your grandpa.'

The telephone had its own low wooden table in the central hall of the bungalow from which all the other rooms opened. Ellen opened her door.

'I'm not dressed...'

'Doesn't matter, there's only the two of us here.'

Ellen rushed to the phone.

'Grandpa, it's me. Where are you?'

'I'm in London, but I'm coming up soon. I've got to find somewhere to stay. Are you OK?'

'Don't know. Are you?'

Then silence. Ellen realised she'd hoped that grandpa could somehow make this better but as she listened to his strangely flat and faraway voice she sensed that he wasn't thinking about her, but about his daughter. Into the silence came the noise of the pips. Grandpa's money was about to run out.

'Look, I haven't any more money. I'll be there soon. I'll ring again.'

And the line went dead. Ellen felt numb. She really was on her own now. Grandpa couldn't save her. Did he blame her? Did he think she should have looked after her mother better? Ellen remembered the time, at the beginning of the school holidays, when she'd asked her mother if they were going to go away anywhere. The other girls at school all seemed to have holiday plans. Spain was a favourite destination, but those who weren't travelling abroad were going to country cottages or heading for the Cornish coast.

'What are you doing over the summer?' Julie had asked, making conversation one day as they found themselves sitting side by side at the lunch table.

'Not sure yet,' Ellen had replied, knowing inside that they weren't going anywhere. Her mother didn't have the money. 'We may go to Filey.'

'Oh, we've been there. I love the rocks, don't you?'

'Yes,' said Ellen, who had never been there. 'I really like climbing up them.'

Afterwards she worried about what she'd say if Julie asked her about her holiday when they came back to school in September. Why had she lied? How could she have been so stupid? It had been the evening after that lunchtime conversation that she'd asked her mother if they could go away somewhere, to the seaside. Inside she knew she was being childish and unreasonable but the words came out anyway.

'Why can't we go? Everyone else goes on holiday. Why do we have to be stuck here? I'm sure you could save a bit of money if you tried.'

Her mother's face had crumpled and then set in a hurt, strained but determined look.

'Don't keep asking me, Ellen. You know I haven't got the money.'

The guilty, frightened feeling this memory evoked settled around Ellen's heart. The world seemed grainy and dark as if she were acting in a black and white film. After she'd put the phone down she went back to her room and got dressed. She had, of course, arrived at Barbara's in her school uniform and she couldn't put that on again, so she hunted through the case that had been packed for her and found a pair of dark blue trousers and a pale blue jumper with a collar. Where had whoever-it-was who had packed her case found those? Where were her favourite clothes? Her jeans, for example? Now what should she do? She opened her door again and looked across the square hall. On the other side she could glimpse a room with a large oval table in it and a tree's branches tapping on the bay window. As she stood and wondered what to do Barbara appeared from another door carrying a teapot in one hand and a plate of toast in the other She was wearing a beige tweed skirt and brown cardigan.

'Ah, there you are, dear. Come and have some breakfast. Don't be nervous, it's only us. Alan is away this weekend. He's working in Bristol.'

Obediently, Ellen sat down at the table, both hands on her knees.

'Now, what would you like, dear? Cereal? Toast? I can cook you some scrambled eggs if you like. Or boiled?'

'I'm not hungry, thanks. I'll try some toast. Thank you.'

Barbara smiled and passed the plate of toast over to Ellen and then a silver butter dish and marmalade. Ellen noticed that the marmalade had been transferred from its jar into a small cut-glass bowl with its own silver lid and spoon. She remembered her mother telling her that it was good manners never to put jam straight from the jar onto your toast but to put a portion of it on your plate and then spread it, a little bit at a time, as you ate the toast. So that's what she did now, carefully removing the lid of the bowl and scooping out some marmalade with the tiny silver spoon. She kept her eyes firmly on what she was doing so she didn't have to look at Barbara. She was aware of Barbara's eyes on her though. It was as if she were expecting something from her.

'Now, dear, I wondered if you'd like to come into town with me this morning? I've got to get some food and take back a jumper I bought that isn't quite right. We could have coffee in Lagenbach's while we're there.'

Half an hour later Barbara and Ellen were sitting in her Austin mini, heading for town. Barbara found a parking space in the central car park and got out of the car. Ellen wandered after her. At the supermarket she pulled the plastic bags off a hook by the till and helped Barbara pack away tins of mackerel, bread, cheese and fruit, and a chicken for their supper.

'Do you like chicken, Ellen?'

Ellen had nodded. She didn't feel she wanted to say anything; talking would force her into this new life and make her accept that what was happening to her was true and real. It was easier to hide away inside and let the dim and grainy pictures of the world around her flicker without getting involved in them.

'Let's go and have a cup of coffee, dear.'

Lagenbach's café was in the centre of town behind a large church built of black stone and surrounded by iron railings. The church looked stern and remote.

Why would anyone want to go there? thought Ellen. Wasn't God supposed to be good? How could he have let this happen?

Ellen followed Barbara silently through the door of the café and sat down with her at a corner table. This was the kind of place her mother would have liked to go to but rarely did. She used to say that they weren't going to waste money on buying coffee out when they could easily make it at home. Ellen felt disloyal sitting there now. She looked around at the brown wooden tables and matching chairs, the prints of old Fineston on the wall, the waitresses with their white aprons, the fading roses on the carpet and the glass vases filled with a few dried flowers, orange and yellow, on each table. She saw the other customers, mostly middle-aged women with greying hair and plastic bags full of shopping. They were chatting cheerfully to each other, as if the world were a benign, normal sort of place, where there was nothing to talk about but the enjoyable things they'd done at the weekend and the achievements of their children.

'Well,' said one with a barely concealed touch of pride, 'Catherine's getting all her things ready to go to university. She's going to Manchester, you know. There's so much to buy...' Ellen couldn't bear it.

'I'm sorry. I can't stay in here. I'll wait for you outside.'

Without waiting for Barbara to reply she pushed her chair back, squeezed through the narrow space between their table and the next and went through the door. For a while she stood there, not thinking anything. It was cold and the people passing her on the narrow street pulled their coats closely around them. Opposite the café a tiny newsagent's shop displayed copies of the day's papers on a rack by the door. *Miners ballot for strike action!* declared the *Fineston Express*. For a moment Ellen thought, I must tell mum about that – her mother had often spoken of the danger that miners faced every day and how their work wasn't valued enough – and then she remembered that she wasn't ever going to have conversations about anything with her mother again. Yet her mother's image in her head was so strong and vivid it felt, almost, as if she were really there. And sometimes, in a crowd of people, Ellen thought she saw her and for the tiniest fraction of a second thought, Ah, there's mum. It's all all right after all.

The café door opened beside her and Barbara came out. She looked concerned and thoughtful. Confused.

'Ah, there you are, dear. I've paid the bill. Let's go home.'

For the first time, Ellen looked at Barbara properly. She saw her grey coat and black scarf and the timid green eyes that flickered a little, as if she were nervous and not quite sure what to do or say.

Of course she doesn't know, thought Ellen. How could she? And for a moment she felt sorry for Barbara. It couldn't be easy taking in a stranger. Ellen wondered why she did it. 'I'm sorry, I just couldn't stay there…'

'It's all right, dear. I understand. Let's go home.'

The rest of that day and the following days were a blur. Barbara's was a comforting presence. She didn't try and talk to Ellen directly about what had happened but Ellen sensed her concern and sympathy nonetheless. It was there in the way she touched her arm gently sometimes and smiled and in the thought with which she planned meals that Ellen might like. Sometimes she wondered what the older woman's story was. How often was her husband away working? How come she'd never had children of her own? Why did she take other people's children into her house?

Ellen was dimly aware of helping Barbara to do things like sweeping up leaves in the garden and tidying cupboards. She offered to vacuum clean the floors and let the roar of the machine ride over her as she pulled it backwards and forwards over and over again. The rhythm was soothing. And they watched television together, though what she had seen Ellen wouldn't have been able to say. At night, she took hot milk to bed and fell asleep with the bedside radio on. A few days after her arrival Ellen woke, as usual, feeling frightened. She forced herself to get out of bed and dress and went to the living room, where the table was laid for breakfast. Now that she was beginning to feel more comfortable with Barbara, she didn't have to try to guess all the time how she should behave and what she should say. As they cleared the plates away together when the meal was finished there was a knock on the door.

'Goodness – that's early. I wonder who it is?' said Barbara as she left her seat and went into the hall. A moment later she called out, 'Ellen, come here.'

Ellen arrived as the front door was closing behind her grandpa.

'Grandpa,' she shouted and then hesitated. She remembered the flat, distant tones of his voice when they had spoken on the phone. Was he angry with her? He looked thinner than she remembered and his shoulders were hunched forward. His shirt, under a beige tweed jacket, was crumpled and his shoes were scuffed.

'Hello, love,' he said. 'I've had to come up for the inquest. I'm going back to London tonight – it's cheaper that way – but I wanted to come and see you while I was here. Are you OK? Come and give me a hug.'

Then Ellen ran to him, put her arms around him and started to cry. This time the tears weren't for her mother; she was crying because her grandpa was here and he still loved her. Barbara made coffee and grandpa and Ellen sat together on the sofa.

'How've you been, love? I can see Barbara's looking after you well. And Ellen, remember this was nothing to do with you. I know your mother loved you, as well as she could. But she was very ill. What happened wasn't your fault.'

Ellen's tears returned. She couldn't think of anything to say, or rather, she couldn't imagine how she would put any of the things that she had thought and felt in the past few days into words. If she did try, it might make them real in a way in which they weren't quite, yet. Best to push them down, float over the top. So they sat in silence for a while, until it was time for grandpa to go.

'I'll be back for the funeral, love. Barbara will look after you, I know.'

THREE

On the morning of the funeral grandpa returned. He wore a black tie, clumsily knotted so that it looked too short, and in his breast pocket a clean handkerchief. 'Your mother would never forgive me if I went to her funeral with a dirty handkerchief,' he said to Ellen and smiled.

As they waited for the car that would take them to the church Ellen remembered a time as a young child when she had walked to the bottom of grandpa's small allotment and squatted beside him while he pointed to a tiny hedgehog snuffling in the leaves at the base of a rose tree. Grandpa's allotment, one of a neat patch of twelve, had been peaceful and carefully cultivated, with a crazy-paving path, a vegetable patch and a couple of apple trees. When Ellen was there, she always felt that things would be just fine. Since her grandmother had died grandpa had lived in an apartment close to London's Elephant and Castle, with just a small flat roof outside the kitchen window where he used to grow pots of vegetables. Ellen sensed he had been lonely since his wife died. And now he was here for another funeral. How did he feel watching his only daughter's coffin?

Barbara had lent Ellen a black dress. It was a bit too tight but if she pulled her coat over it she could leave the two top buttons of the dress undone and move more easily. As they waited, Ellen seemed to sense her mother's presence; it was as if she could see her, somewhere just beyond her gaze, a spirit in a blue dress with a ruff about the neck, floating above her. It was the same illusion that sometimes came to her just before she went to sleep; she felt that her mother was there with her, but her manner was distant, out of reach.

Eventually, the car arrived at the house to pick them up. The undertaker, large, pale and unhealthily bloated, made Ellen shiver. She thought his black suit made him look sinister, like a character in a gangster movie. Barbara climbed into the back seat with them. Ellen found her incessant chat, which she half-knew was designed to distract and comfort her, irritating. She wanted to ask her to stop but didn't know how to do it politely. They drove in through the high metal gates of the crematorium drive. The gates were hung on tall pillars of blackened stone and the driveway itself was flanked by borders of marigolds, planted in tidy rows. Other large black cars rolled into the car park and burly grey-haired men in dark suits and heavy coats opened the doors for their passengers and then stood, feet apart, looking discreetly at the floor as they waited for the cars to empty. Ellen noticed a self-consciousness and falseness about their solemnity that made her angry. What had they to do with her mother?

The square stone chapel at the crematorium was full. Ellen was surprised by how many people had come. There was her Aunt Christabel, whom she found stern and critical, together with her silent Uncle Walter. Some of the people there were neighbours, like Mr and Mrs Boyle, and there were staff from the housing project where her mother had helped out sometimes. Lots of others she didn't know and she felt self-conscious as she and grandpa walked past them to the front row. The coffin rested, high and uncompromising, on a platform ahead of them and a vicar that Ellen had never seen before stood waiting. She sensed her mother's presence in the air above the coffin, and imagined her gentle, loving goodnight self when she used to hover around Ellen's door, smelling of face cream. Now she seemed a different kind of being, not someone dead, but somehow altogether different, mysterious and beyond her understanding.

The vicar put on a pair of spectacles and, reading from his notes, started to talk about her mother. Ellen didn't recognise her. 'She was a quiet woman, uncomplaining, who got on with the business of her life…'

Where did that come from? thought Ellen. She was always complaining, making a fuss.

Everyone sang 'The Lord is my shepherd' and Ellen remembered how her mother had cried when she heard this at home on *Songs of Praise* on the television. Ellen had never known why. Maybe it was because the hymn was supposed to be comforting but could never bring her mother any ease. Ellen noticed grandpa beside her wiping tears from his eyes and she started to cry too. Grandpa passed her his handkerchief, pausing for a moment to smile and say, 'I think it's clean enough.'

The curtains closed around the coffin. The final farewell. There was a scratchy, rattling sound, like a trolley being pulled over concrete. Ellen guessed that this was the coffin being moved away to… where? Ellen knew that the box and the body inside it would be burned but the thought was detached, distant; she couldn't connect it with her mother. Ellen gripped grandpa's hand as they walked out into the mellow autumn sun. They were ushered to the car, people shook hands and then it was over.

– – –

Ellen stared out of the window as the car drove away. There was to be a small gathering at her Aunt Christabel's after the funeral. The thought of this frightened Ellen. She had very few relatives and the only one that she was close to was grandpa. There was no one she wanted to talk to and she particularly didn't want anyone trying to be cheerful or behaving as if this hadn't happened. She wanted to be alone. The car turned into a broad, tree-lined street and stopped outside a house with a bulbous bay window that gave the impression that the sitting room was spilling its contents into the long front garden. On one side of the black front door was a garage with ivy growing over its roof. A dark, tight feeling spread through Ellen's chest. She and her mother had come to visit her aunt here only occasionally after her father, Christabel's brother Geoff, had died. Her memories of coming here were not happy.

She recalled one year, at Christmas, sitting in her aunt's sitting room on a flowery sofa, playing scrabble. She had been squeezed so tightly between her cousin, Marcus, and a loud neighbour that she could scarcely reach the scrabble board. The piano, set against the wall, was covered in Christmas cards. A highly polished wooden side table held whisky, Christmas cake and lemonade. Ellen didn't like lemonade but it was all there was and nobody asked her whether she wanted it or not. Her mother sat opposite her, next to Aunt Christabel's short and heavily built husband, Walter. Her mother looked uncomfortable. She had disapproved of Walter, thought him arrogant and loud. 'He expects women to wait on him all the time,' she used to say.

Aunt Christabel had said something about what a pity it was that Geoff, Ellen's dead father, couldn't be there. She had looked at Ellen's mother in a disapproving, challenging way that Ellen found odd, and her mother had got upset and shouted 'Don't blame me! Don't blame me!' After that the day had been stiff and awkward, with people trying to be polite to each other but feeling angry underneath. These were the main feelings Ellen associated with her aunt's house: rage and disapproval concealed behind tight-lipped courtesy. Although she and her mother had never discussed it, Ellen knew that the anger related to the evening her father had died.

She had been seven, and even though she hadn't really understood what was happening, she had vivid and frightening memories of that night. Shouting had woken her. She recognised her mother's voice and her father's and heard some horrible words: 'drunk… bitch…' and a scream, followed by a shout from her mother, 'Don't go.'

There were some other scraping and banging noises that Ellen hadn't recognised and then the sounds of glass smashing on the floor, the front door slamming, a car engine spluttering into life in the street – and her mother crying. Ellen lay there, stiff with shock but scared to move. Eventually she fell asleep, to be woken again by a loud banging on the door.

'Mrs Wentworth, police…'

Ellen heard the door open and then muffled voices in the hall. A scream from her mother and a man's voice trying to calm her. Ellen had stayed in her bed, rigid and petrified, waiting. She remembered that, later, her Aunt Christabel had appeared in her room and picked her up, wrapping one of the blankets from her bed around her as she did so, and taken her downstairs to a waiting car. It was at Aunt Christabel's house that she was told that her father had been killed in a road accident.

— — —

Now she was at this house again. Grandpa got out of the car first. The low brick front garden wall was covered with ivy. Beyond the black wrought iron gate lay a neatly weeded crazy-paving path and a brick patio. The abundant flowers of a potted geranium overflowed onto the front step. Ellen remembered how her mother had loved geraniums but had never been satisfied with the ones she'd grown. 'They just go all straggly,' she used to say gloomily.

As they approached the door, Ellen pulled back so that grandpa got there first. He rang the bell and the door was opened by Ellen's cousin, Marcus. Marcus was a six-foot-tall seventeen-year-old, with slightly ginger hair, a grey suit and a confident smile that Ellen found condescending. She sensed curiosity in his eyes and something else too. Resentment? Irritation? 'Do come in,' he said. Ellen numbly obeyed. She felt that she was operating like a machine. In the hall mirror she caught a glance of what he saw – a smooth, pale, fifteen-year-old face. Green-grey eyes with dark smudges beneath. Light brown hair brushing thin shoulders. A wary, puzzled expression.

Behind him, in the hallway, Ellen was startled to see the round white face of Andrea, the social worker who had taken her to Barbara's on that terrible day.

'Ellen – could we talk for a few minutes before you join the others?' Andrea exchanged glances with Marcus and led Ellen and grandpa into a small study that opened off the hall.

'Ellen – I do hope the funeral went well. I know this is a very difficult time for you. I wanted to let you know straight away what has been decided about your future. As you know, your stay at the foster home was temporary, so you'd be looked after while a permanent arrangement was made. And I'm pleased to tell you that your Aunt Christabel has offered to take care of you for the next few years, until you're grown up and can live on your own. We always think it best if young people without parents can live with family. Your aunt will make sure that your education continues. I know that you're doing O-levels next year. '

Ellen's head whirred. She felt a knot of red anger and panic, all mixed up together, surging through her body and filling her chest.

'No, no… I can live on my own, I can go back to our house. I can take care of myself. No.'

Grandpa, who had followed her into the room, took a step towards her. 'Ellen, love, I know it's hard, but you'll be better off here. You can carry on with your education, get your GCEs, go to university, just like you planned.'

'Can't I live with you? I'll come to London… I don't mind.'

'I'm not well enough, love. You know I've been under the doctor lately – I've had that trouble with my stomach. And it's best you finish your schooling here. You can come and visit me.'

'No, no, no...' shouted Ellen. 'No.'

Aunt Christabel entered the room. 'Come along, dear,' she said. 'I know this is difficult but we've got a room ready for you. You're my brother's daughter and I know he would have wanted me to look after you. Come with me.' Tall and thin, , Aunt Christabel dominated the room. Her voice was loud and commanding. Ellen could tell she expected to be in charge.

'Off you go, dear,' said grandpa. 'I'll be here when you come down.'

Ellen's new room was at the back of the house. She looked around and saw twin beds, with pink patterned covers, a kidney-shaped dressing table with a matching curtain hanging round the base, a built-in cupboard and a white chest of drawers. This was a guest room, with little space to spread out. On one of the beds lay her school satchel and the same red case that had followed her to the foster home. Now what?

She remembered another time when she had felt lost like this. It was when her mother had been taken to the mental hospital, just a year or so ago, when Ellen was fourteen. The events leading up to her admission were obscure; no one had ever properly explained them to Ellen. She knew that grandpa, who had come to visit, had been there and that he had called the doctor. When she arrived home from school she had found the two of them at home. Grandpa looked haggard, his face lined and, unusually, he paid little attention to Ellen when she came in. Her mother's hair was down and hanging loosely around her shoulders as if she had just got out of bed, although it was the late afternoon. She was wearing her dressing gown. Grandpa said, 'I've called the doctor, Bess, he'll be here soon. Just sit down.'

But her mother couldn't sit down. She walked round the room, clutching her elbows and speaking in clipped sentences. Her eyes were looking beyond Ellen, far away into the distance.

'I won't go to the hospital. I'm scared. I don't know what they'll do to me there...'

'They'll look after you, Bess. And you have to think about Ellen.'

There had been a knock on the door then and a young doctor wearing a tweed suit and carrying a large black bag entered the room behind grandpa.

'Now, Mrs Wentworth. I can see you're very distressed. We will make you better but I need you to go to hospital straight away. They know how to take care of you there.'

The doctor had held her mother's hand and looked firmly into her eyes. It seemed to calm her. Then, somehow, she had been put into the doctor's car and driven to the hospital. Ellen and her grandfather followed in the car behind.

'What's going to happen, Grandpa?' asked Ellen.

'They'll take care of her there, love. Don't worry. And in the meantime I'll come and look after you.'

Ellen felt a warm, comfortable burst of pleasure to think that her grandfather was going to be living in her house with her. He'd make her laugh and help her with her homework and play the piano to her. She'd be able to relax.

Half an hour later Ellen's mother and her companions had driven into the hospital grounds through high gates of rusted orange metal that had sunk so far into the ground they looked as if they would never move again. They were met at the reception desk by a dark-haired doctor who said, 'A nurse will take you to your room, Mrs Wentworth, and make you comfortable and I will see you in the morning.'

Then he had turned away and left her. Her mother had pleaded with Ellen not to leave her there.

'I can't stay here, Ellen. Let me come home with you. Don't

leave me here. You've got to say something.'

So, when a stern, middle-aged nurse arrived to take her mother away, Ellen said, 'My mother doesn't want to stay. I'm going to take her home with me.'

The nurse had looked at her disapprovingly. 'Your mother is very ill. If she was my mother I'd be wanting her to get the best treatment possible.'

Ellen had shrunk away. Was it true that she had been a bad daughter who didn't care whether her mother got well or not? Is that why she was here now? Certainly, she had often felt that she had done something wrong, that she was going to be punished for something she didn't quite understand. What would the punishment be now?

— — —

'Come downstairs,' said Aunt Christabel, hovering in the door of the room. 'There are lots of people there.'

A crowd of people was the last thing Ellen wanted but she numbly followed her aunt downstairs. A large sitting room stretched the full length of the house and ended in a glass conservatory that overlooked a garden full of shrubs. A table was covered in plates of sandwiches, sausage rolls and wedges of cheese. Uncle Walter was circulating around the room offering guests a glass of white wine. Ellen wondered who these people were. Mr and Mrs Boyle weren't there but she recognised some other neighbours that her mother used to talk to sometimes. An elderly couple, who spent a lot of time washing their car; they had never been particularly friendly and complained, sometimes, about her piano playing in the evening. Amongst the other guests were people who Ellen vaguely thought might be distant members of the family, but she had no wish to speak to them.

As she entered the room, an uncomfortable, barely perceptible hush fell. Guests glanced at her, and then looked away, not sure how to greet her.

'Ellen, love, have a sandwich,' said grandpa, who suddenly appeared at her side.

'I couldn't eat anything.'

'I know, it's hard. Let's go into the garden.'

Gratefully, Ellen followed grandpa through the conservatory, across the patio and onto the damp, fresh lawn. He wandered over to a rose bush and reached out to a dead flower, pinching its head between his fingers and dropping the browned petals to the ground.

'Your mother loved roses, you know, Ellen. She was so beautiful when she was young. When you were born we planted a rose bush together in our garden in Camberwell, to remember you by. She loved you very much, you know. But she was ill and had been on and off for a long time. You know that – that's why she had to go into hospital last year. I expect she even thought she was doing this for you – she wouldn't have wanted to be a burden.'

Ellen couldn't find any words. Inside, she was thinking, 'What if I hadn't gone to school that day? Did I leave the house in a mess?' Mum hated that. Had she been rude to her? What had happened the night before? But these things were impossible to say. To give her hidden thoughts the substance of words would have made it more likely that her fears were real. Best to push them away, not to think.

Grandpa said, 'There isn't anything either of us could have done, you know. She was a stubborn woman. I sometimes thought she didn't want to get well. Your Aunt Christabel is a bit scary, I know, but she means well. And it's best that you finish your education at your school – it's a really good one, you know – and get those GCEs, go to university. It's what your mother wanted for you, you know.'

Still no words came. Ellen knew that grandpa was right. Her mother would have wanted her to finish school, get good grades and go on and be someone. Ellen felt grandpa watching her silently but sensed that his thoughts were only partly with her. He seemed far away, lost in a place she couldn't see. Then he shook his head slightly as if forcing himself back to this moment and spoke.

'Tell you what, I came up by car this time – the train's so expensive – and I'm staying at my mate Rob's for the night. So if you like, we could go for a walk this afternoon. Get away from all these people, feel the fresh air in our lungs… like we used to.'

'OK… yes, I'd like that.'

Grandpa led the way back into the house and touched Aunt Christabel on the arm. He leant close to her and whispered something Ellen couldn't hear. Aunt Christabel looked startled and not, Ellen thought, very pleased. Grandpa spoke again, still softly, and Ellen heard her aunt's reply.

'Well – it feels rather improper to me. It is her mother's funeral, after all. But if you insist. What time will you bring her back? She has school tomorrow.'

This time, when grandpa spoke, Ellen could hear him clearly.

'I'll have her back by seven. Don't worry.'

'Very well. There are wellington boots she can borrow under the stairs – it will be muddy out there.'

Grandpa turned to Ellen and said, 'OK love. Go upstairs and put on something comfortable for walking in. Your aunt says there are boots you can borrow under the stairs. Then we've got all afternoon.'

– – –

It felt strange to be sitting in the front of Grandpa's old car. He still had the same Ford Popular she remembered from years before, with its square, upright carriage and long, rounded bonnet. Ellen remembered the large book of maps of England that still lay on the back seat and noticed how worn the leather seats looked now, shiny patches mingled with holes. Often, when he'd been visiting Fineston, they had gone on expeditions to the moors and spent the day climbing the hills. Then, Ellen had always been in the back seat. It felt strange to be sitting in the front, next to grandpa. In her mother's seat. There had usually been a picnic on these outings, Ellen remembered. Or rather, because her mother didn't like making sandwiches, a bag with a loaf of bread, some hard boiled eggs in their shells, a few tomatoes, a tub of margarine and a knife. They each spread their own slices of bread, passing the knife between them, and shelled their own egg.

Today, neither of them talked about food. Grandpa reversed the car out of the drive and drove towards the main road. Ellen looked out of the window at the large houses with steep front gardens that lined the road and felt relief when these gradually grew further and further apart. On either side of the road trees leant inwards towards each other, forming a shield against the sky. Eventually the trees gave way to open fields. It felt good to get away from all the people who seemed to have crowded into her life in the past few days and to be alone with her grandfather. The car started to climb a steep hill that she recognised. When she was younger, she remembered, grandpa would slow the car right down when they got here and explain that he was going to drive in second gear.

'Gears change the ratio of the wheels to the engine,' he used to tell her and she had sort of understood. She had always liked being given his technical explanation for things.

'I hope we're going to make it,' he'd say. 'Lean forward everyone.'

And Ellen would lean forward in the back seat, her heart beating slightly faster than usual as she wondered if they were going to stall before they reached the top. Grandpa must have remembered too. Smiling, he turned to Ellen and said, 'I think we'll make it.'

A few miles further on grandpa turned the car into a small car park, empty today, that marked the beginning of a path through some woods. Grandpa locked the car and led the way through the trees. The path was narrow and they walked in single file. Ellen was relieved that she didn't have to speak, or think, about anything. Instead she focused on her steps, one after the other in the damp, dark earth scattered with browning leaves that had already fallen from the trees. Each foot sank into the mud and squelched a little as she lifted it out. Where deep pools of water had gathered she looked for a drier route round their edges, jumping occasionally from one patch of dry ground to another. The rhythm soothed her and the silence was comforting. There seemed to be no need to talk.

After half an hour they emerged from the woods onto a path that wound backwards and forwards up the side of a steep hill. It was drier now, but more effort was needed to climb. Grandpa slowed down a little and Ellen could see that he was getting out of breath.

'Do you want to stop here?' she asked.

'Certainly not. I have to get out on top.'

And Ellen remembered that he had always said this when they were walking, that he loved being at the top of a mountain, gazing on the world below. It seemed to give him a feeling of lightness and freedom. Ellen liked it too, so they pressed on together, slowing slightly as the climb steepened. They reached a rocky outcrop that, for a moment, Ellen thought was the peak and then, when she got there, realised that it wasn't quite. There was another higher point a few hundred yards away. Grandpa paused for breath.

'One more push and we're there.'

Still silent, they continued their climb, both breathing more heavily now, but determined to get there. When they did, they spread a plastic mac that grandpa had tucked into his pocket onto a patch of rock. Out of his other pocket, Grandpa took a bar of chocolate.

'Here – have some chocolate, you deserve it!'

Ellen slipped the wrapper off the bar and carefully undid the silver paper. She loved chocolate but was careful to offer some to grandpa first.

'No thanks, love. I've been having lots of trouble with my stomach – terrible indigestion, really hurts. So I'm being very careful about what I eat.'

Ellen ate the chocolate slowly, staring down at the town below. It looked so small and insignificant, ribbon roads and neat dolls' houses and yet, she supposed, in each of those buildings there were people who had felt like she did, people to whom terrible things had happened. Human grief seemed to fill the houses and drift into the streets around.

Grandpa broke the silence.

'Things always seem better up here, you know. The fresh air in your lungs.'

A strong gust of wind blew round them, lifting the edges of the plastic mac and pushing Ellen's hair into her face.

'Are you all right, love? Not too cold?'

An aeroplane flew low overhead, drowning her words. They were silent for a few moments longer. Then Grandpa spoke.

'We used to do lots of walking when your mother was a girl, you know. She never seemed to be unhappy then – had lots of energy, skipping up these hills. And even later, after – after the baby died and she got ill, she seemed to be her old self when she was out in the country, walking, away from everything. I bet if I'd been able to get her out here when… when…'

Ellen waited for him to finish his sentence. Would it have made a difference if grandpa had been there last week? She watched him brush aside a tear and waited, afraid, then he turned to her.

'Remember what I said though, love. None of it was your fault. She was my daughter – I should have looked after her better.'

Another tear rolled down grandpa's cheek and again he wiped it away. Ellen watched in a silence that she couldn't have measured afterwards, then she suddenly felt brave, as if the hidden, stubborn thoughts that her throat would not usually allow her to voice found the courage to force themselves out.

'Grandpa, why was mum like she was? What was wrong with her?'

Grandpa paused for a long time before speaking.

'She was a lovely young girl, you know. Lively, always dancing. And the best dressed girl in Fineston. She made all her own clothes, you know. Latest fashion. And she loved children, always did. Played with the children next door to our house in Camberwell. Their mum used to say she was a natural. Then she married Geoffrey. Too young probably and he was away such a lot, being a sailor. When she got pregnant with your brother she was really happy. It was what she'd always wanted, to be a mum. As you know, the baby – your brother – died soon after he was born and she was never the same after that. Got depressed, couldn't do anything. Post-natal depression they call it. She never really recovered. A lot of the time she'd be fine and then, this black mood would take over and she could hardly do anything. Just wanted to stay in bed all day.'

This was a description Ellen recognised. Her mother had sometimes been in bed when she got home from school, and although she said she had been up and about during the day, Ellen had never really believed her. Every effort to move seemed to be too much for her. Grandpa continued.

'I've always blamed those doctors. Women often get a bit low when they've had a baby but this was different. She couldn't shake it off somehow. And your dad was away – he did get some time off and then had to go back to sea. She just seemed to get worse and worse and then they took her to hospital and gave her this horrible treatment. They called it ECT – electric shock treatment. Said it was the only thing that could help her but she was frightened… She was never the same after that. Got depressed, couldn't do anything. She worried about forgetting things.'

Grandpa stopped talking and Ellen waited. She remembered her mother telling her once about the electric shock treatment she had had. They had been sitting in a café in Ryston after a rare shopping trip, rounding off their treat with tea and cakes. It had taken Ellen ages to choose between the chocolate éclair and the cream slice that were brought to their table with a silver teapot, a pot of hot water and a tiny milk jug. As she reached out her hand for the éclair her mother had looked out of the window and allowed one of the uncomfortable silences that sometimes happened between them to continue. Ellen felt as if she should say something, but wasn't sure what. Then her mother, still turned away from her, asked, 'Do you think I've hurt you, being the way I am?'

Ellen froze. 'The way I am?' What did her mother mean? The visit to the mental hospital? The sudden changes of mood? The anger and the silence interspersing the times when they had fun together? What could she possibly say? This uncertainty was all Ellen had ever known and one of the main things she had learnt was that she mustn't say anything to upset her mother. So, still speaking to the side of her mother's head she said 'No.' Her mother turned to her then.

'I have tried, you know, to be a good mother. It's been very hard for me. When your brother was born – when he died – I got very upset, depressed and they gave me this ECT. It was really scary. They put these electrode things on either side of your head and then an electric current goes through you.'

Ellen had gasped. They had electrocuted her?

'Yes – it's supposed to "re-set" your brain or something. But when I came round I knew something wasn't right. I couldn't remember things, got confused. The depression did go for a bit, but then it came back. Don't let them do that to me again, Ellen.'

Ellen recalled the moment her mother had been in hospital and had said, 'You're not to let them give me that ECT again.' Was that why she had always been frightened of going back there?

Grandpa took his hand away from his face and turned to Ellen.

'The thing to remember is that none of it was your fault, love. This is a hard life. I've lived through two world wars, remember, seen my friends die. Seen my own brother die. I sometimes wonder why, when there are so many millions of people in the world, we can get to care about just one or two so much.'

'Yeah, but if I'd been there… if I'd been…'

Ellen paused. She'd never said this to anyone before, or even let herself think it. And now, when her mother still seemed to be present in the air above them, a shape in the clouds, floating like a wisp of air, insubstantial, but angry, she felt guilty mouthing the words. They came out anyway.

'I don't think she really loved me, Grandpa. If she had she couldn't have done this. And sometimes I was bad – didn't look after her properly – so I suppose it's not surprising.'

'Ellen, you mustn't think that. It was her job to look after you. If anyone should feel the blame, it's me. I should have moved up here to be with her – and you. I always thought you had to let your children live their own lives and not interfere. But she needed me more than I thought. She was so lovely when she was young though. And always knew her own mind – a real stubborn streak in her. If she'd made up her mind to do this I don't think anyone could have stopped her.'

A huge buzzard flew high overhead, its fringed wings proud and strong as it circled its prey below. Ellen and grandpa sat silently and watched. Ellen wondered at its freedom and power. There was another question she had to ask.

'That night, when my dad died. What really happened? Mum would never talk about it, though I think she was angry because of what he'd done.'

Grandpa paused. 'Well, I wasn't there, of course, but your mother said that he'd come home drunk and wanted to drink some more and she tried to stop him, but he wouldn't listen and they had an argument and he went out in the car and drove into a tree. The car turned over and he was killed.'

The first bit of this certainly matched Ellen's memories.

'But why would mum say to Aunt Christabel, "It wasn't my fault"? Like she did one Christmas.'

'Well, Aunt Christabel and her brother were very close and I think he talked to her about your mother's illness – her having to go to hospital and the ECT and everything – and your aunt thought she should pull herself together and be a proper wife to him. She thought your mum made your dad's life difficult and that was why he drank too much. But it was hard for your mum – your dad was away at sea a lot and she had to cope with losing the baby alone really…'

A picture of her mother, in her dressing gown, staring out of the window at the back garden, her faced closed and blank, came into Ellen's mind as her grandpa spoke. This was too much to think about now. Later…

Grandpa reached out and touched her hand.

'There are so many things in this life, Ellen. You must go for them. Be strong. Get your exams, go to university, get away from here. Don't get caught up in all these memories.'

'I'm not going to like it at Aunt Christabel's, Grandpa – I know I'm not.'

'You can't give up your schooling now. This is an important year and, remember, you're a scholarship girl. Your mother was so proud of that. You mustn't throw it all away now. And I'll write to you.' Grandpa paused as he reached into his pocket. 'Here, Ellen, here's some money, in case you need anything.' He handed over some ten pound notes.

'No – I couldn't, Grandpa – you've not got much money. You've only got your pension now. I'll be all right.'

'I want you to have it, just in case…'

Neither of them spelled out what 'just in case' might mean. Ellen took the money and put it into the inside pocket of her jacket.

'We should be getting back,' said grandpa and he picked up his plastic mac and rolled it up.

Ellen's feeling of dread deepened as they drove back along the lane and then onto the main road and turned, again, into her aunt's street. Most of the cars that had been parked outside the house for the funeral had left. Grandpa got out of the car with her and rang the bell.

'Remember, I'll be thinking about you. I know you're brave and I'm going to be so proud when you've got those exams.'

Ellen couldn't say anything. Inside, she was thinking, 'I'm really on my own now.'

FOUR

Ellen didn't know what to do when she woke the next day. She had gone to bed early, straight after grandpa had dropped her off, and refused anything to eat. Aunt Christabel had given her a new toothbrush and clean towel.

'Get some sleep, dear. Then in the morning I think we should take you back to school. Take your mind off things.'

But Ellen hadn't slept. The now familiar three moments repeated themselves in her mind – the door, the policeman's face, his shout. Her watch said quarter to seven. What time did people get up in this house? Could she get to the bathroom without bumping into anyone? Would people be annoyed if she locked herself in there? Where was her school uniform? She climbed out of bed and hunted through the clothes that she had taken out of her case hurriedly the night before and left lying on the second bed. Clean knickers, a shirt, navy skirt – but no tie. Where was her tie? She heard a knock on the bedroom door. Aunt Christabel, fully dressed and looking businesslike, came round the door.

'Ellen, here's some tea. Breakfast will be on the table in fifteen minutes. Did you sleep well? Have you got everything you need?'

'Yes, thank you. I can't find my tie. I can't go to school without my tie. I'll get into trouble. I don't know where it is.'

'Don't worry about that, dear. I'm sure people will understand.'

'No, I can't, I…'

Aunt Christabel had gone. Ellen looked again through her bag and found the tie tucked into an inside pocket. She dressed quickly, peeped round the door to see if the bathroom was empty, then, finding that it was, hurried across the landing, went in and washed her face. Now, she had to face the family.

The table was set in the conservatory: a glass jar filled with cereal, toast in a basket, orange juice in a jug. It was what Ellen imagined being in a hotel might be like. She remembered her breakfasts at home. Usually, her mother had been low in the morning and Ellen had looked after herself. She would grab a bowl from the cupboard – sometimes she had to wash one left dirty from the night before – fill it with cornflakes and, if she were lucky, fresh milk. If there was no milk she would pour orange juice into the bowl instead. Sometimes, Ellen's mother would appear before Ellen went to school, wearing a dressing gown and looking grey and resentful, but often she stayed in bed while Ellen gathered up her bag and ran for the bus.

Even when Ellen was younger, at primary school, breakfasts had been uncomfortable. Then, Ellen had worn her long straight hair in pigtails, which her mother usually tied up for her at breakfast. Ellen would be eating her cereal at the red, Formica-topped kitchen table and her mother would stand behind her, pulling a hair brush through her night-tangled hair. She wasn't always gentle and sometimes the plaits were tied so tightly they hurt. Reminded of this now, in this strange house, at another breakfast, Ellen remembered how, when she reached eleven or twelve and started secondary school, her mother had announced that she was taking her to the hairdresser to have her hair cut.

Ellen hadn't wanted her hair cut but knew, somehow, that there was no point in saying so. So, that Saturday, Ellen and her mother had walked down Fossett Crescent, turned into the main road and stopped at a small hairdresser's built at the junction between roads, with glass windows on each side. Ellen could see lots of older women sitting under hairdryers, reading magazines. They went inside and her mother said to the receptionist, 'I have an appointment for a cut and a perm for my daughter.'

A perm? thought Ellen. I don't want frizzy hair.

'Mum...'

'Don't make a fuss, Ellen. I can't be plaiting your hair any more every morning. And you hair is so straight it will look like rats' tails if it doesn't have some curl in it.'

A hairdresser had led Ellen to a stool in front of a mirror and asked her to sit down. She had taken hold of each plait in turn and snipped it off, with a single cut.

'There you are, dear. You can take those home with you if you like.'

Ellen had felt as if she were being punished. She had watched in the mirror as the young hairdresser applied some foul-smelling liquid to her hair and then, painfully and slowly, curled each strand of her hair into a roller. These were fastened very tightly and dug painfully into her scalp. Ellen was moved to a seat under the dryer and the machine's large plastic hood placed over her head. The air that circulated had been too hot and hurt her. Ellen had found a control by the side of the seat and turned the temperature down, bringing temporary relief, but a few minutes later the hair assistant had stopped beside her and turned it up again.

'You'll never set at that temperature. It needs to be hot.'

Later, at home, Ellen had looked aghast at the tight curls she saw in her mirror. What was she going to say at school the next day?

'Ah, Ellen. Come and sit down, dear.'

Her aunt's voice jerked her back into the present and Ellen saw Uncle Walter sitting at the head of the table, reading the *Daily*

Telegraph. The other places were empty. Ellen chose a seat as far away from her uncle as possible and waited for a clue about what to do next. Aunt Christabel supplied it.

'Help yourself to cereal, Ellen dear, then would you like an egg? I usually do one for the boys.'

Before Ellen could answer, Marcus arrived at the table, dressed in a suit, like all the sixth formers at his school.

'Morning everyone. Can I have a bit of the paper, Dad? Two eggs today please, Mum. And I'll be back late, I've got rugger after school.'

Ellen refused an egg. She managed to eat half a piece of toast and then wondered what to do. Could she leave the table? Should she wait until everyone had finished? How was she going to get to school? Aunt Christabel took charge.

'Uncle Walter will drive you to school today, Ellen. I think you need to be there by eight thirty, is that right? In future you can take a number 3 bus and walk up Elms Road. I should go and get your teeth cleaned and make sure you've got your school bag ready. You'll find it in the hall.'

'How did that get there?' wondered Ellen but cared little so spent no more time thinking about it. Instead she said, 'Thank you, Aunt Christabel', and got up from the table.

'Take your dirty plate with you, dear, and put it by the sink.'

'Take mine too if you're going,' said Marcus, not lifting his eyes from the back of his father's paper, where he was trying to read an account of a football match. Obediently, Ellen picked up the two plates and a dirty cup. Marcus didn't shift and said nothing.

Ellen cleaned her teeth, came downstairs and waited by the front door. Her coat was there but no beret. Not wearing the school beret was a very serious offence but she found that she didn't care. Uncle Walter appeared, carrying a shiny black briefcase and struggling into a grey raincoat.

'Come along, young lady. Mustn't be late. I need to get to the office.'

They walked out together and Ellen climbed into the black Rover that was parked in the drive at the side of the house. Uncle Walter was silent as he backed the car out onto the road and set off into town. Then he tried to initiate a conversation.

'Lovely day. Can never tell what it's going to be like in September. Often as hot as high summer. This journey won't take you long by bus, but I go into town quite a lot so I'll be able to drop you off some days. Hear this is your GCE year – lots of work. I remember the boys doing them. Had to keep them at it. Are you a good student? Do your homework and everything?'

'Yes, Uncle Walter.'

Inside, she was thinking she couldn't remember a single thing about any subject at school and couldn't imagine writing a coherent essay about anything. She sat silently after that, watching people hurrying along the street, waiting at bus stops, climbing into cars – as if the world was just as it was before and nothing unusual had happened. It seemed strange and distant to her, as if this grey world had nothing to do with her.

A now familiar flicker of fear began to lick around her heart when they reached school. She wondered if everyone would know what had happened. Of course, they would, it had been in the *Fineston Express*: '*Local woman hangs herself*'. She felt strangely ashamed, as if she had done something wrong. The posh girls at the school – the ones who didn't have a scholarship like she had – would probably sneer and talk about her behind their hands.

Uncle Walter parked the car in the road outside the front entrance to Fineston High School. It was a tall, dark Georgian building that fronted onto the road. Girls entered by a side entrance just past the games court. The stairs down to the fifth years' cloakroom were just inside the door. Ellen breathed deeply, climbed out of the car, walked quickly to the entrance and scuttled down the stairs. The cellar smelled dank. There were only a few coats hanging up so far; the lockers beneath the rows of hooks were empty. Once, girls had to change their shoes when they arrived at school and put their outdoor shoes in a black shoe bag and then in the locker. This was the only rule that Ellen could remember being relaxed during her time at the school.

She was hanging up her navy blue gabardine coat before anyone spoke to her. Jennifer was the daughter of a miner and travelled from a nearby pit village. Like Ellen, she was a scholarship girl. Come to think of it, all Ellen's friends were scholarship girls, a small group that had unconsciously sought each other out on their very first day at the school.

'Hello,' said Jennifer. 'Are you all right? I'm sorry about your mum.'

'Thanks,' replied Ellen.

Neither girl could think of anything else to say. The enormity of what had happened to Ellen seemed to fill their heads and stop any words coming out.

– – –

There was noise on the stairs: bumping satchels, thumping shoes, loud voices talking over and interrupting each other. A group of girls tumbled into the cloakroom. Sheila appeared first. Her hair was long and very straight and her uniform, although the regulation navy blue, looked somehow neater and classier than Ellen's. The skirt was only just knee length, so Sheila would pass a uniform inspection, but it was very tight fitting and revealed her slim figure. The coat she held over her arm was made of a soft material that looked expensive. Her shoes were very highly polished and had the faintest suggestion of a heel. Ellen noticed tobacco stains on the fingers of her right hand. Sheila hesitated when she saw Ellen and half turned towards her friends standing behind her on the stairs. Her eyebrows lifted a little.

She paused for a moment to say hello to Ellen then turned away and carried on with her conversation.

Ellen ran up the stairs. There were lots of girls arriving now, all rushing to their assigned cloakroom. It was easy to slip into the crowd and walk down the polished corridor and up the stairs at the other end to her classroom: 5G. Once there she opened the lid of the old wooden desk and began to remove her books from her satchel and stow them away neatly. She did this very slowly. No one could see her as long she kept the lid up. At 8.50 exactly Miss Harte, form tutor and maths teacher, entered the room and stood waiting by the teacher's desk. Immediately and silently, the girls rose.

'Good morning girls.'

'Good morning Miss Harte.'

'Sit down. I have a couple of notices for you before we go to assembly, girls. First, on my desk are letters for your parents about parents' evening. I know they will all want to come so please give them the letter as soon as you can. Second, tickets for the school play will go on sale next week so please find out how many your family would like. Thank you. Now, line up quietly please.'

Silently, the girls rose. The class was arranged in height order for the walk to assembly, and as Ellen was fairly short for her age, she was near the front. Her partner, Helen, looked shy and embarrassed but tried to smile at her. Ellen stared straight ahead and walked down to the school hall without any conscious awareness of what she was doing. Bleak, cold fear filled her body. Family? What family? Who could she ask to the school concert? She certainly wasn't going to bother picking up the letter from Miss Harte's desk.

The hall was large, with lots of mahogany wall panels and matching furniture. High stained glass windows threw a coloured light, red, blue and purple, onto the polished floor. Girls in their form groups lined up silently, one behind the other and, at a signal from their teachers, sat cross-legged on the floor. Only the sixth form girls had chairs. Miss Hibbett, the music teacher, played a Mozart sonata, ending mid-phrase as Miss Gaunt, the school's headmistress, appeared from the blue side curtains on the generous stage, her gown flowing behind her.

Miss Gaunt always looked stern. She wore her greying hair pinned in rolls around her neck. Slowly and smoothly she walked to the carved table in the centre of the stage. Six hundred pupils, at a sign from their form mistresses, stood.

'Good morning, girls.'

'Good morning, Miss Gaunt'

Ellen's body felt stiff. In her mind, she floated above her fellow pupils and looked down on Miss Gaunt reading a passage from the bible. It had nothing to do with her.

'Please kneel,' said Miss Gaunt, and the whole school bent to their knees and recited the Lord's Prayer together.

There was a further comment about parents' evening, a note of congratulation to the school hockey team on a victory the previous weekend against Townley Girls' School and a reminder about a rule. To deliver this, Miss Gaunt raised herself a little taller. Her hands and arms opened at her sides so that her gown fluttered a little. She looked like an owl.

'Girls must not walk along Hedley Road when they go to games lessons, but use the recognised route of Elms Road. I shall take a breach of this rule very seriously.'

Hedley Road passed the boys' school that shared a governing body with the High School and girls were strictly forbidden from making contact with the pupils there.

— — —

It was nine thirty now and Ellen felt as if the day had already lasted several hours. First lesson was English and Ellen liked Mrs Brown.

She was round and comfortable and liked to make gentle, literary jokes. It was the school custom for a girl from each class to go and wait for their teacher at the staff room door and carry her books to the class for her. On the first day of term Ellen had been given the job of meeting Mrs Brown, but now that she had been away from school for a few days she didn't know if someone else had taken over. She went up to the staff room in any case. It meant she didn't have to sit in the classroom, wondering what to say to the other girls, or getting nervous that they may say something to her. But there was no one else from her class at the staff room door, waiting for the teachers to come out. When Mrs Brown appeared, she touched Ellen's arm lightly.

'Hello, my dear. I'm so sorry. And so glad to see you back in school.'

Ellen felt tears behind her eyes. She breathed deeply but no words formed. What had happened was too big, too fearsome... too embarrassing. She sensed – and understood – that people simply didn't know what to say. So she said nothing to Mrs Brown except, 'Can I carry your books please?'

Mrs Brown looked at her, paused, and then said quietly, 'Thank you, dear.'

They set off together, Ellen slightly behind her teacher, down the stairs and along the corridor to 5G's classroom. As usual, the girls stood when Mrs Brown entered. Ellen slipped back to her desk and hurriedly took out her red English exercise book and her copy of *Macbeth*. She remembered her last English lesson, before the world changed forever. Mrs Brown had read Macbeth's speech, from Act 5, spoken after he hears of his wife's death:

> *She should have died hereafter;*
> *There would have been a time for such a word.*
> *Tomorrow, and tomorrow, and tomorrow,*

Creeps in this petty pace from day to day,
To the last syllable of recorded time;
And all our yesterdays have lighted fools
The way to dusty death. Out, out, brief candle!

The speech had made Ellen's heart tingle and she had gone home and learnt it by heart. Now she hoped that Mrs Brown wasn't going to read it again. The third line crept into her mind, despite her efforts to push it away. She said it differently to herself now, emphasising the 'and'. 'Tomorrow *and* tomorrow *and* tomorrow.' This was never going away.

— — —

Her mind drifted back again to the time her mother had been in the Aston Green mental hospital. After being admitted she had stayed there for several weeks as the doctors tried to alleviate her severe depression. The hospital was near her school, on a wide, leafy street. Ellen used to visit her every day when lessons ended. She always tried to think of something to take that might cheer her up: a magazine, her favourite dark chocolate selection box, a bottle of perfume. One day, she gathered up her mother's knitting that had been left in the sitting room, on the coffee table, and put it in one of the plastic bags given away free at the supermarket in town. Her mother had glanced at it, with a pitying and – Ellen felt – a rather self-important look.

'I'm not well enough to do that. Why did you bring knitting?'

Ellen crumbled inside. She knew her mother's disapproving look well. It made her feel frightened. Panic swirled round her heart.

One day they had stepped outside into the hospital grounds that were about the size of a hockey pitch, but not well kept. The grass was overgrown and interspersed with patches of brown. A few trees

– a beech, an ash – were scattered unevenly around. Stony patches of earth were planted with straggly shrubs. The two of them sat side by side on a bench and Ellen noticed that her mother's face looked set and stern. She saw lines that she had not seen before in a face that was pale without make up.

'I can't stay here, Ellen. It's not doing me any good. You need to talk to the doctor.'

'They won't listen to me, Mum. I'm a child, remember. I'm sure they're doing the best they can. I'll talk to grandpa.'

'I don't like taking all these pills. They make my head feel funny.' Grandpa had been firm.

'Your mother can be very stubborn. I'm sure the doctors know what they're doing. We just have to wait and see.'

That night, they ate potatoes and pork chops. Grandpa wasn't a very skilled cook. The potatoes were lumpy and the chops were tough, but Ellen felt herself unwind as she sat with a tray on her knee watching the news on television. Grandpa didn't make any demands on her. After supper he said, 'I know, let's go for a walk round the lake. The fresh air will do you good.'

Straight away they had put on coats, climbed into Grandpa's car and driven the two miles from the house to Old Wheeler Lake, on the edge of town. Ellen had come here often as a child. Sometimes with grandpa, sometimes with her mother. She even thought she remembered walking round the lake, when she was very small, with her father. Or maybe she just remembered her mother telling her that that is what they used to do. That evening the ground was wet and the path between the trees that surrounded the lake was slippery with fallen leaves. Ellen wished she'd put wellington boots on.

'I used to push you in your pushchair round here when you were small, Ellen,' said grandpa. 'Then, when you got bigger, you used to run around yourself and, sometimes, you paddled in the shallow water at the side of the lake. Look – there are the stepping stones. Do you remember slipping on them and falling in? We had to bundle you into the back of the car and take you home – you were sopping wet!'

Ellen did remember. Her mother had shouted, 'She's in,' and run to the water, but grandpa had got there first. He had waded across the pebbles, grabbed both her arms, pulled her out and put her into the car. Once she was settled in the back seat, with a tartan picnic rug, her mother's relief turned to anger.

'What were you doing, you silly girl, running across those stones, right into the lake? I told you to be careful. You're the clumsiest girl I know.'

Ellen pushed the memory away and tried to return her attention to the class. Mrs Brown was talking.

'For homework, girls, I would like you to re-read the act we have just read and make notes about what you have learnt about the character of Macbeth. I'll be asking you to share your ideas with the rest of the class next lesson.'

Ellen realised she hadn't heard a word that had been said in the lesson. She was going to have to read the act again, at home… no, not at home, at Aunt Christabel's house… but where? At her real home she had been used to doing her homework in the tiny sitting room, resting her books on her lap. Her mother wouldn't let her watch the television as she worked. Sometimes, she would bring her cups of tea. She wouldn't be able to work in the sitting room at Aunt Christabel's. It was too public and large enough to contain two comfortable sofas, a coffee table, several book cases and a television. Ellen couldn't imagine settling down there, with this strange family around her, trying to concentrate on *Macbeth*. What if someone else wanted to sit there? So her room maybe? It was quite small and there wasn't a chair or a table. She would have to sit on the bed.

'Very well, girls. I'll see you next week.'

Ellen remembered that she was monitor and hurriedly put her things away in her desk before moving to the front to carry Mrs Brown's books.

'Thank you, dear.'

Mrs Brown looked shrewdly at Ellen. As they walked up the stairs to the staff room together she said quietly, 'Let me know if I can help in any way, Ellen. These next few weeks are going to be very hard for you.' Ellen felt a tear prick her eye again but managed to hold it back.

'Thank you, Mrs Brown,' she said.

The cold, numb feeling that Ellen was used to now stayed with her. She went to her lessons but heard very little. At the end of the day, she walked down the stairs to the cool, dank cloakroom. Sheila was there again, with her best friend Janice. Janice wore her hair short with a full fringe over her eyes. Like Sheila, she wore a skirt that was very tight, dark stockings and expensive shoes. Ellen watched her pinning her beret as far back onto her head as she could with hair pins. She looked stylish and confident and Ellen was aware again that her own skirt flared too much. Her mother had made it for her, as she made most of her clothes, to save money. Ellen knew it wasn't quite fashionable and made her look dowdy. Sheila and Janice looked at her briefly as she took her coat from the peg and fastened her buttons then they turned away.

'Are you going to the club on Friday?' asked Sheila.

'Probably – depends if Malcolm is going to be there,' replied Janice, looking self-important and pleased with herself.

As usual – or even more than usual – Ellen felt dowdy and unsophisticated. Just after her fifteenth birthday she remembered trying on a dress she had bought, secretly, at a cheap fashion shop in town. At school, she had heard the other girls talking about the shop and describing the new 'midi' skirts they were buying. Ellen's new green dress hung loosely around her. She had used some birthday money that she had saved to buy it. Somehow she felt her mother wouldn't approve so she had waited until the house was empty before trying it on in front of the long mirror in her mother's bedroom. Using a hand mirror she had tried to see what the frock looked like from behind and was turning and wriggling, trying to get a good view of her back, when her mother came in. She had laughed.

'Good heavens, Ellen. Where did you get that? Have you got to the age where you're looking in the mirror all the time? Green isn't really your colour, you know.'

Ellen had felt her face flush and then she had rushed out of the room, tearing the dress off as quickly as she could. She hadn't felt confident about socialising with friends after that and, in any case, her mother had been nervous about letting her out in the evenings. But most Friday evenings Sheila and her racy friends met up with boys from the Queen Mary School. The girls wore low-necked dresses, high heels and strong perfume and seemed completely at ease with the boys. Ellen wondered if she would ever catch up with them. What would Aunt Christabel's rules be about going out? Ellen was sure she would have some.

As she headed for the stairs again Ellen heard a voice. Jennifer was there, looking friendly and comforting in her ordinary chain store skirt and cheap mac. She was sensible, clever and unassuming, and had a mother who quietly supported her while running the household on not very much money.

'Shall we go to the sweet shop and get a caramel whirl on the way to bus?' asked Jennifer. 'I've got some pocket money left. I'll treat you.'

'Yes please, but are you sure?'

Ellen knew that money was tight in Jennifer's household. But her aunt and uncle had given her none. What would happen about that? she wondered to herself. She had the money that grandpa had slipped into her hand before he returned to London. 'For emergencies,' he had said, but she didn't want to touch that. It felt like her only link to independence.

Caramel whirls were their favourite treat. They ate the chocolate at the top first, letting it melt in their mouths, and then sucked out the light whipped cream filling. Then they nibbled the rest of the chocolate shell until only the walnut at the bottom was left. They didn't really like these, but ate them anyway. When they'd finished, Jennifer said, 'Are you OK?'

'It's funny. I feel as if I'm not really here.'

'Do you want to come and stay the night on Saturday? We can go to the youth club.'

'Oh, yes please, but I'll have to ask Aunt Christabel I suppose.'

'What's she like?'

'Stiff, posh. I think she means to be kind, but she's very bossy. I don't know where I'm supposed to be when I'm there, or what I'm supposed to say. There are these two boys – my cousins. David, the older one's at university so I haven't really seen him. The other is really posh too and behaves as if he can have whatever he likes.'

The girls separated at the bus station. Jennifer joined the queue for the number 12 and Ellen walked to a stop on the other side. She was pretty certain that this was the right bus, but not entirely sure she knew which stop to get off at. When the conductor came she asked him: 'Half to Pendal, please. Where do I get off for Southcote Road?'

'I'll tell you when we get there, love.'

FIVE

The journey took twenty-five minutes, longer that her usual ride home, and Ellen sat staring out of the window, watching the shops getting ready to close and the river flowing darkly under the bridge as they left the centre of town. Terraced streets gave way to more expansive roads with large houses set back from the road. This felt like another country to Ellen. Around her, passengers were talking about their day at work, what their children were doing, what they were planning to have to eat. The talk sounded ordinary, solid, relaxed. Ellen wondered if she'd ever feel like that again.

'Your stop's next, love,' said the conductor and Ellen stood up, swaying with the bus. As she walked up Southcote Road she realised that she didn't have a key to her aunt's house. Presumably there would be somebody in? A light was on when she reached the house and she knocked, tentatively. Marcus opened the door. He was still wearing his school suit, but his tie was undone and he had no shoes.

'Oh, hello. We must ask mother to get you a key. Do come in.'

Marcus seemed neither pleased nor displeased to see her. She felt that he scarcely registered her presence. What should she do now?

'Is Aunt Christabel here?' she asked.

'No, she's gone to the shops, back in a minute. Make yourself a cup of tea if you want.'

Marcus disappeared back into the sitting room, from where Ellen could hear sounds of some loud music she didn't recognise. She didn't know what to do, so went upstairs to her bedroom. At home, she would have changed out of her uniform into something more comfortable so she hunted through her clothes and found some old trousers and a warm jumper. She wondered what time Aunt Christabel served dinner and what they called that evening meal here. At Jennifer's house it was a pretty hearty meal – sausages, eggs, beans – but called tea. Ellen had noticed that some of the girls at school called it 'supper'. She didn't know what to do while she waited. At home, she would have allowed herself to play some music, or read a magazine or watch television for a while before starting her homework. None of these were options here so she pulled out her copy of *Macbeth* from her school bag and started to read the scenes they had been working on in English that morning. She lay on the bed, a notebook next to her, and was just getting involved when there was a knock on the door.

'Ellen, are you in there?'

Before Ellen could answer, Aunt Christabel appeared.

'Ah, there you are. Come and give me a hand with putting the shopping away and getting the dinner on, will you, dear?'

'OK,' said Ellen and followed her aunt downstairs.

As she walked past the sitting room door Ellen could see that Marcus was still sprawled on the sofa, arms above his head, a glass of what looked like beer by his side.

'Right, dear,' said Aunt Christabel. 'I've got the bags out of the car, we just need to carry them into the house. If you could put the things away, I'll make a start on preparing the chicken.'

So Ellen obediently picked up two of the carrier bags and carried them through to the kitchen. A pale evening sun shone through the conservatory windows onto the dining table. The kitchen, by the side of the house, was dark in contrast. Ellen put her bags down and wondered what to do next. Where did things go?

'Now, dear, I'll put the food away that needs to go in the fridge. Could you take this bag – and this – and empty them in the pantry. You'll see where things go.'

Ellen picked up the two bags and opened a door. It led to a small cupboard, with brooms and a vacuum cleaner inside. She closed the door hurriedly and tried another. That was it. A small room, like a corridor with a door, was lined with shelves and on each shelf were stacked groceries: cereals, rice, tins, packets of spaghetti. She started to empty her bag and match the contents to those of the shelves. As she did it, she recalled the shopping habits at her house. Often her mother had been too tired or depressed to shop and would wait for Ellen to get home from school and ask her to go to the tiny shop at the bottom of her street that also served as a post office.

'Right,' said her aunt. 'You'll soon find out where things go. Now, let's get started on dinner. You peel the potatoes and I'll start cooking the chicken.'

An even louder beat of music emerged from the living room.

'Hey, Mum, when's dinner ready? I'm starving,' shouted Marcus.

'Not long now, darling,'

Ellen wondered what to do. At home, her mother had always used a small, sharp knife to peel potatoes – if they had really needed peeling. Mostly she left the skins on. What should she use here? She felt too nervous to ask. Aunt Christabel, her grey patterned dress covered in a pink floral apron, looked as if she expected Ellen to know. Ellen found she had to pluck up her courage to speak to her.

'Is there a special knife to use, please?' she stammered.

'Good heavens, no, use a potato peeler. It's in the drawer beside the sink.'

Ellen had no idea what a potato peeler looked like, let alone how to use one. What was she going to do? Eventually she said, 'I'm sorry, Aunt Christabel, I've never used a potato peeler before. What does it look like?' Aunt Christabel looked irritated and, Ellen thought, a little scornful.

'Good heavens. Didn't you peel potatoes at your house? Leave it to me. The meat will be cooked before the potatoes are ready if we don't hurry up.'

Aunt Christabel opened the drawer, took out the potato peeler and expertly peeled the vegetables.

'You go and set the table.'

Ellen walked through to the conservatory and wondered what to do. Where were the knives and forks? Did she need to put out table mats? Plates? She heard the door slam and the sound of her uncle's voice. Her aunt went out into the hall to greet him so she was alone. What should she do? There was a dresser at the side of the room and she opened all the doors and shelves hurriedly. She found some heavy, silver forks and knives with yellowish handles and set them out round the table, one knife and fork at each of four places. Then she found some small plates and put them next to the forks. It was nearly seven o'clock. At home, she would have been half way through her homework by now.

'Ready boys,' called Aunt Christabel from the kitchen and Marcus and her uncle walked into the conservatory and took the same seats that they had at breakfast. Aunt Christabel entered the room carrying a large dish.

'Ellen – I need a table mat. Quickly please.'

Ellen went back to the sideboard and started hunting through drawers.

'In the right hand drawer,' said Marcus, not moving from his seat.

Ellen found the mats and put one on the table.

'More than that,' said Aunt Christabel. 'I'll need somewhere to put the vegetables. And I see we haven't got side knives. Could you get those at the same time?'

Ellen hunted through the cutlery drawer and found four more knives. She walked round the table, putting one at each place.

'I can see you're going to need a bit of education, Ellen,' said her uncle.

Aunt Christabel served the meat and passed the plates round the table. As soon as he received his, Uncle Walter began to help himself to vegetables. Ellen thought again about the suppers she'd had on a tray in front of the television. Was it going to be like this every night? She remembered the homework waiting for her and felt helpless and scared. How could she get it done? What trouble would she be in if she didn't do it? And if she lost control of her work what else would she lose control of? Would the life she had known until now slip away completely?

'How was work, dear?' asked Aunt Christabel, turning to her husband.

Her Uncle Walter had recently taken a new job, working for the council in a neighbouring local authority. He was responsible for the housing department and had been brought in to make cuts to services and reorganise the department. Before supper, he had loosened his blue tie and removed the jacket of his grey suit. A short, broad-shouldered man, with thinning hair, he seemed to Ellen to take up more than his fair share of space at the table.

'The place is a shambles,' he said. 'No work ethic, far too many staff, secretaries with nothing to do but paint their nails all day. I'm going to need to make some big changes.'

'Well, just the sort of thing you're good at, dear,' said his wife.

Marcus said, 'People should be providing their own houses, not expecting tax payers to give them free homes for life. It's time people got off their backsides and did a proper day's work.'

Ellen thought of her own council house and her neighbours, many of whom were coal miners who worked long hours for little pay. She wanted to say something, but couldn't find the words.

Towards the end of the first course of the meal she glanced at her watch again: a quarter to eight. When was she going to get her homework done? She felt a tightening panic around her chest, a bubbling, resentful feeling. She had to say something. Why was she so scared? Eventually, she plucked up some courage.

'Excuse me, Aunt Christabel, but I need to do my homework. Please could I leave the table?'

Aunt Christabel looked surprised and not pleased.

'I do like the family to be together at the evening meal, Ellen. And then there will be the dishes to do.'

'What homework have you got?' asked Marcus.

'English mainly. We're doing *Macbeth*. I need to read an act and answer some questions. It will take at least a couple of hours.'

'Goodness – I never spent that long on English.'

Aunt Christabel frowned.

'Well, just this once. But in future it would be best if you got down to your homework straight after school. What time do you finish? Three-thirty?'

Her aunt's irritation frightened Ellen. It reminded her of times at home when her mother had been feeling bad and got annoyed with everything. Once, she remembered, when she was quite small – about six or seven – she had sensed her mother's misery. They had been getting ready to go shopping together and her mother couldn't find her purse. In her irritation she had thrown her bag across the room. Ellen's memory of her mother then was of a dark, looming figure who might at any moment do harm. When they had returned from the shops, Ellen tried hard to think of something to cheer her mother up. She had gone into their small back garden with the blunt scissors from her pencil case and cut some bright red peonies from the garden; they were her mother's favourite flower. In a kitchen drawer she had found a paper doily and wrapped it round the flowers to make them look like a proper present. Then she had gone to find her.

'Got you a present, Mum.'

Her mother had stared furiously.

'You stupid child. You should never pick peonies – they don't last. You've ruined them now. And they're my favourite flower. You're a very naughty girl.'

The same fear and sense of being wrong overcame Ellen now. She continued to sit at the table, saying nothing, while the rest of the family finished their chicken.

'Right. Help me with the plates, Ellen, and then I'll get the apple crumble out of the oven.'

'Wow, apple crumble, Mum!' said Marcus.

He and his father continued their conversation about football as they ate. When they had finished eating, Ellen silently gathered up the plates and took them into the kitchen. Along with the fear a cloud of resentment, green and misty, was filling her chest. Was it going to be like this always?

'I'll wash and you dry, Ellen,' said Aunt Christabel.

Ellen didn't reply. It was as if her anger and frustration were blocking the words. What would happen if she let them out? For a moment, she imagined a flame leaving her mouth and tearing round the kitchen, setting everything alight. But she didn't speak. Instead, she picked up a tea towel and began to dry the pots. She was learning quickly where everything went. As she was finishing, her aunt made coffee and took it through to the sitting room where Uncle Walter and Marcus had settled down in front of the television again. Ellen wondered what to do. Should she just slip away to her bed? Or go and say goodnight? What would her mother have said? She was always meticulous about social etiquette. 'If you go and stay in another person's house you should always strip the bed before you leave,' she used to say. Ellen took a deep breath, opened the sitting room door and put her head round it. She tried to make her words sound polite.

'I'm just going upstairs. I'm going to finish my homework and then go to bed.'

'Very well, dear,' said her aunt.

'You'll need to get the bus to school in the morning,' said her uncle. 'I won't be driving that way. Goodnight.'

'Goodnight.'

It was late – quarter to nine – by the time Ellen got up to her room and started her homework. She was tired, and although she finished answering all the questions, she realised that her work was superficial and not properly thought through.

'It'll have to do,' she said to herself.

Her clock said eleven when she finally got into bed. The light out, she lay waiting, eyes closed, for the same three terrible moments, the sharpest memories of that dreadful night, to pass in front of her eyes.

– – –

The next day, Thursday, Ellen arrived at school a little late. She hadn't been sure how long the bus journey would take. She rushed down the stone steps to the basement cloakroom and found Jennifer there, putting her coat on a peg. It was so good to see someone she knew and could trust.

'Can you come on Saturday?' Jennifer asked.

'I hope so. I haven't dared ask yet. Aunt Christabel is funny – I don't really know how to talk to her.'

'Ask her as soon as you get home and tell me tomorrow.'

Lessons were a blur for Ellen that day. The teachers seemed far away and she couldn't focus on what they were saying. The other girls, apart from Jennifer, seemed wary of her, as if they didn't know whether or not to speak. Ellen, for her part, felt as though she wasn't really there. The world around her looked grey and misty. Her only experience of colour came from a sense of her mother's presence, which seemed to drift around in the space above her head. Everything felt wrong and dangerous.

As she got the bus home, she imagined taking that other journey, the one she'd taken every night since she started at the High School. The number 20 from the bus station, the walk past the shops up Ashley Road, the key in the door of 11 Fossett Crescent, the moment's hesitation while she found out whether or not the door was double locked and therefore whether or not her mother was in. If she were in, the trepidation. What mood was she in? Would she be greeted with a cheery 'Hello darling, shall I make you a cup of tea?' Or would she be angry about something – something which, Ellen felt, was certain to be her fault?

Ellen thought about how she had often felt frightened as a child. There was one time when she had been selected to join a gym team that was going to do a display for some distinguished visitors to the school. Ellen was good at gym, fearless. She loved the feeling of power the leap over the box on her hands gave her, and the sense of mastering her body that came from leaning over backwards into a crab. She had put her blue Aertex gym shirt, with her other dirty washing, into the laundry basket a few days before. Her mother normally did the wash on Tuesdays. This was Thursday. As usual, she went home for lunch. She was feeling cheerful that day. Her English essay had got a good mark and she would be getting out of lessons that afternoon because of the gym display.

'I'm home, Mum,' she shouted cheerfully as she walked in. 'Can I collect my gym shirt for this afternoon? Is it ready?'

Her mother's face had become contorted with anger.

'What do you mean "is it ready?" Is what ready?'

'My gym shirt. You remember, Mum. We're doing a display this afternoon. I'm on the team. I told you.'

'How dare you?' her mother had shouted. 'No, it's not clean. Do you realise how busy I am?'

And then her mother had swung her arm wide and hit Ellen on the back, hard. Ellen had gasped. She was determined not to cry. She went into the kitchen, rummaged through the dirty washing basket, found her dirty gym shirt, folded it as neatly as she could and immediately left the house. At the bus stop, her heart thumped. What should she do after school? Should she find somewhere to stay?

– – –

Tonight, though, she had no reason to fear what she would find at home. She wasn't going home. She was going to Aunt Christabel's house. She felt the dread work up from her stomach to her chest, where it settled, crowding the air from her lungs. Would anyone be in the house? What should she say if they were? She had her own key now and she put it tentatively in the deadlock. It wasn't locked: that meant someone was in. Ellen took a deep breath, readying herself to meet whoever was there. She hung her coat on the rack and tried to work out who the other coats hanging there belonged to, but couldn't. Then she pushed the sitting room door to her left tentatively. No sound. She went in but the room was empty. As she left, heading up the stairs to put her school bag in her bedroom, she heard her aunt calling from the kitchen.

'In here, dear. Let's have a cup of tea. I think it's time we had a talk.'

Ellen's heart, already beating too fast, began to pound even harder. A talk? She turned round on the stairs and walked through to the kitchen, her satchel still hanging over her left shoulder.

'There, dear, I've just made some tea. Come through to the sitting room. I've put a spoonful of sugar in yours.'

Ellen didn't take sugar and hated sweet tea, but unable to find the words to say so politely, she took her cup and followed her aunt into the sitting room.

'Now, dear. I know it must seem very strange to you being in a new house and I know that what has happened has been very distressing. But you know your mother was very ill. It's perhaps not so much of a surprise. I want you to be very brave and not get too upset. Look forward. Never any point dwelling on the past. You're at a good school – you'll be able to get some further training when you leave. Perhaps you could train to be a secretary next year? Or maybe a nurse? Have you thought about what you want to do?'

Ellen opened her mouth to protest. In her head she said, 'I'm not leaving school now. That was never the plan.' But the words wouldn't come so her aunt carried on.

'You're very lucky to be living in a lovely house like this and your uncle and I will take care of you until you can go out to work and earn enough to keep yourself. I think you do your GCEs this year? So, maybe secretarial college after that. We'll see. In the meantime, treat here as your home. I expect you to help with the chores and keep your room clean and tidy. Your uncle, as you know, has just got a new job and is very busy. He mustn't be worried about anything – we girls must look after him. And the boys, of course! Marcus is doing A levels this year so he'll be working very hard. We must try and keep the house calm and cheerful so he doesn't get stressed. Now, do you have any questions?'

Ellen felt panic surge in her chest, together with resentment and anger. Secretarial college! Nurse! She was going to read philosophy at university. She and her mother had discussed it often. What should she say…? In her head, the words came fast and furious.

'I'm as good as any boy. Why should you assume that I can't go to university? Or be a doctor if I want? Or a nuclear physicist? What you're saying is wrong. Mum wouldn't have stood for it. I'm not going to be put down like this. You can't tell me what to do. I'm just as clever as your sons – cleverer probably. Neither of them got scholarships. You had to pay for their education and I know that Marcus had to retake his O levels because he didn't do well enough. Everyone assumes that boys are best and cleverer and deserve everything. But it's not true…'

None of the words came out though. Instead, Ellen sat silently, looking at her tea. She couldn't bring herself to look at her aunt. Eventually, she said, 'No… oh, one thing. My friend has invited me to stay with her on Saturday night and I'd like to go. Is that all right?'

Her aunt looked taken aback. 'Oh, I'm surprised you want to get away from us so soon. Where does your friend live? How will you get there?'

'Dartwith. I can get the Grisley bus. It stops near her house.'

'On second thoughts, I'll ask your uncle if we can drive you over. I think we should meet your friend's parents if you're going to stay the night. What's her name?'

'Jennifer'

'And what does her father do?'

'He's a miner.'

Ellen could tell that her aunt was a little thrown by this. She knew, because her mother had told her how some people in Fineston, people who lived in big houses like this one and who tried to talk without the flat northern vowels that Ellen was used to, looked down on miners. This time, her fury gave her a flare of courage and she was able to speak through her resentment.

'Jennifer is my friend. She's been the best friend I've had. She's going to be a doctor. Her dad is a lovely man, kind and clever. He makes me laugh. I'd really like to go and see them.'

Aunt Christabel looked taken aback.

'Well, I'll see what Uncle Walter can do. But I can't promise. I've told you how busy he is at the moment.'

'I can easily get there myself. I don't need to trouble anyone.'

Aunt Christabel's chest rose and her lips narrowed.

'I've told you already, Ellen. I think we should meet the parents of anyone you are going to stay with. I'll talk to Uncle Walter after we've eaten. Now it's time to start getting dinner ready. We're having a casserole tonight so it needs to go in the oven straight away. Please come and help me peel the vegetables.'

After the meal was prepared Ellen went up to her room and spread her homework out on the bed. Maths tonight and history. History was reading, so she could do that later in bed. She took out her maths text and exercise books and spread them on the bed. Usually she enjoyed solving the problems, focusing her mind hard until she could almost feel her brain working. But this evening she couldn't concentrate. She kept imagining what it would have been like at her house at this time. Mum would have been making something to eat and listening to the radio. On a good night she would just get on with it and present Ellen proudly with a steak and kidney pie, ham with cheese sauce or mince. If it were not such a good night there might be irritated shouts from the kitchen and fish fingers, possibly slightly burnt, with baked beans and sliced bread. Tonight, Ellen felt she would have enjoyed even very burnt fish if she could have been back on the Winslet Estate. Home.

It wasn't her home, though, not any more. It was the place – she had to somehow believe – where her mother had taken a piece of rope, tied a loop in it, put the noose around her head and, she supposed, jumped from the stairs. Most of the time this thought didn't penetrate the cloud that surrounded Ellen, the dark and heavy fog that separated her from the rest of the world. When it did, like a tiny thrust of light, she wondered about the practicalities. Didn't the knot on the rope need to be a slip knot, the sort that she'd learnt to do in her short time as a girl guide? Otherwise, how would the rope close tight around her mother's neck? How did she fix the rope to the stairs? How did she get into the right position to jump? It seemed impossible that her impractical mother, who knew nothing of ropes and knots, would have worked out how to do this. So it couldn't really have happened – even though people said it had.

Ellen had thought about hanging before. She had been eight or nine when the death penalty was abolished and she remembered her mother talking about it with a neighbour, a man who lived two doors away and worked as a dustbin man for the council. The discussion had grown heated; her mother had been strongly in favour of the abolition and the neighbour against.

'Death's too good for some of these buggers,' he'd said.

The argument was fiercely fought in Fineston because executions were carried out in a nearby gaol. Ellen recalled one day, at primary school, hearing the other children talking in a scared but excited way about a hanging scheduled for that day.

'They're going to hang someone today,' they whispered to each other. To Ellen, it had seemed as if an invisible mist hung over the town that everyone sensed.

— — —

Eventually she had to go downstairs. She understood now that it was her job to set the table and help carry the dishes through from the kitchen. Her uncle was not in a good mood. He and Marcus were, as usual, watching the television as Ellen set the table. She could hear her uncle talking to the set.

'Bloody ridiculous. Why make us close perfectly good schools for some socialist notion that everyone can be the same?'

Ellen understood that he was talking about the Labour government's commitment to closing grammar and secondary modern schools and replacing them with comprehensives. Her mother had talked about this often. Ellen remembered when Joyce from next door had got the results of her eleven-plus exam, a couple of years before she herself had taken the test. Joyce's mother and her own had had an unusually long conversation over the fence between the two houses.

'She wasn't herself that day. It was t'day after our Arthur had gone off with his regiment for t'first time. She were right upset,' said Mrs White. 'It's not fair – Joyce is a clever girl. She's brains of family – always got top marks.'

Ellen's mother had sympathised. She had told Mrs White that she thought it was wrong that children should be separated out at eleven on the basis of a single test. Ellen remembered her mother telling her that a system that depended on a test meant that children from well-off families always had an advantage because their parents coached them, or paid for tutors. Working class kids were just as clever as middle class ones. Why shouldn't they have a chance to succeed? Ellen knew that her mother had had to leave school at fourteen and resented it all her life. Uncle Walter was still muttering when he came to the dinner table.

'Bloody socialists. We've got damn good schools here in Fineston and this Labour council is going to do what the government says and destroy them. Grammar schools for bright children whose parents can't afford to send them to private schools. Secondary moderns for those who are never going to be academic. Perfectly good system. Why waste all that money? And how are the bright ones ever going to succeed when they are being held back by the thickies? You wait, now I'm chair of our Conservative Party here in town, those Labour idiots are going to get a run for their money.'

'I know, dear,' said Aunt Christabel, 'but you know what this council is like. Things would be very different if you were in charge – or me for that matter.'

Marcus grinned at his mother.

'Definitely different if you were there! Things would be properly organised then! Why didn't you do something like that, ma?'

'Oh, women didn't go out to work when I was young. We stayed at home and looked after our children…' Aunt Christabel's voice trailed away and Ellen noticed a thoughtful look in her eyes, which disappeared as Marcus continued.

'Well, anyway, I can't imagine what it must be like being in a class with thickos. How would you ever learn anything? And we need people to mend the roads and sweep the streets. People like us aren't going to do it, are we?'

'They'll be wanting to turn your High School into a comprehensive next, Ellen!' said Uncle Walter and the others laughed. Ellen knew that her school was a bit different. It was a direct grant school which meant it was partly independent, and girls like her only got there because they won scholarships. The parents of most of the girls there paid fees. She couldn't see why her school shouldn't become a comprehensive too.

Ellen felt her heart race faster. She strongly wanted to disagree with her uncle. There was so much she could say. Words circled round in her head, but she couldn't get them out. She looked at the table as Uncle Walter held forth.

'And the expense. Do they realise how much it is going to cost to convert schools, or even build new ones? Not to mention the upheaval of reorganising all the staff. The cost to the rate payers will be huge. This is England, not the Soviet Union.'

Once or twice there was a fraction of a pause in the conversation and Ellen tensed, ready to speak, feeling, as she did so, that her face was turning pink. No one was looking at her though so the conversation continued without her.

Later, as Aunt Christabel and she were clearing the dishes from the table, she remembered that no one had mentioned her visit to Jennifer's on Saturday. This time she was determined to speak. She chose her words carefully.

'Aunt Christabel, I wonder if you'll be able to ask Uncle Walter this evening if I can go to Jennifer's on Saturday please?'

Her aunt looked cross. 'Well, I suppose if you're determined to go, we'll have to drive you there.'

Ellen was discomfited but her desire to see her friend was so strong that she was determined to stand her ground. 'Thank you. Can I let Jennifer know what time please? I need to let her mother know.'

'It will have to be about five, after we've been shopping. I hope it's not too far away.'

SIX

It was five o'clock on Saturday afternoon. Aunt Christabel, newly returned from shopping, closed the door behind her.

'Ah, Ellen. Just help me with these. You know where things go now. When you've finished your uncle and I will drive you over to your friend's house.'

Ellen obediently began to put away the food. It was more a question of doing it than 'helping' her aunt who was in the sitting room urging her uncle to get his coat.

'Do we have to take her?' Ellen heard him say crossly. 'There are plenty of buses and she's not a child.'

'Yes, Walter, we do. It's important that we know who she's mixing with. This friend of hers may be at the High School but she lives on a council estate – and a rather rough one. If that girl gets in with the wrong sort she could cause us no end of trouble.'

Ellen seethed, thinking of her clever, kind, hardworking friend. But she was to get away tonight, so she said nothing. When she'd finished putting the food away she went upstairs and put her toothbrush and nightdress into her school bag, after emptying out her books. She didn't have another bag. Then she went downstairs.

'I'm ready, Aunt Christabel.'

Uncle Walter, looking irritated, took the car keys from the hook by the front door and went out into the driveway. Ellen followed and got into the back of the car, watching as Uncle Walter drummed his fingers on the steering wheel. Aunt Christabel joined them a few moments later and they set off.

The car soon picked up the main road and the route of the bus that Ellen had always taken when she went to visit Jennifer. The houses, set back from the road, were protected by high hedges beyond which you could glimpse broad drives and carefully planted gardens. They passed the lake where Ellen and her grandfather had walked when she was young then, after a right turn, they began to climb a hill into a small village. The houses on each side of the narrow streets were small, semi-detached and pebble-dashed. They reminded Ellen of her house, her home. The houses here were identical, all built as 'homes for heroes' after the First World War. From the top of the hill, the huge black wheel perched on a stern scaffold at the pit head could be seen clearly in the evening light.

Uncle Walter's Rover was too big for the narrow street and when he parked it outside 52 Garton Crescent Ellen worried that no other vehicle would be able to pass by. Aunt Christabel didn't seem at all concerned.

'Come along, Ellen,' she said as she walked briskly up the path to the front door.

Ellen paused to collect her bag. She heard the house door open and her aunt's loud voice.

'Good evening. Mrs Sugden, I presume? So pleased to meet you. I'm Mrs Ash, Ellen's aunt. So kind of you to invite her to stay. Is your husband at home?'

Ellen had reached the front door by the time this speech was over. She saw the nervous, shy and puzzled look on Mrs Sugden's kind face. She felt her dear friend's mother's discomfiture as if it were her own. Mrs Sugden smoothed down the floral patterned apron she was wearing and then ran her fingers through her permed grey curls.

'Oh, 'ello,' she said. 'Very kind of you to bring Ellen over.'

There was a pause and silence. Ellen waited for Aunt Christabel to move, to say goodbye and leave, but she did not.

'Jennifer'll be back in a minute,' said Mrs Sugden eventually. 'She's just finishing up a delivery. We've got this big job delivering leaflets for that new mail order factory.'

Ellen knew that Mrs Sugden made a little money putting leaflets advertising local businesses through people's letter boxes. Jennifer sometimes helped her mother and Ellen had too. The money had been useful and it was fun working with her friend.

'There's another job coming in next week, Ellen,' said Mrs Sugden. 'If you're interested in earning a bit of extra pocket money you could help us.'

Aunt Christabel cut in quickly. 'I don't think so, thank you. That wouldn't be suitable for Ellen.'

A look of hurt passed across Mrs Sugden's face and her cheeks coloured slightly. Ellen's anger at her aunt's rudeness and her desire to protect her friend overcame her fear.

'I'd like to, Aunt Christabel. It's fun and I could do with some pocket money. Mum used to let me.'

Aunt Christabel's eyes flashed. She looked furious.

'We'll talk about this later, Ellen,' she said, turning briskly away. 'Goodbye. I assume you'll make your own way home. Be back by six – and no later – tomorrow.'

She walked down the front path without a backward glance. The car door slammed loudly and the Rover set off too quickly down the narrow street. Ellen turned to Mrs Sugden, determined to try to make up for her aunt's rudeness.

'I… I… I'm sorry…'

'Don't worry, love. Come in and mek yourself at home. I'll put t'kettle on.'

The two of them settled into the worn armchairs. The patterned covers were a little frayed but clean. A small television was propped high in one corner of the room and a folding table was set back against one wall. In another corner a budgerigar perched on a swing in its cage.

'Are you all right, love?' asked Mrs Sugden. 'It's terrible what 'appened to yer mum. Such a lovely woman. And you such a good daughter to her. She can't 'ave 'ad an easy life.'

Ellen felt the tears rising. Mostly in the days since the death she had been numb, not even having to make an effort to not think about what had happened. It was as if her body were encased in a steel frame that held her together. The greyness of the metal echoed the greyness of the world around her. She didn't think about the past. That was a different world, a different place, and what had happened had probably happened to someone else.

'Remember though, lass,' Mrs Sugden was talking again, 'people mek their own decisions. There's nowt you could have done – and you mustn't go thinking there were. None of it were your fault.'

Ellen did start to cry then. Mrs Sugden passed her a handkerchief.

'It's a'right love. You 'ave a good cry.'

Mrs Sugden put a hand on Ellen's shoulder and the two sat quietly until her tears had quietened. Jennifer arrived soon afterwards, fresh-faced and bubbly after her exercise. The two girls smiled at each other and then went up to Jennifer's room to listen to their favourite Buddy Holly LP.

Jennifer said 'Shall we dance?' And she put two straight-backed chairs in the landing at the top of the stairs – a partner each. They kept bumping into each other in the tiny space and that made Ellen giggle.

'There's a band on at the youth club tonight,' said Jennifer tentatively when they sat down on the top stair to have a rest. 'They're supposed to be good. I wondered if you'd like to go. Or...'

Ellen sensed her friend's hesitancy and thought that she should try and please her, even though listening to music in a crowded hall was the last thing she wanted to do.

'OK – I can't go like this though.' Ellen was wearing old jeans and the grey round-necked jumper she always put on when she wanted to be comfortable.

'You can borrow something – what about my tie dye shirt?'

Normally, Ellen and Jennifer loved trying on different clothes. They were more or the less the same size and often swapped garments. Ellen remembered how that had felt and tried to behave as if she were enjoying herself in the same way they always had, but she felt as if her real self was far away, observing what was happening without any feeling. The friends tried on several outfits, and when they'd agreed on a blue and green shirt for Ellen, they set out for the youth group, which met in the community hall next to the Methodist church.

Ellen had been to dances there several times before. It was a scruffy room, with blue paint peeling from the walls and a rickety stage erected at one end. This evening the trestle tables and folding chairs had been stacked by the sides of the room and the lights had been dimmed. A single spotlight, covered in red cellophane, was positioned above a microphone stand. The band had started when they arrived. Two young men with long hair and guitars slung round their necks were shaking their heads as they sang 'It's just rock 'n' roll. It's just rock 'n' roll'. A drummer pounded behind them and Ellen felt the beat thud through the floor and up through her body as if it were her own heart thumping. All around, young people swayed and waved their arms, reaching over to shout into their friends' ears when they wanted to be heard. As more people arrived and the crowd pressed more tightly around them, Ellen felt a wave of panic surge through her.

'Jennifer – I'm sorry – can we go?'

Her friend looked at her but said only 'OK'.

— — —

That night, as usual, Ellen slept on a rubber mattress on the floor of Jennifer's tiny bedroom. With the two of them as well as the wardrobe and a chest of drawers there was no room to walk about or even to put a foot on the floor. Ellen felt safe and comfortable. She had stayed here often before and for a moment it was as though none of this had happened, as if time hadn't lurched forward and changed everything for ever. As she lay there she could hear voices, animated after a Saturday evening in the pub, and she imagined their owners strolling cheerfully home. Probably they'd watch television and make tea before going to bed late. She felt as if she were locked out of an ordinary life like that. Jennifer's voice broke into her thoughts.

'Ellen – are you OK? I've been thinking – since it happened – I haven't known what to say to you. Nothing seemed right. I just didn't know what to say... I'm sorry.'

'There isn't anything. I don't know what to say either. I can't really talk about it. Except it's horrible at my aunt's house so it's really nice to be here.'

'Well – come when you like. Mum won't mind.'

'Thanks.'

Soon afterwards, Ellen fell asleep, warmed by her friend's concern and the glimmer of a feeling it gave her that she wasn't completely alone.

SEVEN

Monday morning began as usual. Marcus came down after his parents, wearing his suit but with no tie.

'You're late, darling,' said Aunt Christabel as she placed a boiled egg in a silver cup onto his plate.

'Two please, ma, I'm starving.'

'There's another one coming. Here – have some toast.'

Ellen watched her cousin silently as he sliced the top off the egg and sprinkled salt liberally into the yoke. She felt invisible and found that comforting; she wasn't really here at all. When the phone rang, it seemed very far away, and she was only dimly aware of her aunt pushing her chair back and getting to her feet as she spoke.

'Good heavens, who can that be at this time of the morning?'

In the hall, Aunt Christabel picked up the phone. Ellen cut her slice of toast into two and then into four pieces. Maybe she would be able to eat one of them. She was lifting a piece to her mouth when she heard her name. Aunt Christabel was talking about her. Ellen immediately stiffened and began to listen intently to what her aunt was saying.

'Yes… I see… but Ellen does have school today. Are you sure this is wise?… I see, yes. In that case… Very well, ten o'clock… Goodbye.'

Uncle Walter and Marcus were discussing Saturday's football match when Aunt Christabel returned to the room.

'Well – that was rather unexpected. Ellen, that was Andrea – you remember, the social worker. She wants to take you round to your old house today, to see if there's anything there you want to keep. The council needs to relet the house and will have to have everything cleared.'

Ellen felt a dark, frightening shadow, like a fierce black bird, pass over her heart. Go back to Fossett Crescent? She couldn't. How could she open the gate, walk up that path, see the front door again… walk through it? But all her things were there – her books, her clothes, her records, her teddy bear. Not to mention her mother's things. She couldn't think about that. How could she decide what to keep? And what would happen if she didn't go? Would everything be piled into dustbin bags and thrown away? Her life… her mother's life…thrown out as rubbish?

Ellen became aware that there was silence in the room and the figures round the breakfast table were watching her. It was Aunt Christabel who spoke first.

'Would you like me to come with you, dear?'

'Thank you. No… yes… maybe…'

'I'll come and wait in the car. You can get me if you need help. Now, try and eat something, it will make you feel better; and then get your teeth done and everything before Andrea arrives.'

Time passed slowly. Ellen obediently cleaned her teeth and then sat on her bed. Afterwards, she couldn't have said how long she waited there, staring out of the window. At the bottom of the garden a wood pigeon nestled in the lower branches of an apple tree. A ginger cat turned over onto its back and wriggled in a patch of sunlight. How could these creatures be at such ease with themselves? In the distance Ellen heard the screech of a police car and remembered the time the emergency it signalled was hers. A few moments later there was a knock on the door. Ellen waited; Aunt Christabel was in charge here. Sure enough, a few moments later, she heard her aunt's voice.

'Ellen, dear, it's Andrea, the social worker. Come down.'

Ellen felt unsteady, as if everything inside her were loose; she was having to force herself to breathe. Downstairs in the hall, on the other side of the open door, the world looked colourless and jagged. Only Andrea's red Mini, come to take her back to Fossett Crescent and now parked in the road outside the house, had a clear form.

'Ellen – you remember me. How are you?'

Unable to speak, Ellen stood with her eyes lowered, saying nothing. Andrea continued.

'As I'm sure your aunt told you, I wanted to give you a chance to collect your things from your old house. The council need to put another family in there now, but it's important that you take what you want. I think, Mrs Ash, you're coming with us?' Andrea turned to Ellen's aunt. 'Shall we go? Do you mind sitting in the back, Ellen – your aunt will need more leg room.'

Obediently, Ellen followed her aunt and Andrea down the front path to the car and waited while Andrea unlocked it and pulled the back of the front seat forward so that Ellen could climb into the back. There was only just room for her knees. It felt strangely comforting to be in such a small space, as if she were in a safe hole, hiding from everything. She was aware of Andrea and her aunt discussing the plans for a new shopping centre in Fineston but made no effort to join the conversation and they didn't try and include her. Relieved, she stared out of the window. As the car passed through the centre of town and took the road out to her estate, following the same route that her bus from school had taken every day – that her bus had taken *that* day – she began to feel frightened. Would she be able to walk through that door again? Step into the house? The same illusion that had accompanied the funeral returned: her mother's presence seemed to be in the air around her.

A mile or so out of town, Andrea turned right into the estate and then left into Fossett Crescent. The street was so narrow that she had to park the Mini, small as it was, partly on the pavement to allow other cars to pass. Andrea held the door open as Ellen climbed out, leaving Aunt Christabel in the car.

'I'll be here if you need me,' her aunt called, so loudly that a man pushing his bicycle down the street in front of them turned round.

Ellen didn't reply but stepped forward to the unvarnished, dry wooden gate of number 11; it was as she remembered it, slightly loose on its rusted hinges. An old newspaper had blown over the fence onto the bare earth of the front garden. As she walked through the gate and up the path Ellen felt as if an angry grey shark was snapping at her heart with fierce, jagged teeth.

At the side of the house two stone steps led into a small porch. Ellen stared at the space where her front door had been. It was covered now in a sheet of corrugated iron held secure with a large padlock. The fear that had accompanied that last attempt she had made to open the door to her home overwhelmed her. She remembered the sound of the policeman battering the door and took a deep breath to steady herself.

'Ellen,' said Andrea gently, 'I've got the key to the padlock here.' And she passed Ellen, climbed the steps and put the key into the padlock. It didn't open immediately and Ellen heard Andrea muttering quietly to herself, 'Drat… come on… come on…'

Finally, the key turned and the padlock sprung open. Andrea removed it and pushed the door open. She went in first, and turning, held a hand out to Ellen. 'OK, Ellen – come in.'

It seemed strange that it was all still there. The small hall with the stairs that turned onto the landing above, the door to the cupboard in the stairwell that never shut properly, the low-hanging fringed lampshade. Andrea's voice jerked Ellen back to the present.

'Where would you like to start, Ellen? I think it's important that you take away anything you want to keep because we are going to have to empty the house. If you put it all by the door, here, I'll make sure it's packed up and sent to you at your aunt's house. Though if there's anything big, tell me and I'll put a label on it.'

'I don't know, I...' Ellen couldn't think. It was so strange being here again. Everything was so familiar and yet so, so far away, as if she had stepped into a dream. 'I'll go upstairs first.'

'OK. I'll wait here. If you need anything, just call.'

The bathroom seemed like the easiest room to enter first. There couldn't be too much to upset her in there. As she pushed the door open, though, the first thing she saw was the red, yellow and green striped towel she used for swimming hanging over a washing rack under the window. That towel had been her swimming towel for years, ever since her mother had first taken her to the Fineston Baths. Her swimming costume, she remembered, had been green and ruffled. It fastened with a bow at the back of her neck that sometimes came undone when she was in the pool. Her mother's costume had been black, with a halter neck. It had been such fun, having her mother pull her through the water at the shallow end of the pool, gradually encouraging her to try a stroke by herself. When she had finally learnt to dog paddle a whole width they had celebrated with an ice cream in the café that overlooked the water. She had been so proud – and her mother had been too. Did she need a towel? Probably not, but the feel of it was so familiar and just looking at it brought back so many memories. Ellen took it down from the rack and hung it over her arm.

Without making a conscious decision to do so, Ellen turned towards her bedroom as she left the bathroom. She pushed open the door slowly and stood still as the familiarity of the room seemed to pull her back to her old life. So much had changed since she had last been here. How could it still look the same? The single bed, with its blue nylon cover with the frill around the edge slipping off the bed. The dark blue curtains were drawn and the doors to the cupboards built in next to the boarded-up chimney breast were open. The bookcase that her father had made before he died stood against the wall opposite the window. By the bed stood a small table that was his handiwork too. On it was the black alarm clock that had woken her for school that morning. What if, for once, it hadn't gone off and she had stayed at home…?

Where to start? Ellen knew that this was her last – her only – chance to save the things she wanted. She would never step in this room again. Moving over to the window she opened the curtains a little and a beam of sunlight settled on the bookcase. Ellen saw the books she had loved, each one with its own atmosphere and memories. Her mother had read her *Peter Pan* over and over again at bed times and Ellen had flown to the Neverland with Peter and Wendy before falling asleep. Ellen reached out and took her copy of *Alice in Wonderland* from a bottom shelf and let it open at the page still marked with a folded piece of paper. A drawing of Alice holding the pig met her eyes and Ellen recalled how callous she had thought Alice to be, apparently not caring too much that a baby had been transformed into an ugly piglet. *'If you're going to turn into a pig, my dear, I'll have nothing more to do with you.'* Ellen had felt for the baby. It wasn't its fault that it had turned into a small ugly creature. Just as it wasn't her fault that her hair was too straight to do anything with other than plait, or that her feet grew too quickly and a new pair of sandals had to be given away soon after her mother had bought them. Her mother's annoyance had scared Ellen and the feeling swept over her again. It had been part of her life here, the fear that she would do or say something wrong, that she would make her mother angry and she would be alone.

Almost every book on this shelf, though, had been bought for her by her mother, who had wanted her to love reading and encouraged her to keep trying something new. Each week when she was younger they had gone together to the public library and she had chosen the four books she was allowed to borrow and read during the week.

The books were about lives that were so different from hers. There had been stories about young girls who owned ponies and won prizes at gymkhanas or who went to ballet school in London. With groups of adventurous teenagers who were seemingly free of adults she had climbed mountains, camped and rowed boats on lakes. Her mother had chosen books too; she would disappear up the wide wooden staircase to the adult library after leaving Ellen to explore the children's section. Afterwards, if her mother was in a good mood, the two of them would walk up the High Street to Frank's Café and order a coffee and an orange juice.

'Let's see what you've got, Ellen,' her mother would say, picking up a book. 'Ah, *Ballet school in London*! Time we went to see your grandpa again. I could do with some bright lights and the big city. Next time we go, shall we try and see some dancing?'

Excited, the two would plan a visit, adding things to the list of what they wanted to see: the zoo, Buckingham Palace, Madame Tussauds, before her mother laughed and said, 'Time and money, Ellen. We don't have enough of either – but let's go anyway.' Planning trips had been fun, and remembering her mother's elation on those occasions made Ellen ache even as she recalled how uncertain those good spirits were and how they could change in an instant to gloomy depression.

There was a child's shout outside the window, 'Mam, mam…', and Ellen roused herself from her memories and tried to focus on her task. She definitely wanted to keep all her books. Her clothes were next. As she opened the door of the cupboard by the window she saw the long maxi dress, deep blue, with short sleeves, that had been her most recent purchase. Of course, she had to take that. She began to rifle through the rest of the clothes and then stopped. This was ridiculous; she wasn't going to choose which of her things to keep or not keep. As well as her books and clothes there was a stiff cardboard box with a lid. In it were her 'treasures' – letters and cards, pictures she had painted as a child. There were the toys she'd kept from childhood because she loved them: the teddy bear with the button eyes and the patch on the back where the stuffing had started to leak that had been her father's; her favourite doll, Lucy, with the gingham dress that her mother had made; the set of playing cards that her mother had taught her to play Rummy with. She wanted all of them.

At the bottom of the case lay a small blue hard-backed notebook that had belonged to her father. In it he had divided each page into three columns, the first with the date, the second with the number of gallons he had put in the tank of his car and in the third the cost of the petrol. Every few pages he had listed the total miles he had done, the cost of the petrol he had bought and the miles per gallon the car had used. Ellen loved this book. It gave an insight into her father's meticulous and practical mind; seeing his writing there seemed to connect him to her and she stood silent and unmoving for a moment until a noise downstairs roused her from her memories. She heard her aunt's voice and then, as she moved out of the room to the top of the stairs so that she could hear properly, Andrea's.

'Yes, Mrs Ash, I'm just leaving Ellen to go through her things upstairs. We should give her as long as we can and, yes, I think it would be very helpful if you could take some of her personal things back to your house.'

This was the moment. Ellen went down the stairs, took a deep breath and spoke as confidently as she could. She wasn't at all sure how her aunt was going to react to her request.

'Thank you, Aunt Christabel. I'd like to keep all the things in my room – my clothes and books and the case under my bed. I don't know how to choose what to leave. I know I can't take the furniture… but my dad made the bookcase and the bedside table. Could I have those? Then there'll be just bits of other things I think.'

'Good, I can arrange that. You go back and look in some of the other rooms.'

Ellen was surprised by the speed with which her aunt agreed and then thought that maybe she was relieved to have something practical to do.

At the top of the stairs that Ellen had just descended there was, of course, another door: the one that opened into her mother's bedroom. She couldn't face that yet. Instead she turned to the kitchen and saw, at the far end of the room, the deep square sink with its scrubbed wooden draining board and, resting on that, an odd metal mesh contraption that Ellen's mother had used to mash the remnants of tablets of soap together so that they could be used for longer.

Pinned to the wall above the sink was a picture of the seaside, with bright yellow sand, a round sun and a red bucket next to a large white shell. Ellen had painted it years ago after a rare day's outing. Her mother had been in one of her elated moods and insisted that the two of them went to the public toilets and change into their bathing costumes so that they could swim in the sea. It had been freezing cold, Ellen recalled, but her mother had just laughed and said, 'Don't worry, you get used to it. Just swim fast.' And Ellen, who had just learnt to dog paddle across the swimming pool, did. She kicked and kicked and found that her mother was right. After a few minutes she felt only the sting of the salt and the intermittent warmth of the sun on her back. A baby seagull bobbed up and down on the water next to her and made her smile. Later, wrapped in that same striped towel she had found in the bathroom, she had begun to shiver but her mother had rubbed her back and helped her dress. This picture, she wanted to keep.

Next was the living room. A large oak table with curved legs dominated one side of the square room. It looked too big and grand for here, but Ellen knew that it had belonged to her father's family and that, when he died, her mother had found it impossible to get rid of it. She had placed a strip of lace along the centre of the table that had, she said, belonged to her own mother. On a sideboard, at an awkward angle, stood the small box of the television, its aerial resting on top. Ellen had always found it easiest to sit on the floor when she was watching anything, while her mother sat in a high-backed chair under the window. Television had been strictly rationed though: homework and piano practice came first.

Pushed against the wall opposite the table was an old upright piano with a hard wooden stool that you could lower or raise by turning the handle at each side. This was where Ellen had done her music practice, and a book of Mozart sonatas still rested on the stand. Ellen remembered that lately she had been able to skip her half hour of playing without her mother reminding her. At the time, she had thought that was good luck and been relieved. Now she wondered what it had meant. Had her mother, who was so keen on her practising and who had been so proud when she had passed a piano exam, just lost interest in her? Maybe she should keep her music. Who knew, there might come a time when she would want to play again. She gathered up the pile on the top of the piano and took it out to give to Andrea. The only room left now was her mother's room.

'I'm just going upstairs again,' she said to Andrea. 'Then I've finished.'

Her mother's bed was neatly made, with the sheet turned back over the green cover. In the window the dressing table was unusually tidy and looked strangely bare. The blue plastic-covered jewellery box that held her mother's favourite string of pearls, a present from Ellen's father, was placed neatly in the centre. Often her mother had hung necklaces over one of the table's three hinged mirrors, but there were none there now. Nor were there any earrings tumbling together in the glass tray that also held a hair brush and hand mirror. Losing one of her earrings had been a common occurrence for her mother and had led to outbursts of irritation that made Ellen feel as if losing a piece of jewellery was one of the worst things that could happen.

'Have you been playing with them again, Ellen?' her mother would say, and Ellen would feel that somehow the loss was her fault, even though she would have been much too frightened to play with her mother's jewellery. Even now, she felt scared to touch the jewellery box. Everything was so tidy as if carefully prepared for... For what? Did her mother ever imagine that Ellen would come back here? And what could possibly happen if she did take the box with the pearls now? Tentatively, she stretched out a hand and picked it up. She would give it to Andrea and then decide whether or not to keep it.

Ellen turned and looked around the room. On the table next to the bed stood a collection of photographs. They were so familiar that Ellen felt she knew them, but as she stopped to look at them again she realised that she had never really studied them closely. One was of her mother as a young woman: carefully posed she was turning to look over her shoulder at the camera, smiling tentatively. On her head she wore an elegant straw hat decorated with flowers and ribbon. In another, Ellen was sitting next to her mother on a low wall, behind which the outline of a pleasure steamer could be seen. Ellen wore a gabardine mac with the hood pulled over her head, her top lip pulled over her bottom one as if she were thinking hard about something. Next to her, her mother was grinning, despite the grey sky. They had both loved being close to the sea when the weather was stormy and surging waves crashed onto the beach. These were pictures from another life. Ellen picked them up and tucked them under her arm. She could think about them later.

On the wall opposite the bed, in a white frame, was a poster with a picture of the homeless shelter where her mother used to volunteer. Printed above the picture, in red letters, were the words:

HOMELESS AND HUNGRY?
THERE'S ALWAYS HELP AT THE NOOK

Handwritten at the bottom of the poster was the message, '*To Bess – thank you for all your help at Nook – we all appreciate it. You've made a difference to the lives of the homeless in Fineston.*' After the message there were lots of signatures, names she didn't know. Ellen remembered how some of the workers from the homeless project had come to the funeral; they must have really cared about her mother. It seemed odd now that Ellen knew so little about this part of her mother's life. She had visited the Nook occasionally with her during the school holidays.

The project was based in a former café in a shabby street to the south of the town. The front window was covered with posters advertising the help available: hot food, clothes, shoes, the occasional services of a doctor who volunteered there, and a day room where the clients could sit during the day instead of walking the streets. At night, they were directed to a hostel a few miles away. Ellen's mother's job had been to help cook and serve the food. On the occasions she had visited, Ellen had sat with the project users and listened to some of their stories. She'd found out how easily a life could slip from comfortable security to a life on the streets: a difficult divorce, a lost job, a drink problem... And she had watched as her mother cheerfully juggled boiling potatoes with chopping carrots and stirring soup.

A sudden, vivid memory sprang into Ellen's mind. Her mother was standing behind the counter where the food was served. An old man, dressed in worn brown corduroy trousers tied with string around his ankles, moved closer to the stack of plates waiting to be filled with food. Bald, apart from some wisps of grey hair around his ears, he had a dirty blanket thrown around his shoulders. He shouted, 'Heyup missus, get a move on there, some of us are starving here.'

Ellen's mother had laughed and replied, 'You wait your turn, young man!'

Amused, assured, lively – this was a mother Ellen didn't really see much. Later, she remembered, a young man, blond hair falling over his eyes, had shuffled through the café door, looked around warily, then half turned as if to leave. Immediately Ellen's mother had put down the dish she was holding, moved out from behind the counter and walked over to the boy.

'Jamie – stay…'

Ellen couldn't hear anything else that was said but she watched as her mother put a hand on the boy's arm and led him over to a table in the corner. She had felt, she recalled, a pang of jealousy.

– – –

The bulky mahogany wardrobe was next. Dare she open that? Ellen reached for the ornate brass handle and pulled it open. As she did so, the key fell out of the lock and she spent a minute or two searching for it on the dusty floor. Crawling around she saw, at the bottom of the wardrobe, a large clutch bag that Ellen remembered well. It was made of dark blue leather and had a square clasp at the front that opened and shut with a spring. Her mother hadn't used it recently, but Ellen remembered that when she was very small she had loved to play with the fastener. 'Stop that, Ellen, you'll wear it out,' her mother used to say as Ellen opened and closed it with a snap. The bag looked stuffed full and Ellen reached out to pick it up, adjusting her position on the floor as she did so, before undoing the clasp. Inside was a collection of papers and Ellen flicked through them rapidly. There were drawings that she had done as a child, photographs, letters. This was more than she could bear just now, but she knew she had to take this with her. She closed the bag and continued her search.

Above her, on the wardrobe rail, hung a line of clothes: the dresses that her mother had made herself, carefully following patterns that they'd bought together in Harold's in Fineston. Ellen had often watched as her mother laid out the tissue paper shapes on sheets of fabric and cut them out with a pair of especially sharp scissors. At the front of the line was a sun-dress in cream linen with a square neck and shoulder straps. That had been a dress for outings and was associated, by Ellen, with fun. A black fur coat, protected by a plastic cover, had been worn by her mother on special occasions, like the time they had gone to see a ballet in Ryston. The tickets had been a gift from her grandfather, to celebrate passing her scholarship. When they came out of the theatre, Ellen, buoyed by the grace and energy of the performance, hadn't been able to resist practising some of her dance steps on the pavement, floating her arms above her head and turning. Water from a recent rainfall reflected the yellow street lights and danced with her. She remembered the smile her mother had given her and felt a renewed thud of pain around her heart.

But she couldn't take these clothes with her. She didn't want to. She was done here.

EIGHT

Ellen was sitting by the window in a maths class. Miss Harte was her usual, abrupt self. She liked the girls to sit neatly in rows, their feet positioned symmetrically under the desk.

'Don't slouch, girls, please. Ellen, face the front – and are you wearing patterned tights? See me afterwards, please.'

They were doing quadratic equations and Ellen, who liked maths, was finding it hard to concentrate. She knew she would be in trouble for flouting the school's tight uniform code, but that morning there had been no clean plain tights, so she had put on a pair with a distinct diamond pattern. She hadn't yet worked out how best to get her washing done and ironed at her aunt's. The school uniform was a navy skirt with white shirt and, because she was now in the fifth form, a striped dark and pale blue tie. Last year it had been a plain navy tie. A couple of days ago she had washed a white shirt in the bathroom sink and let it drip-dry in her room. She felt nervous about using the machine and didn't, in any case, know how it worked. Her aunt, she was sure, would raise her eyebrows and look exasperated if she asked, as if she were expected to know everything without being told. The machine was much more complicated than the one they'd had at home where you just put the washing into the tub and pressed the lid down.

'Ellen, come to the front and show us the next step in solving this problem for me, please.'

Ellen started. She had heard nothing that Miss Harte had said for the last few minutes. But she rose from her seat and took the piece of chalk that her teacher held out to her. She looked at the problem:

$$5x2 - 3x + 3 = 0$$

And had no idea what to do. Silently she stood by the board, aware of everyone in the class watching her.

'Well,' said Miss Harte, 'I used to think you were a very clever girl. Go back to your seat.'

Ellen could feel the colour rise in her face. She went back to her desk and looked out of the window at the tree whose branches were rising and falling in the late autumn sunshine. It was true. Miss Harte was horrible but she was right. She couldn't do anything now. It was all too hard. She didn't have the energy. She wasn't clever enough. In order to think clearly she needed to see clearly, above the swirl of the dark feeling that filled her head. She couldn't do it, not any more.

At lunch that day the girls went to queue up outside the low-ceilinged dining hall that had been constructed as a temporary building years before and had never been demolished. The rule was that you had to fill up the tables in the same order as you had queued, so you couldn't choose who you were going to sit next to. As a result, there was always much calculation and jostling in the queue. Ellen couldn't be bothered to join in and found herself sitting on a table with girls she hardly knew from one of the other fifth forms.

As she sat down, she sensed a flutter of hesitation in the air. A small girl with glasses looked across the table at her friend and raised an eyebrow. No one spoke to her. Ellen wondered if they knew what had happened and then realised that of course they did. Scandal always travelled quickly through the school. The other girls knew and they would be feeling awkward and curious and sorry for her all at the same time. Maybe they thought it was her fault and were thinking that they would never let such a thing happen to their mother. None of them knew what to say. Days were mostly silent for Ellen. She felt as if she were drifting on a cold sea in a tiny circular boat, drenched and stung by spitting waves and harsh rain that fell from a sky indistinguishable from the waves.

It was only with Jennifer that she felt comfortable; whenever her friend suggested that Ellen went back to her house after school she always agreed. Aunt Christabel and Uncle Walter thought she was doing homework in the library at school so asked no questions about her arriving home rather late. And she and Jennifer did do some work together. It was companionable, sitting on the sofa in the front room with Mrs Sugden in the tiny kitchen behind them.

'There you are, love,' she'd say, bringing in a cup of tea and a piece of home-made lemon cake and touching Ellen's arm.

'Look at you two – all them brains. You're going to be someone in the world, both of you.'

'Oh, Mum,' said Jennifer, 'don't be silly.' But Ellen sensed that deep down she loved her mother's attention and admiration.

NINE

Uncle Walter was cross. Ellen sat quietly at the dinner table, as usual, speaking only if she were spoken to. The meal was steamed plaice with rice and spinach. Ellen hated steamed fish – it was so tasteless – but she mixed it up with the rice and forced herself to swallow each mouthful. Uncle Walter addressed the family.

'It looks as if they're really going ahead with this absurd plan to close all our excellent grammar schools and turn them into comprehensives. It's ridiculous. All those thick kids with the bright ones – they'll just drag them down. And why should the clever ones have to put up with having their lessons disrupted by children who don't want to learn? What will happen to standards? But these loony Left councillors are determined to have their way. At least the Fineston paper has some sense. They're running a "Save Fineston's Top Schools" campaign. I'm planning to get in touch with them next week – get them to print some of our campaign literature. Let's hope they whip up lots of support and those councillors will have to think again.'

'Goodness, that's dreadful, darling. I'm so glad we were able to educate our boys privately,' said Aunt Christabel. She obviously thought none of this was anything to do with her. 'Would you like more fish, dear?'

'Gosh yes – more fish, Ma, please,' said Marcus. 'Glad I don't have to go to school with those yobbos from the estate.'

After supper Ellen saw the *Fineston Express* with its headline *'Save Fineston's Top Schools'*. Ellen thought of her own friends from the estate, the children she had been at primary school with, before she'd got her scholarship to the High School. Pat, who was bright as a button and got one of the top marks in the eleven-plus; Anthea, who was so kind and creative – always making things from empty cardboard boxes and bits of material; Janet, who was so brilliant at playing make believe games. How dare her cousin call them 'yobbos'? She felt really angry and sad too.

Again, she remembered the conversations she'd heard her mother have sometimes about the importance of giving every child a chance and treating everyone equally. She used to talk about how unfair an education system was if it allowed some families, but not others, to buy an education that would help their children get on in the world. What would her mother have done just now? She'd probably have got cross and said what she thought and everyone would have looked at her as if she'd been rude and raised their eyebrows in a sort of 'there she goes again' way. They would have ignored her and gone on passing potatoes around the table as if she hadn't spoken. The thought of this made Ellen even angrier, but the other faces around the table showed such confidence and talked with such speed and apparent authority she couldn't think how she might begin to say what she thought.

That evening, after dinner was finished and Ellen was released from her chores, she excused herself and went and sat in her room. Ideas were whirring round her head. She would write a letter to the *Fineston Express*. That would have made her mother proud. She was sure she could get the arguments together – it would be like writing an essay at school – and her mother had been right. An education system that gave everyone an equal chance to learn and get exams was better than one that decided what a child was going to be on the basis of a single test at the age of eleven. What if you were ill on the day you had to take it?

Ellen sat down and took out her notebook from her school bag. As she wrote, she found that some of the phrases she had heard her mother use when she had discussed the plans for education in the town with their neighbours, seemed to be lying in wait in her mind:

Dear Sir,

I have followed the discussions about the future of the schools in Fineston and I am writing to say that I think that all the schools in the town, including my school, Fineston High School, should become comprehensive.

All children should have a fair chance to do well. It is wrong that a decision made at 11 on the basis of a test result should affect someone's whole life. After all, a child could have been feeling ill that day. I know that when I passed my scholarship to the High School I lost touch with my friends from my junior school. It can't be right that society is split into people who go to grammar schools and those who don't.

At my junior school I learnt that children of all backgrounds can get on and do well together. I think a teacher needs to adapt what she is teaching to the individual and if she does this, everyone can do well.

I know that I would have liked to go to a school that did not divide children up into rich and poor, or clever and not so clever.

Yours faithfully,

When she had finished writing this Ellen paused. She felt good. She realised that while thinking of what to say and scribbling it down, she hadn't thought of anything else. She had been completely absorbed. As Ellen read through this rough first draft in her notebook a spark of excitement ran through her. She would send it, but she'd wait a few days to see if she could think of anything else to say. Ellen went to sleep that night feeling more relaxed than usual. The thought of her letter kept her going during the following days. She concentrated as well as she could in class, but mostly it was a blur. At the back of her mind, she worked and re-worked her letter until it said exactly what she wanted it to say. Ellen didn't mention the letter to anyone, but at night, before she went to sleep, she thought about it and felt a tiny spur of excitement. She felt rather proud of herself.

The following Wednesday, after school, she went into a newsagents and bought a copy of the *Fineston Express* and a pack of blue Basildon Bond writing paper with matching envelopes. Back at home, she hurried up to her room and wrote out her letter. She addressed it to the editor, wrote out the address and then realised she didn't have a stamp. Never mind, she could post it tomorrow. She kept the letter in her school bag, tucked away in the front pocket. On Thursday she called into the post office after school and posted it.

Ellen knew her letter wouldn't be in time for the next edition of the *Fineston Express*, but the following Thursday she went into the newsagent and bought a copy anyway. Even though she was prepared, she was disappointed to see that it wasn't there. There were lots of letters though, complaining about the plans to turn Fineston's schools into comprehensives, under a headline '*Save Fineston's Top Schools*'. She could think of nothing else whilst she did the rounds of school, home, cooking, cleaning up, going to bed, getting up… A week later, when Jennifer asked if she'd like to go to the coffee bar after lessons had finished, Ellen made an excuse and raced to the newsagents and bought a copy of the paper. She sat on a seat by the bus stop outside the shop and started to turn the pages. At last she found the letters' page. And there it was, under the heading '*Pupil at Fineston Girls High School wants Comprehensives*'; her letter, not changed at all, but just as she had written it and, at the bottom, her name, Ellen Wentworth, and her uncle's address below. Ellen felt very proud. She wanted to tell someone but could think of no one. Would anyone see it? Would her mother have been pleased with her?

- - -

Ellen was sitting in a geography lesson. Geography was Ellen's worst subject, partly, she thought, because she found it hard to read the place names on the maps they used. She was staring out of the window as an unusually fierce autumn sun turned fallen leaves into golden flakes when the classroom door opened. Lessons were never interrupted. Twenty-six curious faces turned and watched as the school secretary, who was smiling apologetically, entered the room.

'I'm so sorry to interrupt, Miss Gladwin, but the headmistress would like to see Ellen Wentworth in her study now.'

A flutter, quiet but palpable, ran through the class. What on earth had Ellen done? Ellen's first thought was that something else terrible had happened. Her grandfather? He was really the only person she cared about – or, she thought, who cared about her. She was interested, and mildly shocked, to discover that she would feel no anguish at all if her aunt or uncle or cousins were hurt.

Ellen followed the school secretary, who was looking away from her and not speaking, across the polished floor into the dark, panelled corridor that led to Miss Gaunt's room. The door was heavy and had a brass knob. Ellen stepped forward.

'One moment, please,' said the secretary, rather tartly. Then she knocked lightly, twice, on the door.

'Come.' Miss Gaunt's deep, commanding voice could be heard clearly in the corridor.

'Ellen Wentworth to see you, Headmistress.'

'Very well. Show her in.'

Ellen entered the room. She had never been in the headmistress's study before. Like the corridor, the walls were panelled in dark, lustrous wood. A rug of red and blue patterns had that slightly worn look that Ellen recognised from her aunt's house: it meant it was precious – old and expensive. There was a large, shiny table with dining chairs around it in one corner. On the walls were prints of old Fineston and photographs of earlier generations of High School girls. A cut-glass vase of yellow roses stood on a low table by an empty fireplace. Miss Gaunt herself was sitting behind a large desk, her elbows resting firmly on its red leather top. Ellen stood inside the door, unsure what to do next.

'Come in,' said Miss Gaunt icily.

Ellen walked slowly towards the desk. There was a chair positioned by it, presumably for visitors, but Miss Gaunt did not invite Ellen to sit on it. Instead, she raised her eyebrows and looked hard at Ellen. There was silence for a full five seconds. Then: 'Well. Could you explain yourself, please?'

'I'm sorry… I'm not sure…'

'This!' said the headmistress loudly, lifting up a copy of the *Fineston Express* with Ellen's letter marked in red. 'What do you think you've been doing?'

'I… I…' Ellen had no idea what to say.

'It is a great privilege to come to this school. You were given a scholarship so are particularly fortunate to be here. You have the benefit of the finest teachers and opportunities opened up to you that someone in your position in life could not otherwise hope for. And this is how you show your gratitude – by calling for the school to be destroyed and embarrassing us all in the local paper. What do you have to say for yourself?'

'I…' Ellen hesitated again and then, from somewhere deep inside, the words came. 'But I believe in fairness. In everyone having a fair chance. It doesn't seem right for some children to have all those opportunities and others not.'

Miss Gaunt drew a deep breath. She stood up and the academic gown she always wore at school flowed out around her. Ellen could tell that she was furious.

'I see you have no concern for the reputation of the school. I shall be contacting your uncle about this. I'm sure you understand that he is a big supporter of the school. Now, go back to your lesson.'

Ellen left the room without speaking. She looked at her watch. Ten minutes to go before geography ended. No point in going back there, she thought. After looking around quickly to see that no-one was watching she turned right instead of left, ran along the corridor and down the stairs to the basement cloakroom. It was peaceful there, just row after row of empty coats and empty shoes. No one to criticise her, or tell her what to do, or make her feel small. She sat there numbly for a while, deliberately not thinking about what had just happened. Five minutes passed, then ten, and she realised that she was too late for the start of the history lesson. Her mind seemed to empty as she sat, not feeling anything, during the next lesson too.

Ellen was still there when the final bell of the afternoon went. She knew that girls would be coming down to the cloakroom shortly and didn't want to be found sitting on the bench, so she slipped into one of the toilets and locked the door. When she heard the first footsteps on the stairs she came out, went to her peg and started putting on her coat. It was then that she realised that she had no books for her homework. Her geography exercise book was probably still open on her desk and her school bag hanging on the chair. Should she go back for them? Then Jennifer appeared, carrying Ellen's bag as well as her own.

'Shall we go for a coffee?' she asked. 'I picked up all your books for you. What did Miss Gaunt want? You were gone for ages.'

'I can't tell you here but, yes, I'd love a coffee. Shall we go to Paradiso's?'

Half an hour later the two girls were sitting at a corner table in Fineston's new coffee bar. They'd chosen the Beatles to play on the juke box and were scraping the foam from the tops of their coffees with spoons.

'So what happened?'

'Well, last week I wrote a letter to the *Fineston Express* saying I thought that all the schools should go comprehensive – not just grammar schools, ours too – and they published it. Miss Gaunt was really angry, said I was "attacking the school's reputation". But it is what I think – aren't we supposed to have opinions?'

'Golly,' said Jennifer. 'You're brave. What will your uncle say? Isn't he heading the campaign to stop the council doing it?'

Ellen hadn't thought of that. She'd vaguely known, she supposed, that her uncle was a Conservative but she hadn't thought about his reaction. It was the Labour councillors who were trying to make the changes to the schools. It was one reason why her mother, who always voted Labour, hadn't got on with him. Now she thought about it she could see that he probably would have something to say. She suddenly felt in even less of a hurry to go home than she usually did and suggested to Jennifer that they had another coffee. Jennifer had plenty to tell her. She had met a boy on the school bus; his name was Paul and she really liked him. He was a pupil at Queen Mary's, which was a direct grant school for boys – the twin school to theirs – and they had started to say hello to each other when they met in the mornings.

– – –

It was nearly six o'clock when Ellen eventually put her key in the lock at her aunt's house. She still thought of it as 'Aunt Christabel's house', not her own home. Her aunt was in the kitchen, putting several bags of shopping away. Ellen could see straightaway that she was cross; her mouth was tight and her eyes narrowed as she looked at Ellen.

'Where have you been, young lady? Your uncle and I need to have a serious talk with you. Miss Gaunt rang your uncle earlier today and told us what you've done. Go into the sitting room and wait for us.'

Ellen's initial response was 'Why should I?' She wanted to tell her aunt, 'Get lost'. But she didn't. She put her bag down in the hall and hung her coat up on its usual hook by the door. Then she went into the sitting room. It was empty so she went to stand by the window. A low evening sun cast a deep yellow beam into the garden. Huge leaves, patterned in orange, yellow and fading green, lay in swirls on the lawn. It was beautiful and sorrowful at the same time. The year was dying, along with the life Ellen had always known.

The door behind her slammed. Her uncle entered the room. He had removed his coat but still carried his brown briefcase. As he sat down in the middle of the large sofa he started to hunt for something. Ellen didn't need to wait to find out what it was.

'What,' he said, 'is this?' And he held up a copy of the *Fineston Express* and waved it backwards and forwards in front of her. Ellen was still standing and not sure whether or not she should sit down. Something inside prevented her from moving though. She didn't want to get too close to this red-faced, angry man.

'Have you any idea how stupid this makes me look? In case you have forgotten I am the leader of the Fineston Conservative Party. I have made it my mission to oppose this appalling idea of closing our grammar schools and turning them into comprehensives. Years of tradition just thrown away. Excellent schools destroyed. Ruining our education system. And, in my very own house, a member of my family says publicly that I am wrong! Do you realise how rude and ungrateful you have been? And how disrespectful to a school which, my girl, you are very lucky to attend. Your aunt and I took you in here out of the goodness of our hearts. You could have been in a children's home. And this is how you repay us. With contempt. I shall be talking to your aunt about what we're going to do about this. In the meantime you can write a letter of apology to Miss Gaunt.'

Ellen could feel her breath quickening and the tight red feeling in her chest that she was getting accustomed to spreading throughout her body. Why should she write something she didn't mean, just to please her uncle? He was wrong, she knew he was. And she wasn't going to be told what to do by him. In her head, the arguments in favour of comprehensive schools were swirling. But she said nothing. She couldn't think how to start.

'Well, young lady?'

Still Ellen was silent. Determined not to agree and too scared to disagree, she said nothing. The silence lasted for several seconds. Ellen started to count them in her head: 'One elephant, two elephants, three elephants, four elephants, five elephants ...' Unable to countenance the silence Uncle Walter called out to his wife.

'Come in here, Christabel.'

Aunt Christabel appeared promptly in the doorway, still wiping damp hands on a kitchen towel. She seemed unsurprised by what she saw. Ellen realised she had almost certainly been listening at the door.

'This young lady,' said Uncle Walter, 'is refusing to answer when I speak to her. She hasn't said she will write a letter of apology to Miss Gaunt. She is treating us with contempt.'

Still Ellen remained silent. It had started to feel like a very powerful thing to do. She could see that her relatives were becoming increasingly frustrated and angry. And that they were helpless. They couldn't force her to sit and write a letter, could they? The silence continued ('six elephants, seven elephants, eight elephants, nine elephants...').

Then Aunt Christabel spoke.

'You are a wicked, ungrateful child. We take you in, after such an unfortunate occurrence, out of the goodness of our hearts and in memory of my poor dear brother, whose life, I'm sure you realise, was made a misery by your mother. I'm sure it was her fault that he had drunk too much that night – the night of the crash – and this is how you repay us. Your uncle has his reputation to think about. He was fully expecting to be elected a councillor soon. This is most embarrassing for him. If you must have ridiculous radical views then you can kindly keep them to yourself in this house. Now, go and sit down at the table and I'll bring you some writing paper.'

Ellen didn't move. She felt strangely exhilarated to have discovered the power of doing absolutely nothing at all. The room was still. Ellen could hear the noise of children playing in the tiny park at the end of the street. They sounded so innocent and carefree.

'Very well then,' said Aunt Christabel. 'If you continue to be so rude and obstinate I shall write the letter myself and you can sign it.'

Not likely, thought Ellen to herself. But still she said nothing.

Aunt Christabel walked over to the long cupboard that stood opposite the sofa and took out a small portable typewriter and a pack of paper. Ellen watched her fingers moving swiftly over the keys and remembered her mother telling her that Aunt Christabel had once trained to be a secretary but had married soon after she finished the course and never really used her skill.

'That's probably why she's so bossy,' her mother had said. 'Frustrated. She'd have been better off doing a job instead of stuck at home all day interfering with other people's business.'

When she had finished typing, Aunt Christabel pulled the sheet of paper from the typewriter and put it on the table in front of Ellen.

Dear Miss Gaunt,

This letter is to apologise for my foolish action in writing to the Fineston Express about the plans to change the High School and the grammar schools into comprehensives. I did this without thinking through the arguments carefully enough and I can now see that I was wrong.

I am sorry that I embarrassed you and the rest of the school. Please forgive me.

Yours sincerely,
Ellen

'When you've signed that, you can come and join the rest of the family for supper, Ellen,' she said. Then she and Ellen's uncle left the room.

Ellen had little sense of time as she sat there. The shadows in the garden lengthened. The glow of the leaves dimmed. The chatter of the birds ceased. In the conservatory next door she could hear her aunt, uncle and Marcus eating and talking but paid no attention. She didn't hear her name spoken. She thought of the times when her mother had punished her. This feeling – as if she'd done something bad and that something terrible was going to happen as a result – was familiar.

— — —

She remembered one day, sitting in class at Sanderswood Primary School. Her desk was on the left by the window, with the clever children. She wasn't sure how old she had been – seven or eight she guessed. Her teacher, Miss Shaw, tall and thin with her greying hair tied back, was wearing her usual flared skirt with a neat shirt and cardigan. Her flat shoes were well-worn but shiny. Ellen had been watching the motes of dust in the beam of sunlight that passed through the high windows and wondering how the air could be dirty like that. Miss Shaw was handing back arithmetic exercise books. Ellen liked arithmetic and was usually very quick and accurate. She enjoyed the feeling that she got from seeing the answer to a sum quickly and getting it right. Then her book arrived on her desk. She opened it, looking for the usual row of ticks on her last piece of work, but found, instead, a large cross and a line through her answer. Ellen could still remember the cold feeling of panic that had seized her chest. She had got a sum wrong. What would her mother say?

Ellen went home for lunch. She was used to crossing the main road by the school and walking down the hill past the council houses that looked just like hers. As she turned into Fossett Crescent the feeling of dread returned. What was her mother going to do when she found out about the wrong sum? Ellen knew that it was her job to make her mother feel proud. She had to do well and come top of everything, otherwise the dark moods might descend and Ellen would feel guilty and lost and alone. She knew it would be her fault.

This was her fault too. She had done something she believed in – something that might have made her mother proud – and she had only succeeded in making her aunt and uncle angry with her. It was true that she didn't like them, but maybe they were trying to be kind. Ellen picked up the pen and signed the letter. She folded it into the envelope and sealed it. Then she went next door. The family had cleared the plates for the main course and were eating fruit salad and ice cream.

'I've signed the letter,' she said. 'I'll take it to school on Monday.'

Uncle Walter and Aunt Christabel exchanged looks. Ellen noticed her aunt's raised eyebrows and waited.

'Very well,' said Uncle Walter. 'Make sure you remember to give it to Miss Gaunt first thing.'

'There's some chicken on a plate in the kitchen for you, Ellen,' said Aunt Christabel.

The food was cold but Ellen scarcely noticed. She ate a few mouthfuls in order to be polite but wasn't really hungry. She waited for the others to finish their puddings and then she helped to clear the table.

'Do you want ice cream, Ellen?' asked her aunt.

'No thank you. I'll help clear up and then I must do my homework.'

As soon as she could, Ellen disappeared upstairs. No further word had been spoken about her letter, or the letter she had just signed. Part of Ellen continued to feel angry but she sat very still for a while and let it subside. It was as if part of her mind was telling the rest of her that what had just happened hadn't happened at all. It felt safer that way.

TEN

Saturdays were always difficult for Ellen. She never knew where she should be in the house and often spent much of the day in her room. This one was going to be even worse; now she was in disgrace the air of disapproval and irritation she always felt about her would be even less bearable. She knew that her elder cousin, David, who was at university in Newcastle, was coming home for a visit but she wasn't sure whether that would make it better or worse. Her memories of him were dim and confused. It had been a long time since she had seen him and now he was grown up, so the boy she remembered would have changed completely.

At eleven o'clock she was sitting by the front window in the sitting room when she heard her uncle's Rover pull up outside. The passenger door opened as the car was coming to a halt. David climbed out. He seemed very different from his brother, and not just because he was older. His hair was long and a dirty blonde colour. Ellen could see that he was wearing jeans and a leather jacket, and as he climbed out of the Rover he flung a rucksack casually over his shoulder at the same time as he reached onto the back seat and pulled out a guitar. He looked up and saw Ellen watching him through the window. He smiled and Ellen, embarrassed, looked away. Ellen heard the front door open and her cousin saying to her uncle, 'It's OK Pa. This is the 1970s. Everyone wears their hair long now and, no, I'm not going to have it cut. You have to get used to the idea that I'm grown up.'

'Well, I don't know what your mother will say. You might think about her feelings.'

Aunt Christabel hurried out of the kitchen when she heard the voices in the hall. 'David! How lovely…'

She threw her arms around her elder son and then pulled back, still holding him by the arms, and looked closely at him.

'You look tired, darling. And your hair needs cutting.'

'Not you as well, Mum. Long hair is in fashion these days. You have to keep up with the times, you know. And I am almost 21!'

'Yes dear. I know. It's just that your father needs to keep up appearances if he's to be elected to the council this year. But come on, bring your bag in. Let's have a cup of coffee. I've put the pot on.'

David tucked his bag away in a corner under the stairs and went into the sitting room to greet his brother. Ellen noticed how different the two boys looked. Marcus, carefully dressed in pressed trousers and a shirt, even though it was Saturday morning, was sitting in an armchair reading the *Daily Telegraph*.

'Hi, little brother,' said David, 'how's it going? Reading that Tory rag still I see.'

'Hello, good to see you,' replied Marcus, ignoring the taunt.

Coffee arrived and Aunt Christabel handed out cups from the tray. Uncle Walter followed her and poured the rich, aromatic liquid from a chunky earthenware pot.

'Well, young man,' said Uncle Walter. 'Finals this year. Lots of work – I hope you're getting down to it.'

'Of course, Father.'

Ellen watched David closely and thought she saw a slight twinkle in his eye. Was he making fun of Uncle Walter? If so, what would happen? David turned and caught Ellen's eye for a moment. She saw him looking at her closely, a slight smile around his lips, as if he knew what she was thinking. Then the conversation slipped on. Aunt Christabel wanted to know whether David was comfortable now that he'd moved out of the university hall of residence. Uncle Walter asked some more about the papers David would be taking for finals. David answered politely and then suddenly stood up.

'I think I'll go and look at the garden. See what's happened to my apple tree. Why don't you come too, Ellen? You look as if you could do with some fresh air.'

Surprised, Ellen stood up, and feeling that she needed permission to leave the room, looked enquiringly at her aunt.

'That's fine, dear. Off you go.'

There was a slight mist outside that was not quite rain but made the air feel wet. The sky was a uniform pale grey, one huge cloud. David led the way over the lawn through damp green and gold leaves and Ellen followed him into a corner of the long garden, next to a wooden shed, where they couldn't be seen from the house. Ellen saw the fat green apples that still hung from a nearby tree. She looked closely at the dark and pale brown patterns on the tree's rough bark and saw a raised doughnut shaped scar where a branch had been chopped off. The bark here was shiny and smooth, like the skin on a baby. Ellen wondered if the tree had felt any pain when the sharp saw had cut through one of its limbs and how long it had taken for the new bark to grow and cover the cut.

David was reaching into his pocket for something. He took out a packet of cigarettes and offered it to Ellen.

'I don't expect you smoke, Ellen. At least, I hope not. But they're a bit much sometimes, aren't they, those two?'

Ellen said nothing, fearing it would seem rude. David took out a cigarette for himself and lit it, standing with his back to the house to make sure he wasn't seen.

'They mean well, though. Trouble with ma is she's frustrated. She's been stuck at home all these years looking after us two. She should really have been out doing something. She sometimes says she thinks she would have been really good at running a hospital – or doing a job like dad's. I think she secretly thinks she'd have been a better housing director than him – and she's probably right! When we were young it was OK, I guess. She made a job out of bringing us up – used to organise all sorts of activities. We were always off to cubs or swimming or archery or chess – or having friends for tea. It kept her busy. And I think she enjoyed it – though secretly I think she hoped one of us would be a girl.'

As David spoke, Ellen, only half consciously, turned her attention away from the tree and started looking at him.

'They wouldn't have wanted a girl like me though.'

David looked at her intently. 'So far as I can see you're a perfect daughter.'

Tears came to Ellen's eyes and she turned away, to hide them.

'It's OK. Cry if you want – here, have this.'

And David handed Ellen a neatly ironed and folded white handkerchief from his pocket. Ellen looked at it, surprised. David didn't look like the kind of person to have a laundered handkerchief in his pocket. He smiled.

'I know what you're thinking. It's been there for yonks. Ma always slips hankies into my pockets when I'm not looking. God knows why.'

Ellen smiled too and dried her eyes.

'Come on – we'd better go in. Ma will be wondering what we're doing.'

The weekend was easier after that. All attention was focused on David and Ellen was able to sit unobtrusively in the corners of rooms, or, better still, disappear into her bedroom and read. He left on Sunday evening, squeezing her hand before he climbed into the car.

When David had gone, she felt exposed. On Monday morning, she walked cautiously down the stairs to breakfast. She dreaded having to spend half an hour trying to be polite to her aunt and uncle. Her shoulders always tensed up as she sat there and she found it difficult to eat. As she neared the bottom stair she could hear their voices, lower than usual, talking intensely to each other. She knew without hearing the words that they were talking about her. Part of her knew, too, that she should probably have given a signal of some kind, a cough, or a heavy tread on the stairs, to let them know that she was there and to protect herself from anything they said that might upset her. But she didn't. Her curiosity was too strong. So she tiptoed a little nearer to the door, as quietly as she could, and listened.

'Well, I don't know what we're going to do with her if she carries on like this,' said her uncle. 'There's bad blood in that family. Her mother's difficulties must have affected her in some way. I don't want our household disrupted.'

Then her aunt's voice, tight, indignant. Ellen imagined the self-righteous look in her eyes.

'Well, I do wonder if she really wants to be part of our family. It's not just that letter. She never really wants to join in. Sits there like a mouse at meal times then scurries off to her room. And she can't wait to get out of the house. I don't know what we're going to do either.'

Ellen's stomach lurched. It was true that she didn't like it here, but she was trying her best. And what would happen to her if her aunt threw her out? She remembered from her primary school days that there were children who lived 'in care' – who were looked after in big houses without their parents. It had happened to a girl in her class at primary school, Roberta Lavery. For a long time Roberta had come to school in dirty clothes, looking pale and forlorn and lonely. The other children had called her Roberta Lavatory. Ellen experienced a painful shaft of remorse as she remembered that; her heart ached with pity for that small girl she had failed to defend. And now she knew what it was like to have no one to care for her. Well, she wasn't going to beg and fawn. If they didn't want her here that was OK by her; she'd be fine on her own. So she went into the room with her head held high, imagining that she had a protective ring of steel around her.

'Oh, Ellen, there you are,' said Aunt Christabel, exchanging a flustered glance with Uncle Walter. The look seemed to say, 'How much did Ellen hear?'

'Good morning, aunt, good morning, uncle.' Composed, distant, untouchable.

'Remember to give the letter to Miss Gaunt, won't you, dear?'

'Yes Uncle Walter.'

That was that for conversation that morning. Ellen ate her cereal, which was all she could manage, in silence. She got up, took her plate into the kitchen, washed it and then, without waiting to help clear the rest of the things from the table, went up to her room. She picked up her school bag and left the house.

— — —

The autumn was still gloriously rich. The sun, which seemed alarmingly low in the sky, went on shining brightly day after day. The remaining apples on the trees grew large and sweet. The leaves that floated down from the branches were now huge, subtly patterned in rich gold, brown and green. Ellen felt as if the world was accommodating itself to her grief, her loss amplified in the dying beauty around her.

She was early for school. The cloakroom was empty, so she removed her coat and beret and hung them on her assigned peg. Then she went to the toilets and stared at herself for a long time in the mirror. Who was she now? She could see something of her mother's eyes and also imagined that she could see her father's mouth, but she had only a handful of photographs of him and her memories were too fleeting to see his face clearly. One of her last memories of him sprang into her mind. They had been walking together, on a country path somewhere. He had shown her a tiny frog hopping between the plants and the two of them had squatted down together to watch. It must have been soon after that that he had died.

Ellen heard footsteps on the cloakroom stairs and pulled herself back from her memories. She took the letter out of her bag, climbed the stairs and walked along the dark, polished corridor to Miss Gaunt's room. Outside the door of the secretary's office was a tray marked 'FOR THE HEADMISTRESS'. Ellen looked round, saw that there was no one in sight and put her letter into the tray.

Quickly, she turned back down the corridor. Eight forty, ten minutes to go before tutor time. But instead of turning left at the end of her corridor to go to her form room, which was in the new wing behind the school, she turned right and walked back down the corridor towards the cellar steps. She climbed down to the cloakroom for the second time that morning. A few girls, worried about being late, were tearing off their coats and gathering their things together before they rushed to their form rooms. As Ellen tried to slip past them one of the girls tossed her long hair back and said loudly to the group, 'THAT'S the girl who wrote a letter to the paper saying our school should be abolished. Stupid girl.'

The others joined in. 'I don't know why she came here if she doesn't like it. She should go to that other place down the road – what's it called? Where the boys fight a lot. She'd fit in there.'

'My mum says that's what comes of giving girls scholarships. She should be made to leave if she can't appreciate the privilege she's been given.'

Ellen felt herself flush. She looked away and rushed past the girls into the toilets. They were starting to feel like the safest place in the school. She chose the furthest cubicle, went inside and locked the door. Her watch said eight forty-seven. At eight fifty-five she came out. It was peaceful down there now. The girls had gone. She could hear muffled footsteps above, the occasional sharp voice, a door banging. Mostly, though, it was quiet.

All the girls were in class. They'd be answering their names on the register politely.

'Yes Miss Harte…'

There'd be a reminder about some aspect of school policy: 'Please remind your parents not to enter the staff car park when they drop you off at school. Use the Beech Street entrance.' Or: 'Miss Gaunt has noticed that some girls are wearing shoes that have a buckle. Please note that these are not allowed.'

Then there would be lining up at the door, in size order, before the trooping down to assembly in the big hall. Ellen thought that no one would miss her and, if they did, they'd probably be glad she wasn't there. She knew she made people feel awkward; they didn't know what to say to her. Now, she expected, the story about her letter to the *Fineston Express* would have flown round the school and all the daughters of members of the Fineston Conservative Party (of whom there were many at school) would be tut-tutting and whispering about her. She could just sit here for as long as she wanted and nobody would know. She noticed her breathing – in – out – in – out – and felt her mind go blank. She felt more peaceful than she had since before her mother had died.

After an hour or so, her mind jerked back into activity and, without thinking – as if an unconscious impulse in her head were controlling her – Ellen stood up, put on her coat, stuffed her beret into her bag, raced up the stairs, looked both ways, saw that the corridor was deserted and slipped out of the school.

It was so easy. No one saw her. The side door that she had exited from led into a narrow passageway, with high walls on each side.

This in turn led to a quiet street at the back of the school. The town centre lay to the left; to the right the road passed a square of grey brick Georgian houses. Beyond that, the buildings thinned out. There were the long gardens of semi-detached houses and then the road that led to the river at the north of the town. Ellen continued along the path until she smelt the damp earth of the river bank. Her heart felt lighter than it had for ages. She felt free.

This wasn't the first time Ellen had thought of truanting from school. When she was nine or so her mother had had one of her special days, shopping in Ryston. This was an adventure for her. It was rare for her to have any spare money to spend, least of all on herself, so the times when she had saved up enough were exciting. Ellen watched her that morning put on her best coat with the big collar and make up her face with rouge and red lipstick. She had a raffia shopping basket with her and a handbag with two handles that she slung over her shoulder.

'I'm going to Ryston today, Ellen,' she had announced at breakfast. 'Time I had a new dress. Janey will be coming to give you lunch.'

Ellen didn't like Janey. She was a distant cousin of her mother's and always seemed resentful when she was asked to help out, but as she had neither job nor family of her own Ellen's mother seemed to think it was Janey's duty. Ellen walked to and from school by herself in those days. The road wound through the estate and then up the hill on the main road to the three-storey Victorian school. On the day Janey was looking after her, Ellen walked home as usual, dawdling a bit to look in the sweet shop window and decide whether she would spend her sixpence pocket money on a chocolate bar or a sherbet fountain. She was in no hurry to get home. When she did arrive, her lunch was already on the table.

'You're late,' said Janey, 'it's getting cold.'

Ellen looked at the plate of thin sausages and cabbage and felt rather queasy. She hated cabbage. She knew, though, that she'd have to eat it, and so slowly, washing it down with copious sips of water, she made her way through the food. Janey watched her silently. After Ellen had finished she got up to go to the bathroom and find her coat, eager to get out of the house. As she came downstairs Janey looked at her sternly.

'Don't think you're going to leave me to clear up. I'm not your family's slave. I don't know who your mother thinks she is.'

Ellen didn't know what to say. Then, 'Shall I take the plate to the kitchen?'

'Yes. And then wash it up.'

Ellen had played at washing up before, with her dolls' tea set but had never done it properly, after a grown-up meal. She had seen her mother do it though, so she took the plates to the kitchen, filled the sink with water, squeezed in some washing up liquid and started to wipe the plate. The water was much too hot.

'Ouch,' she said.

Janey, impassive, looked on, and said nothing. Ellen put some cold water into the sink and then carried on rubbing. Janey inspected the plate.

'There's a bit of dirt there. Wash it again and then rinse it.'

Ellen did as she was told and then said, 'I've got to go to school now.'

Quickly, she darted past Janey, picked up her coat and left the house. Once on the street she looked around and thought, do I really have to go to school? No one would know. She walked to the end of the estate's narrow street and then, instead of turning right, turned left down the road that led to the park.

I'll walk round the lake and feed the ducks and then get home for tea, she thought to herself.

Shortly afterwards, though, she found herself face to face with Jo's mother. Jo was in her class and found it difficult to do things by himself so his mum always took him to and from school.

'Ellen, what are you doing here? You're going the wrong way! Are you getting lost? Come on, you can walk with us.'

It was a relief in a way. School was, after all, safe and predictable, and her teacher, though stern, was fair and seemed to quite like her. This school didn't seem quite so safe.

ELEVEN

Ellen walked along the narrow, muddy path beside the river and watched the water eddy and swirl over smooth, grey boulders. The trees on the other bank were dense and scrubby but still held some of their leaves. There was no one else in sight. Ellen was alone, as she had been in the cellar cloakroom at school. Focusing on the rhythm of her footsteps as she tramped along helped her to stop thinking.

'Hello,' said a voice behind her.

Ellen jumped. She turned round and there was a boy she recognised. It was Stuart, Jennifer's friend, who she'd met at the youth club before her mother had died. He was seventeen, a couple of years older than the girls, and they'd had coffee together, the three of them, in Paradiso's one evening. Ellen remembered Stuart's sharp profile: the straight nose, the sensitively sculptured lips. Much taller than her, slim and fair-haired, he was wearing a Queen Mary's school blazer under his coat, but he had no tie and his shirt was open at the neck. His school bag was slung over his shoulder.

'Hello.' Ellen's voice came out higher than usual.

'We're both going to say, "What are you doing here?" next, aren't we?' said Stuart, smiling. 'Shall I go first?'

'OK'

'Before I tell you, would you like a cigarette?'

'Er, no thanks. I don't...'

'Ah – you're a good girl, I see.' Stuart paused while he took a Woodbine out of a rather battered packet and lit it with a match. 'Well, my story is that I can't stand rugger and it's a special tournament today. Some ridiculous school tradition. Once a year, we take a day out and play loads of matches between different years and old boys. If you're not playing, you're supposed to watch and cheer and stuff. But I refuse to spend the day being cold and bored. So I ran away! Now, your turn.'

'Won't you get into trouble?'

'They'll never notice. And if they do, I don't care. But don't divert attention from yourself. Why are you here and not learning how to be a proper young lady?'

'I don't know. I…' Ellen's words wouldn't come, but she looked up at Stuart for a moment and saw his eyes focused intently on her. She saw something in his expression – sympathy and kindness – that made her think she could maybe tell him what had happened.

'I got into trouble. I wrote a letter to the *Fineston Express* saying I thought that all the schools should become comprehensives. And my uncle – who I live with – is a big Tory and he got cross, and the headmistress, she was cross too, and she called me into her office. They made me write a letter saying I was sorry, so I signed it and took it in but I didn't mean it. And then I couldn't stand the thought of spending the day with everyone looking at me and talking about me. So I just ran out of school. It was an impulse really. I didn't think about it.' The words came out too quickly.

'Gosh. You're brave. And I agree with you about the schools. I hate my snobby school. Everyone so stuck up and superior. But what are you going to do now? They're going to ring your home when they realise you're not there – unless they get a message to say you're ill.'

'Oh no, I didn't think about that. I didn't think about anything. I just walked out.'

'Would you like me to ring and pretend to be… to be who? Who did you say you live with?'

'My aunt and uncle. Yes. You could pretend to be Uncle Walter and say I've got pneumonia or something. Then I could be off for ages!'

'Tell you what, let's go back to my house. It's not far. I can make the phone call there. Then we can have a cup of tea and I'll play you some of my records.'

So the two of them retraced their steps. Stuart, Ellen discovered, lived in one of the houses with the long back gardens leading down to the river. A gate in the wooden fence was only just clinging on to its hinges and had to be lifted up before it could be coaxed open. Once through it, Ellen saw a garden that had been allowed to grow wild. Very tall rose trees that hadn't been pruned clambered up the garden walls and mingled with the tangled twigs of a Russian vine. Ellen compared it to the trim lawns and neatly weeded beds of her aunt's garden. She liked this better. The back door of the house led into a kitchen that was big and bright with a large window. Breakfast pots were piled in the sink.

Stuart followed her eyes. 'Sorry about the mess. Mum and dad go out to work early. They're both solicitors and have always got too much to do. What would you like? Tea or coffee?'

Stuart put the kettle on to boil and then remembered.

'Before I do that though, I'd better make this phone call. What illness do you want to have? And how long are you going to be off school?'

'I should say a week. Otherwise they'll get suspicious. And it will give me a bit of time to think. Say I've got flu.'

'OK. Don't suppose you know the school number? No? Never mind, I'll look it up in the phone book.'

Stuart took down the thick Fineston telephone directory and found the number. He picked up the black receiver on the phone, which stood on a table just outside the kitchen in the hall, and started to dial.

Then, 'Hang on a second, what's your uncle's second name?'

'Ash.'

'OK.'

Stuart dialled the number. Ellen could hear the ring and felt herself tensing up. 'Brrr-brrr, brrr-brrr.' Then, finally, a voice: the school secretary.

'Good morning, Fineston High School here. How can I help you?'

'It's Mr Ash here,' said Stuart in an artificially deep voice. 'Ellen Wentworth's uncle. I'm just ringing to say that Ellen is ill. She has flu and won't be in school this week.'

'Very well. Thank you for letting us know, Mr Ash.'

And it was done. Ellen had been given a week free of school. Stuart came back into the kitchen and returned to the kettle. He made a pot of tea, put milk into two mugs and then put everything onto a tray. He looked practised and at home in the kitchen. Ellen couldn't remember ever seeing her cousin Marcus in the kitchen at her aunt's house – she couldn't call it home – let alone making a cup of tea.

'Come on. Let's go through to the sitting room.'

Ellen obediently picked up her bag and walked out of the kitchen after her new friend. The room they entered was long and thin, with a window overlooking the short front garden and a road into town beyond that. There were two large sofas, covered in a creamy coloured fabric with dark red stripes, a plain beige carpet and dark velvet curtains. Beside the chimney piece were shelves of books and on the walls hung several paintings that looked as if they were real and not prints.

Ellen looked at Stuart as he said, 'My dad did those – do you like them? He's an amateur artist. Mum takes the photographs.'

Ellen turned her attention to the two low tables in the room. They were covered with photographs. Several of Stuart as a young boy; one pictured him with his arm around a huge toy lion, looking proud and happy. It was a calm and peaceful room and, although ordered, she didn't feel that anyone would mind if it were untidy. She thought about her aunt's house again. There, she was always worried about whether or not she'd put everything back in its right place. If she didn't her aunt would give her the despairing, disapproving look she hated. 'Ellen can't be expected to get anything right,' it seemed to say.

'So, what shall we listen to?' said Stuart, 'Bob Dylan?'

'Er – OK. Yes.'

Ellen didn't really know much about Bob Dylan. She hadn't had a record player at home. She watched Stuart take the record reverentially out of its sleeve and set the needle down carefully. He came and sat at the other end of the sofa. Dylan's throaty voice captivated her. Its tone of restless rebellion, underpinned with a slightly menacing hope and a confidence that change was coming, was exciting. It echoed the feeling she'd had when she written her letter to the *Fineston Express*. She'd wanted to capture this indignation and determination when she tried to explain her beliefs to her uncle. This was her life and times were certainly changing for her. She hadn't asked to live with her aunt and uncle. They couldn't dictate her life or make her believe things she didn't want to believe. She was herself and she could think – and do – what she wanted.

They listened to the whole album in silence together. When the final notes had been played they smiled shyly at each other and then looked away. Ellen found herself noticing again Stuart's delicate, sharply defined profile. His lips were slightly pursed together in a thoughtful expression.

'What will you do when you're not at school, Ellen?'

'Don't know. Don't care really. So long as I'm out of the house and don't have to face everyone at school. Maybe I'll go to the park. Or get a bus to Ryston. Or the library… I could read all day.'

'What's it like at your house?'

'My aunt's you mean? I feel out of place. They're really strict and they don't care about me. They just took me in when Mum died. Felt they had to I suppose. And my aunt makes me do stuff around the house. I feel like a servant sometimes. My cousin – Marcus – he just sits around after school and watches telly. I have to help make supper, put food away, tidy up. He never helps. It's horrible.'

Ellen hadn't put any of this into words before. Stuart was listening intently. This felt reassuring and safe but it was also disconcerting – having someone focus hard on what she was saying and feeling, as if it really mattered.

'When did your mum die, Ellen?'

'A few weeks ago. I can't remember exactly. Term had just started.'

'Ellen, I'm so sorry. I didn't know it had only just happened. That's terrible. Was she ill?'

'No – yes – yes, she was, but it wasn't cancer or anything. She was depressed. She killed herself. I came home from school one day. I couldn't get in. She'd stuffed the locks with something, and…'

Ellen paused. She could feel anguish tearing through her chest and wasn't sure how she was going to carry on.

'Ellen, don't say if you don't want to.'

But Ellen found that she did want to. She hadn't spoken about what had happened to anyone. It felt scary, but was also a relief to do so now.

'It's OK. She'd hanged herself. I'm sure she didn't mean me to find her.'

Stuart gasped, but said nothing. Ellen felt as if she had been impolite. She had said something shocking and could see that Stuart didn't know how to respond. They both looked at the floor for a few long moments. Stuart looked awkward and confused. Then he spoke.

'Ellen, I'm so sorry. So then you had to go and live with those Tories. What about your dad?'

'He died too. A long time ago. When I was about seven. He was in a car accident. People – or at least my aunt – say he was drunk and that it was my mother's fault because they'd had a row before he left the house. She says my mum drove him to drink because she was so difficult.'

'You poor kid. I can see why living with your aunt must be so horrible. I think you're really brave.'

Brave wasn't a word Ellen had used about herself before. She had got used to thinking of herself as someone who was often in the way, who could be difficult and upset people. It was her job to try and mitigate the effect she had on people: to please others, to make them feel happy. She knew she had failed with her mother.

'Tell you what,' said Stuart. 'Let's go somewhere. I passed my driving test a couple of months ago. Let's get out of town.'

'Won't your parents be cross?'

'Possibly. But they won't be back until late – they work really long hours. Sometimes I scarcely see them. I know what they do – setting up the law centre – is important, but...'

Stuart paused for a moment, looking uncertain and, Ellen thought, a little sad. Then he seemed to bring himself back to the present moment and turned his attention again to her.

'We'll need to be back before school finishes though, so you can get home on time. We don't want to arouse any suspicions! Where shall we go?'

Ellen had no idea but she followed behind Stuart as the two of them left the house by the side door and climbed into his parents' Vauxhall Viva that was parked in the narrow drive. Stuart edged the car out of the gateway and manoeuvred into the road. The car was facing north, out of town.

'Ok, let's just see where we get to.'

They passed the last edges of the town and joined a wide road leading out to the hills beyond. Ellen was always surprised by how close the countryside was to Fineston. She and her mother hadn't usually ventured much beyond the confines of the town. Soon the road was bordered by fields, sloping up and down the gentle hills. There were sheep and the occasional horse grazing. It was easy to sit in silence. Ellen felt the relief of not having to think about anything at all. After half an hour, Stuart slowed the car down, turned left and drove down a narrow lane overhung with branches. The hedges brushed the side of the car. Eventually, he stopped in a muddy layby at the entrance to a footpath.

'Come on. I'm going to show you something.'

Ellen opened the car door and stood waiting.

'This is where we used to come when I was small. I think you'll like it.'

Ellen followed Stuart down the narrow path. She breathed in the damp autumn soil. Soon her feet were wet from the moisture retained by the fallen leaves. Eventually, she heard water.

'Nearly there,' said Stuart. 'Now, look…'

A final corner and Ellen found herself staring at a waterfall that gushed, full and joyous, into a fast-flowing river. She stood and watched the energy of the water that seemed as if it would go on for ever: a life force that spurted and hissed and gurgled, delighting in just being.

'It's wonderful,' said Ellen.

'I know. My dad and I used to climb up the side of it when I was small. Shall we give it a go?'

'I'm not sure – I'm not really dressed properly – and my shoes…'

'You'll be OK. You're brave. It's fantastic at the top.'

Stuart led the way. The rocks by the side of the waterfall were broad and flat but they sloped down the hill and were, of course, wet. Ellen the gymnast loved challenging her body and feeling that it would do what she asked of it. Her spirits rose as she started to climb, hands reaching for holds in the rough earth above. Very soon, they were both soaked from the fall's spray, but Ellen liked that. It felt cleansing and healing. Once she slipped and grazed her hand but she patiently set off again, hand, foot, hand, foot, like a cat. When Stuart reached the top he leant down and, taking Ellen's hand in his, pulled her up. They grinned at each other, triumphant.

'Well, what do you think? Was it worth it?'

Ellen smiled. 'It's wonderful.' And she sat for a while, watching the water rush downwards from the upper stream. She felt the energy and delight of the spray; it seemed so carefree. What would so much energy feel like?

When you're climbing a hill, thought Ellen, you always look forward to the ease of coming down. But the reality of the downward path is that it is often more difficult. Stuart went first. He turned over, so that his stomach faced the ground, and, moving feet first, reached for a firm place for each foot in turn. Occasionally he slipped but was able to grab a nearby branch from the bushes to save himself from falling further. Ellen did the same. She focused on one foot at a time, all her thoughts concentrated on placing her feet on a secure piece of ground. They edged downwards slowly and carefully. The sound of the rushing water made it difficult for them to hear what each other was saying so they worked in silence. Suddenly, Ellen's foot slipped. She reached out to grasp a bush but it wasn't strong enough to hold her. She slithered down on her stomach and felt her foot collide with Stuart's shoulder and the two of them slid down the remaining slope. Stuart reached the bottom first and Ellen landed on top of him. They disentangled themselves and looked at each other. Stuart started to laugh first, then Ellen joined in.

'That was fun,' she said. It had been a long time since she had laughed without feeling guilty, without being aware of herself. They were both covered in mud and bits of grass. Ellen knew it was difficult to get grass stains out of clothes and that she should be worried, but she wasn't really. She thought, what will Aunt Christabel say? And realised she didn't care.

'OK – better get you home now,' said Stuart.

They walked back along the path until they reached the car. Stuart found an old blanket in the boot and they spread it out on the seats to keep them clean. Back at the house, they wondered what to do with their filthy clothes. It was easy for Stuart. He went upstairs and changed and put his dirty things in the washing machine. They wiped Ellen down with some old rags as well as they could and then, suddenly hungry, made baked beans on toast. When they had finished, it was nearly three o'clock.

'I should go home,' said Ellen. 'I'll need to get these clothes in the washing machine, preferably before anyone sees them!'

Before she left, Stuart put his hand on her arm. 'Ellen, be careful these next few days. You don't want to get caught. Tell you what, on Thursday we have rugger all afternoon. No one will notice if I'm not there. I'll come and meet you if you like. Be at the bus station, near the Ryston stop, at twelve thirty. I'll see you there.'

'I'd love that,' said Ellen.

When she got back her aunt's house was empty. Ellen breathed a sigh of relief. She changed into an old skirt and jumper and put her school things in the washing machine. With a bit of luck she'd be able to hang them up before anyone got home. She could tell them she'd slipped on the road – they needn't know quite how dirty they were. Alone in the house, she sat silently on her bed, focusing on nothing, her muscles, for once, relaxed.

TWELVE

Next morning, Ellen got up as usual and left the house with her school bag. She had a plan. She would get her usual bus to school but remove her beret and button up her navy blue gabardine so no one could see her school blazer. Then she would just stay on the bus until it reached its destination, Butely, a small mining town a few miles from Fineston. She liked being on the bus. Two women behind her were talking about their children who had just started nursery school.

'It was awful leaving her,' said one. 'She started to cry and wouldn't let go of me. But the teacher made her and I had to go. I worried about her all day.'

Ellen listened to their conversation and, at the same time, watched the drifting leaves out of the window. Stray thoughts passed through her mind. How had her own mother felt when she left her at school for the first time?

She remembered it slightly. There had been lots of children sitting at low tables with paint palettes in the middle. They were chattering loudly and all seemed to know what they were doing. Ellen had felt very small and a bit confused but also interested in what was to happen next. She hadn't been aware of her mother going out of the room.

When the bus reached Butely she got off and looked around. She was in a small bus station: two lines of bus stops with scattered benches. An old woman, her white hair covered with a lopsided purple beret, sat on one of the seats clutching a bag of vegetables. A road sweeper in a navy council uniform was picking up litter with a gloved hand. On the other side of the road Ellen saw a small café and she crossed over and went in. The café was tiny, with only four tables, pressed close together, all of them empty. She approached the glass-covered serving counter and looked at the plates of doughnuts, pork pies and chocolate cake.

'I'd like a cup of tea please,' she said to the kindly looking woman behind the counter.

'A'right ducks. A'll bring it over t'yer.'

Ellen sat down on the plastic chair and looked at her watch: half past nine. That meant she had five hours to spend before she got the bus home. She had time to sit here for a while. In her bag she had *Northanger Abbey*, one of her O level set books, and she took it out and opened it but didn't really feel like reading. It was peaceful just sitting there, sipping the hot comforting tea and knowing that no one knew who she was. Nobody would order her to do anything, or talk about her behind her back, or complain about something she had or hadn't done.

When her tea was finished she thanked the waitress and went out into the street in search of the library. She saw the High Street on her left, almost empty at this time of day. There was a butcher, with huge slabs of meat hanging from hooks in the window, a dress shop selling long dresses and tweed suits, a toy shop with an array of wooden trains, and then, almost at the end of the street, a large building of blackened stone, with steps up to the front door. Over the entrance the words 'Butely Town Hall' were etched. A sign at the gate pointed to a door at the back of the town hall and read 'Butely Public Library'.

Ellen followed the sign and entered the hallway. Immediately she felt at ease; libraries had always been a place of peace for her. She passed the door to the Children's Library and paused to read the notices on the wall that advertised local events – the Butely choir, the keep-fit class, the play group – and then went into the main room. It was almost empty, with a polished wooden floor, high stained glass windows and oak tables. A librarian was shelving books in a corner. Ellen thought it beautiful. An old man, in rather worn clothes with a duffle bag on the floor beside him, was reading the *Yorkshire Post*. It felt like another world to Ellen, this time when most people were at work or school and public places were deserted.

Ellen sat down at a table under one of the windows, so that the autumn light fell onto the surface in front of her. She took off her coat and laid her bag on the chair before setting off to browse round the shelves. In the poetry section she found T. S. Eliot's *Four Quartets*. Mrs Brown had read some of this to her class in English and she had loved the sound of it. She took the book back to the table and started to read. Soon, she felt the same sharp thrill that she had in the lesson:

> *Footfalls echo in the memory*
> *Down the passage which we did not take*
> *Towards the door we never opened*
> *Into the rose-garden*

The ache in the words made Ellen want to cry. Her mother had never found her way into the rose garden – and neither had she.

Ellen sat for a while reading the words over and over. Then, to stop herself crying, she got up and wandered over to the shelves. In a far corner, at the opposite end to the librarian's desk, she paused in front of a noticeboard fastened to the wall. A sign saying 'WOMEN'S RIGHTS – FROM THEN TO NOW' was pinned to the board above a picture of a determined looking young woman wearing a long fitted coat and a large hat. High above her head the woman was holding a banner that said 'VOTES FOR WOMEN'. Ellen had learnt about suffragettes at school and been impressed by the bravery of the women who had endured repeated imprisonment and forced feeding during the hunger strikes they had staged while campaigning for a woman's right to vote. An arrow below the poster led her eye to an open display case of the kind Ellen remembered from the book corner at primary school. Elastic strings held the books in place on narrow shelves.

There were lots of copies of a book on show here. The first that Ellen saw had a picture of a smiling young woman with cropped blonde hair and a high-necked shirt on its cover. Her name, Andrea Fookes, was printed in large white capitals on a black cover and her book, called *Men and their Attitudes*, promised to offer 'MY CASE FOR A WOMEN'S REBELLION'. Andrea Fookes didn't look much older than Ellen herself.

Intrigued, Ellen picked up a copy of *Men and their Attitudes*, went back to her seat and opened the notebook she had brought with her so that she could pretend to be working and, she hoped, avoid drawing attention to herself. The book was dense and difficult but she leafed through it determinedly and found a sentence that intrigued her:

'If we are to believe what we are told, we live in a world where the great scientists, artists, poets, novelists and explorers have all been men.'

As she read, Ellen remembered a discussion they had had in school about a government report, 'The Newsom Report', which her civics teacher, Miss Lawton, had quoted in preparation for a class debate about 'A woman's place is in the home'. Ellen remembered it well:

'We have not overlooked the fact that probably one of the easiest approaches, even with the most difficult girls, to more critical work in both housecraft and needlework lies in their natural interest in dress and personal appearance and social behaviour.'

In her class discussion, Ellen had been strongly on the side of those who had disagreed with the idea that women had no place in the world of work but should be content to stay at home and be housewives. She thought about that now and it brought back memories of how her mother used to say wistfully that she would like to work; she had been at her happiest when working in the Labour Exchange before Ellen was born. Ellen wondered if her mother would have been more fulfilled if she hadn't spent her life looking after her daughter, making do with the small pension she was awarded after her father's accident. What if she had had a career, rather than doing odd bits of voluntary work?

The house was empty when she got home that evening. Ellen breathed a sigh of relief and went up to her room. She had got away with one day off school. It had been great; she hadn't had to keep looking around to see who was talking about her. She hadn't had to find somewhere to hide at playtime. She hadn't had to worry about whether her teachers were going to be cross because she hadn't done her homework or wasn't concentrating properly in class. Being alone had enabled her to breathe more deeply and to think without being interrupted.

For most of that evening she was able to escape the family. When her aunt arrived home Ellen went down dutifully and offered to help prepare dinner. She scraped the potatoes, scrubbed the carrots, laid the table. Aunt Christabel didn't seem to want to talk very much so the two of them, standing side by side in the kitchen, listened to the six o'clock news instead. A child had been killed in another shoot-out between the IRA and the British Army in Belfast. Aunt Christabel gasped but stayed silent. Ellen wanted to understand more about what had happened but something stopped her asking. A pang of loss and pain shot through her; her mother would have wanted to discuss this with her. But her aunt was silent. Indeed they both, Ellen felt, seemed a bit relieved not to have to interact. After the meal was over, Ellen silently cleared the table and washed up. Then she went up to bed. The next day followed the same pattern. She set out, apparently for school, but stayed on the bus until she reached Butely. In the library she found the book by Andrea Fookes and struggled to make sense of it before taking some history homework out of her bag and trying hard to concentrate. Even though she was truanting, she didn't want to get behind with her school work.

It no time at all, it seemed to Ellen, it was Thursday, the day Stuart had offered to meet her at the bus station. Ellen wasn't sure what to do in the morning. Staying around Fineston was risky; someone might see her. So she got the bus to Butely again, had a cup of tea in her usual café and then caught the bus straight back. It was twelve o'clock when she arrived at Fineston bus station. Thirty minutes to wait. What if Stuart didn't come? Ellen chose a seat in a corner behind the Ryston bus stop. Her coat was done up so that nothing of her school uniform could be seen and she bought a copy of the *Fineston Express* and opened it in front of her so that her face was covered. She felt she couldn't be too careful. A few minutes before Stuart was due to arrive she peeped round the edge of the paper and saw him casually dodging in between the buses as they set off and returned from their journeys . He guessed immediately that the paper concealed Ellen and slid into the seat next to her.

'Well, agent X. Are you ready for your next assignment?'

Ellen giggled. The bus to Ryston had arrived and was waiting at its stop. They climbed on and went to sit on the back seat upstairs. Stuart had taken his cap off too and had an overcoat buttoned up to his neck. He was carrying a duffle bag which he slung off his shoulder and placed on the seat beside them. There was a moment's silence and Ellen felt a surge of apprehension mixed with excitement. She glanced at Stuart and saw his mouth turned down with thought, his eyes half closed. Then he turned to her and smiled, his eyes twinkling.

'How's it been? Escaping the rat race? What have you been doing?'

Ellen told him about the book she had been reading and found herself talking about her mother. He was the only person who she had been able to do this with.

'It made me think about my mother. She spent her life at home, after my father died, not much money. She used to plan meals really carefully and make all my clothes. Once we went away in the summer, to Southport – she'd been there when she was small. We stayed in a boarding house and had a big breakfast so we wouldn't need lunch. Then she'd buy stuff for us to eat like a picnic in our rooms in the evening. It wasn't allowed – you were supposed to eat their food – so we had to be really careful about getting rid of the rubbish. I think she worried about money a lot. She worried about everything actually, all the time. Especially me. She kind of wanted me to grow up and be successful but a bit of her didn't want that at all – she wanted me to stay with her. I think she'd have been much happier if she'd been working.'

Stuart listened carefully, nodding and saying 'um' from time to time. Then he said, 'My mum works all the time, and my dad. What they do – giving legal advice to people who can't afford to pay for it – is really important. But I don't get to see them very much.'

Ellen saw a look in his eyes that she thought she understood. It was loneliness. But neither of them spoke again until the bus arrived at the bus station in Ryston. Stuart said, 'I'm starving – let's go and have a bacon sandwich. Then, what about the cartoon cinema?'

For the rest of the afternoon the two of them sat at the back of the tiny cinema next to the station that showed non-stop cartoon films. They watched strange creatures flying through the air and, for a while, Ellen forgot what had been happening to her. Too late they realised that it was three o'clock and they should have been on their way home.

'Let's go,' said Stuart and they ran out of the cinema, along the High Street to the bus station. By the time Ellen had changed buses and reached her aunt's house it was nearly five o'clock. As she drew closer to the house she saw her uncle's car in the drive and felt a surge of fear. What was he doing home at this time? She turned her key in the lock and entered the house as silently as she could, holding the latch as it closed to prevent it clicking loudly. Before she could walk up the stairs there was a command from the sitting room.

'Ellen. Come here at once.'

Uncle Walter and Aunt Christabel were standing side by side in front of the window. This made her aunt's greater height particularly noticeable. Uncle Walter's face was red, his greying hair fluffed around his ears.

'Well, young lady. And where have you been?'

'At school, Uncle. I'm sorry I'm late. We had a debating club meeting after school.'

'Don't lie to me! I know you haven't been in school for three days. Miss Gaunt asked me how you were at the Party meeting last night. You're a wicked irresponsible girl. Your aunt and I have taken you in out of the goodness of our hearts. We've housed you, fed you – and this is how you repay us. Making me look a fool. Wasting your education. What have you got to say for yourself?'

'I... I... I'm sorry. I...'

'Sorry hardly suffices. Well, if you don't want to go to school you can leave. You've made your ideas about that school clear. If you don't like it you can get a job. I've spoken to Miss Gaunt today. You're fifteen now, nearly sixteen – old enough to go out to work. Your aunt will start looking for something for you tomorrow. There's bound to be some shop girls wanted in Woolworth's – they're always advertising. Then you can start paying towards your keep here until you're old enough – next year – to live on your own. We should have known that any daughter of your mother's would come to no good.'

Ellen tried to listen but she couldn't take in what her uncle was saying. Leave school? Of course she couldn't do that. She was a scholarship girl. She was going to university. She was going to write books. But maybe it was true. Maybe she was wicked and ungrateful. Maybe she wouldn't come to anything. The feeling of doing something wrong, of not being the girl she was expected to be, felt familiar. She could think of nothing to say. There was a long silence.

'Well, girl, what have you got to say for yourself?'

Still Ellen couldn't speak. She felt as if she wasn't really there, as if part of her was trapped in a black and white world with two angry figures looming over her. Her real self was somewhere else – back in the cinema with Stuart, reading in the library, walking round the lake with her grandfather. The silence continued until, hardly aware of what she was doing, Ellen turned, left the room and walked up the stairs.

'Leave her,' she could hear her uncle saying. 'She'll come to her senses. But no girl is going to stay in my house and behave like that.'

In her room Ellen sat for a while, unable to think clearly. Anger and fear swirled like a cloud around her heart, as if something terrible that she couldn't understand or control was going to happen to her. Too frightened to go downstairs she didn't go to supper. Instead, she crept to the bathroom when the others were eating and cleaned her teeth.

— — —

She thought again about walking round the lake with her grandfather and took his letters out to read. The idea came to her suddenly, without conscious thought. She would go and find him. She'd leave this horrible house, where no one wanted her. If she was going to have to work to keep herself she could do that just as well in

London. The idea had such clarity and force that she acted on it immediately. It was as if the person doing these things were someone else, someone from whom she felt curiously detached. There was an old rucksack in the cupboard in her room. She took it out and packed underclothes, nightdress, a pair of trousers and a couple of jumpers. The money her grandfather had given her was at the back of the drawer in the cabinet next to her bed, together with a letter he'd sent her and his address. For some reason she wasn't quite sure about she had never told her aunt and uncle that her grandfather had given this to her. She put it in the purse she kept in her school bag and lay on the bed, waiting.

Time went very slowly. She was too nervous to concentrate on her book. Instead of getting undressed properly she just took her shoes off and lay fully clothed under the silky cover on her bed, just in case anyone came into her room. Then she waited. At twelve the house seemed silent apart from her uncle's snores. As she lay, unable to sleep, her eyes fell on the blue bag that she had taken from her mother's wardrobe. Almost without thinking, Ellen got out of bed, took hold of the bag and opened it. Her eye immediately fell on a photograph.

Once black and white, the photo had faded now to dirty cream and brown. A girl aged about six, whom Ellen recognised to be herself, stood, bird-like, on one leg while the other straddled a pier's circular post. The child had a hand at eye level, her elbow jutting out as if saluting. Or maybe she was shading her eyes as she stared out over the sea. Calm water, ruffled lightly with snakes of white and grey and black, shimmered in the reflection of an unseen sun. Light glinted on the girl's ribboned plaits. Below her, pillars of wood plunged far down into the dark sea bed. The stark masts of three yachts, their sails stowed away, reached high into a dim sky – a vast and cloudless pallor above the low curves of distant mountains.

As Ellen stared at this photograph it was the photographer, out of sight, that she remembered most intensely. Her father had taken this picture and, later, developed and printed the film in the cupboard under the stairs. Looking at the photograph, Ellen remembered the feeling she'd often had at home when she was small that even when her merchant sailor father was absent, as he often was, his presence permeated the house.

'When your father is next home, we'll see...' was a common response to Ellen when she asked to buy something for herself.

Ellen wasn't sure at which seaside resort this picture had been taken. When her dad came home on leave they had often driven to the sea for a day out. Always, Ellen and her father would take their shoes off and paddle. Her father would stride out to sea, carrying Ellen and lifting her up over the waves. The three of them would build sandcastles together and Ellen's mother would produce a packet of small flags fixed to wooden sticks to decorate their creation. Afterwards, there would be cups of tea in a wooden hut on the promenade and a huge cotton wool ball of pink candyfloss for Ellen.

As Ellen sat there, the picture resting on the bed beside her, lots of memories of her father flooded back. In the evenings, after she had got ready for bed she would go and kiss him goodnight. 'Nighty nighty' he'd say, and Ellen would reply, 'Pyjama, pyjama' and they would both laugh. One winter, it had snowed very heavily and he had made a sledge out of some scrap pieces of wood he'd kept in the garden shed and taken her to the nearby golf course to try it out and she had fallen off and rolled to the bottom of the hill in the snow. When she was very small a special treat had been to sit on his shoulders as they walked through town. 'Hold on tight,' he'd say and Ellen would squeeze his hands that were reaching up to hers as firmly as she could.

Usually, when her dad arrived home there was a present for her: a black ivory elephant with cream tusks, a teddy bear, a silver egg cup and, on his last visit – the one when the accident happened, the time he'd died – a bracelet of intricately engraved small silver ovals linked together with a delicate chain. These were all stored away in the case she had brought with her from the old house.

Thinking about those visits now Ellen felt some uncomfortable memories seeping into her mind, memories she didn't really want to face. They often started badly. Ellen and her mother would wait in excited anticipation for his return. 'Your father will be home soon,' her mother would say, with relief. On the day he was expected her mother would make sure the house was clean and tidy, put on one of her best frocks and paint her lips with bright lipstick. As they heard the key in the lock, she would rush to the door to welcome him. He would put down his bag, hug her and then reach out for Ellen.

'Where's my big girl then?'

One occasion flashed sharply into Ellen's mind. Her present on this occasion was a necklace of tiny pink beads. After her father had taken it out of his bag and given it to her he had removed a package wrapped in brown paper and given it to her mother, who smiled with anticipation. The smile changed rapidly to an expression that Ellen didn't properly understand: maybe it was hurt, disapproval – or fear. She followed her mother's eyes and saw her father remove a large bottle of rum from his bag.

'And this is a present for me,' he had said with a grin.

Her mother was silent but Ellen sensed the tension that had built between her parents and wondered what it meant. She thought again about the night her father had been killed the argument that she'd listened to as she lay, frightened, in her bed. She recalled other times too when there had been raised voices downstairs, when she had crept to her bedroom door and opened it slightly so she could hear. It was too long ago to remember exactly what had been said, and she had been too young to understand properly. But she felt as if she had always known that her parents couldn't talk about money or drinking without getting angry and shouting at each other.

Ellen returned the photograph to the blue bag and took out a piece of paper, folded twice and curling at the edges. The opened sheet showed a drawing in thick green crayon of a spider with an egg-shaped body, two round eye sockets, a triangle nose and a straight line for a mouth. A forest of legs grew from the body. At the bottom left hand corner of the page 'Ellen' was written in large, wobbly red letters; in the top corner, a neat label in her mother's writing: 'A Spider: November 1958'. Ellen remembered the little girl who had drawn that – how it felt to hold the fat wax crayon in her hand and have the satisfaction of seeing the lines form on the page and her pride when her mother pinned the picture to the wall. Had her mother thought about those days before she had… before she had done what she did. Ellen couldn't put this into words, even in her head.

A beige folder, with the inside papers held together with a tag, was tucked at the back of the bag. Ellen pulled it out and opened it. She knew that this was her writing, but couldn't remember anything that was written there. It had been important enough for her mother to save this though. The first page was headed 'My Holiday, summer 1965'.

We went to Wales for the holiday to stay in the house of a friend of mummy's. On the first day we went into town to do some shopping. In the afternoon we went to a little stream and mummy and me paddled for a bit then we went home.

The next day we went to this big river and we paddled and sat down in it but then it started to get cold so we didn't stay long

On the third day we climbed up a mountain. We took something to eat for when we go to the top. When we got to the top all the sheep ran away.

It was sunny the next day so we went to the seaside and I had a ride on the donkeys that were there, but the water was too cold to swim.

Some memories of that visit came back to Ellen as she read. It had been just the two of them, the first time they'd been away since her father had died a couple of years before. They hadn't talked about him but Ellen recalled imagining that he was with them, encouraging them up the mountain, splashing her in the stream. She had been constantly aware of his absence. Had her mother felt like that too?

Ellen put the bag back inside her case and stowed the case under the bed; she would have to think about how to get her possessions back later. It was impossible to sleep. The thoughts that had been aroused by seeing and touching those remnants of her childhood had awoken a jumble of feelings. Since her mother's death, a resentment and anger had built inside her, and Ellen had found herself often remembering the times when her mother had been depressed, too ill and tired to bother with her daughter. There was the occasion she had woken her mother from an afternoon nap to tell her that her eye was sore and bloodshot. Her mother had said crossly, 'Go away, I'm sleeping.' Now, looking at these pictures, Ellen was forced to recall the mother who had looked proud and pleased when she had been given one of her daughter's paintings, who had read her work with interest and enthusiasm. Who was the real person? It was no easier for Ellen to say now than it ever had been.

– – –

At two thirty Ellen was still awake; the house was silent. It would take her a couple of hours to walk to the railway station. If the first train was at six she'd need to leave the house at four thirty. Make it four to be sure. She kept her eyes fixed on her watch from three o'clock, then at exactly four o'clock she slipped out of bed, tiptoed down the corridor and started down the stairs. She'd read somewhere that if you stood on the side of the step it was less likely to creak so she clung close to the banister as she made her way down.

In her hand she had a note that she had written in her room: 'gone to school early today for hockey practice'. As she reached out to leave it on the hall table she saw a brown envelope half hidden under a leaflet advertising a local estate agent. On it was stamped 'OFFICE OF HER MAJESTY'S CORONER'. Ellen knew what the coroner did; her grandfather had explained it to her. When someone died – like her mother had – from 'unnatural causes' there was an inquiry, called an 'inquest', into what had happened. Her grandfather had travelled up from London so he could attend it. This must be the report. On impulse, Ellen picked up the letter and put it in her pocket. It might be addressed to her aunt, but it was about her mother. She had a right to see it.

Ellen turned the latch on the door and closed it behind her very, very slowly to avoid any sudden bangs. She was out! Now she just had to get to the end of the drive and turn left past next door's high hedge and she would be invisible from the house. Rain covered the pavements and it was hard to see in the dark. She slipped once or twice before turning into the main road. Street lamps threw out a yellowy haze. Headlights from occasional passing cars loomed in front of her but the pavement was completely still. She was the only person walking. Her head buzzed with her plan: get to the station before, well before, the household woke up. She knew from consulting the timetable pinned to the wall in her aunt's kitchen that there was a train that left just before six thirty. If she caught that, she would be well on her way to London before anyone noticed that she had gone. In London, buy a map that would show her where her grandfather lives. Knock on his door – and see the delight on his face. She knew he would be pleased to see her and would understand why she had had to leave.

Quarter past five and Ellen was approaching the factories to the south of the bridge into Fineston. She felt as if she were making good time. She kept her pace though as she walked up through the main shopping street, past the closed stores and the occasional early shift worker who hurried past her, eyes to the ground. It was six o'clock when she reached the empty station car park and walked through to the ticket office. The indicator board said 'London King's Cross, 6.20, platform 1'. In the ticket office, a large, white-faced assistant, scarcely looking up from his desk, sold her a one-way ticket to London. A few moments later she was waiting on the platform for the train that would take her away. She stood behind a pillar, out of sight of the three other people waiting; she didn't want them to notice – and later remember – that she was there. The train appeared in the distance, snaking through the factories that edged the town. When it slowed, she darted forward and looked quickly to find a compartment that was empty. She chose a corner seat and tucked her bag beside her.

'Hurry up, hurry up,' a voice was saying inside her head. She found that she was leaning forward in the seat, as if that might make the train move away more quickly. At last, a harsh whistle, a shudder through the carriage and they set off slowly, gradually gathering speed. Ellen stared out of the window as the concrete factory buildings gave way to the golf course and the strips of housing with their tiny lawns. Her watch said half past six. All would still be quiet at her aunt's house in Southcote Road. No one would realise she had gone until seven thirty.

Ellen had brought her copy of *Northanger Abbey* with her but couldn't concentrate on reading. Instead, she looked out of the window as the landscape changed. Neat housing estates gave way to fields and, in the distance, gentle hills topped by misty clouds. As Ellen stared her mind emptied and she focused on the regular rhythm of the train, until a slight noise disturbed her. She turned her head and saw the shadow of a guard in the corridor outside the compartment. Fear surged through her. Had he come to find her? The man paused and then opened the door. Ellen's heart pounded harder, but the guard simply reached out a hand, said 'Ticket please, Miss' and, when he had taken it from her and punched it with the machine that hung round his neck, stepped outside and carried on his way. Ellen relaxed. She was, after all, technically old enough now to leave school; there was no reason for him to be suspicious.

After an hour or so, Ellen's eyes started to close as a drowsiness resulting from the lack of sleep the night before caught up with her. When she awoke, she felt her chest contract as terror like a greyish green wave, swept through her and made her acutely aware of being alone. The train stopped at a station and her carriage filled up with people. A mother settled two small fair-haired boys into the seat opposite her and took out a box of LEGO pieces and a colouring book. A man in a dark blue suit sat in a corner seat and immediately began to write in a black notebook with a fountain pen. No one seemed to notice Ellen and this disregard, though welcome, emphasised her loneliness. All these people had family, connections, a network of people who cared about them. Who did she have? She looked out at the station name: Peterborough. Not far now to London. Back in Fineston, they would know she had left. Would they have called the police yet? Would they bother, or just think, 'Thank goodness she's gone'. She shrank into her corner, trying to make herself invisible. It was important that no one remembered her.

The train slowed as it slid through the office blocks and the dense housing estates that fringed the track as they approached London. When it finally jolted to a halt Ellen picked up her bag and, looking down to hide her face, slipped in between the other passengers as they stepped onto the platform and headed for the ticket barrier, which seemed far away. The train was a long one and she had been in a rear carriage. Above, dusty beams of light shone through dirty glass between high steel arches. The brick walls of the station were black. Pictures of the first railways and the Industrial Revolution from a school text book came into Ellen's mind. Textiles from Fineston's factories, woven by mill girls earning a pittance for long hours of labour, their hair bound in cloth, had travelled to London this way and been employed to fashion expensive clothes for rich southerners. Now it was Ellen's turn to make that journey. Her ticket was in her coat pocket and she held onto it firmly until she reached the barrier and was able to hand it to the collector. Then she was free. On the other side of the gate the station ceiling was much lower. There was a ticket office in the corner, next to a few seats and a café. A boy was selling newspapers. The people scurrying about seemed small and anxious, rushing this way and that. No one had the slightest interest in or concern for her. Ellen breathed deeply. Now what?

Ellen had been thirteen when she had last visited her grandfather. That was two years ago. The more regular visits of her early childhood had, she now realised, become less frequent as she had got older. Ellen remembered the last trip here that she had made with her mother. Grandpa lived near the Elephant and Castle and provided she could negotiate the tube, she thought she would be able to work out how to get there. His address was on the letter he had sent to her. She reached into her pocket and touched the envelope, as she had done several times already that day, checking that it was still safe. Now she was here, actually in London, it was as if waves of panic that had been partially held at bay by her determination to get away were suddenly released to wash over her. For a few moments she stood still, her rucksack beside her on the ground. People milled past as they rushed to catch an out-going train. The crowd receded but Ellen stayed motionless, her breath quickening as she wondered which direction she should take. As she stood there she became aware of a shape slightly behind her on one side, someone standing rather close to her. She turned and saw a man with a missing front tooth and long hair tied in a ponytail, smiling. There was something odd about his smile, as if he were just using his mouth and not his eyes. Ellen stiffened. The man spoke.

'Are you OK? Just arrived in London? I wonder if I can assist?'

For a moment, Ellen felt relief that someone was going to help her. 'I'm looking for the tube... I...' Her voice faltered.

'Don't worry, love. I'm Frank. I run a project to help kids who arrive in London on their own. Do you have anywhere to stay?'

'I'm staying with my grandfather... I need to find the tube.'

The man was too near to her again. Ellen shrank back, feeling uncomfortable now. She wished he'd go away, but he stayed close and went on talking.

'Tell you what, come and have a coffee, then I'll show you where the tube is. You must be tired after your journey. Here, give me your rucksack.'

The man reached down as if to pick up Ellen's bag. She felt a sudden surge of fear and grabbed her rucksack herself.

'No – it's OK. I can manage.'

But the man continued to pull at the bag.

'Give it to me! Give it to me!' His voice was less friendly now.

'No, no,' she shouted as she held onto it. For a moment both their hands tugged at the rucksack. He was stronger, but Ellen was determined. She started to shout.

'No, no. Give it to me. Give me my bag,'

Passers-by turned to look. The man saw that the pair were attracting attention and suddenly let go of the rucksack and walked back into the crowd. Too scared now to ask for directions to the tube Ellen put her bag on her back and wandered round the station, trying to look as if she knew where she was going. She was intensely aware of people around her – was anyone watching her? Following her? Where was that horrid man now? At last, near the station exit to the street, she saw a large sign saying 'Underground' and, beyond that, a flight of stairs leading down to the tube. Ellen scrambled down the steps and found the Elephant and Castle on a large underground map. She bought a ticket and headed towards the platform, checking that she was on the right branch of the northern line and going south, not north. So far, so good.

On the train, she watched the stations slip by: Angel, Old Street, Bank, London Bridge. An elderly woman with a string bag full of vegetables sat opposite her; she was talking to herself under her breath. Beside her a young woman held onto a pushchair and rocked it awkwardly from side to side, attempting to soothe a crying toddler who was pulling on the hood of her jacket. At the other end of the carriage an elderly man with long grey hair was wearing jeans with holes at the knees covered by fraying strands of cloth. With one hand he played with the beads around his neck and with the other he clasped the strap of an incongruously smart leather briefcase.

Finally, the Elephant and Castle. Ellen stood up to leave the train; she moved aside to let the old woman off first. Three young men with large boots pushed past her as she stepped over the gap between the train and the platform and she nearly lost her balance. She stood for a moment waiting for the crowd to ease. Now she had to find her way out. On the stairs she was distracted by the elegant brass strips that edged each concrete step. For a moment she was taken back to the sparkling concrete stairs that she had climbed every day at school. That seemed a long time ago now.

Signs led her to the lift and as its doors opened she shrank into a corner as the dark cave creaked its way to the surface. A few minutes later she was through the ticket barrier, watching the buses pull up at a line of stops on the road between two large roundabouts. The noise from the cars and lorries that braked and accelerated in turns as they negotiated the wide roads was startling. Behind and above her, a small pink elephant, with a yellow rug across its back, topped by the kind of castle you find in chess sets, perched on top of a shopping centre. Opposite, there was a further cluster of bus stops in front of a sprawling, dirty, yellow stone building partly hidden by a large billboard urging passers-by to 'COME AND BE SAVED'.

Ellen thought she recognised the roundabout she needed to get to, but which of the four roads that converged there should she follow? She took out her grandfather's letter and read the address again: 24 Watley Buildings, Paster Street. Her memory was of a short street leading off a busy main road. But how to get there? Next to her, by the tube entrance, an old man, wearing a long scarf and mittens that left his fingers free, was selling newspapers.

'Excuse me,' said Ellen. 'Do you know the way to Paster Street?'

'No love, but I can sell you a map. Here's an A-Z. You can look it up.'

Ellen scrambled through her rucksack and found her purse. She took the book and leafed through it, not quite sure how this was going to help. There was a different map of criss-crossed streets on every page. How was she supposed to know which one to consult?

'There's an index at the back, love. You look it up there.'

Ellen followed the instruction and found the page, then the square that included Paster Street. The writing was small and it took some time to find the road amongst the criss-cross of others. But she did find it and was able to trace the route back to the Elephant and Castle. It didn't look far. She turned south as the map suggested, past huge black railway arches and onto a busy main street. On her left were block after block of high-rise flats, with a walkway and a row of front doors at every level. Ellen wondered what it was like to live there, so many feet above the ground. Would each of the walkways be like a street? She thought it probably wouldn't feel like that, but wasn't sure why. On her right, there was a parade of shops: a grocery store that seemed to sell everything, a bookies, a yard filled with part-used tyres that were spilling out onto the pavement and a tiny second-hand furniture place that displayed mismatched wooden chairs, second-hand fridges and lamp stands.

Eventually, she reached Paster Street and, on its corner, the Old Red Lion pub, where she could see the staff inside wiping the still empty tables ready for the lunchtime business. She walked on past a dingy terrace of neglected houses and a square of garden that had a broken children's swing in the corner. Turning right, beyond the square, she saw Watley Buildings and they looked just as she remembered them, four storeys of solid Victorian flats, with elaborate stonework on the arched lintels over the entrances to each flight of stairs. Ellen checked her letter again. Number 24. The numbers to the flats were written on plaques at ground floor level beside each staircase. 1–8, 9–16 and 17–24. Ellen shifted her rucksack on her shoulders and began to climb the stairs. Number 24 was on the fourth floor. She was here. A feeling of excitement tinged with relief overwhelmed her. The bell was to the right of the door and Ellen rang it and waited – and waited. Nothing. She rang again. And then again. Still no reply. Now what?

She would wait a bit longer. Probably grandpa was at the shops; he'd be back soon. So she placed her rucksack on the concrete floor and sat down beside it. She wondered whether to take out her book and read but realised she was too agitated to concentrate so she simply sat there, feeling a tightness around her chest which made her more aware than usual of her breathing. Her watch said ten to one. Nearly lunchtime. She would wait for half an hour and then go and get something to eat and come back. He was bound to be back soon. Ellen counted the number of green tiles running up the stairs and then the orange ones. She wondered what was happening in Fineston. Would her aunt and uncle have contacted the police? Would the police have gone to the station to check if a young girl had caught a train that morning? Should she send a note, telling them she was alright so that they wouldn't come and find her? That, she decided, was a good idea, but she needed to cover her tracks a bit. If she sent a postcard from here they would know straightaway that she was at grandpa's and might come and take her away. No, she needed to post it from another part of London. Maybe she should do that now, while grandpa was shopping, and she could come back and see him later. It was still early, after all.

THIRTEEN

Ellen picked up her rucksack and set off back to the tube. She had seen a post office on the main road and she knew she would be able to buy a postcard and stamp there. Her message had to be simple and give nothing away. Standing at the long counter that edged the wall of the post office she wrote:

Am safe. Please don't worry about me
Ellen

Ellen put the postcard into the front pocket of her rucksack and set off for the tube. It didn't matter where she went as long as it was a different postcode from grandpa's. While waiting for the train, she studied the map on the station wall. Some of the names were familiar: Piccadilly Circus, Oxford Circus. She would go to Oxford Circus.

It looked just like it did in pictures of London. Ellen climbed out of the tube station and saw the tall curved stone buildings circling the roundabout. Red double-decker buses slowed down as they turned. One of them came to a halt in front of Ellen and a passenger jumped off the back, ignoring the crisp command of the conductor to 'wait until we get to the stop'. There were four roads to choose from. Ellen walked down the busiest of them, looking for a post box. Expensive looking shops sold shoes and clothes. A scattering of market stalls on the pavement offered scarves and hats and watches. A hundred or so yards down Ellen saw a post box and put her card in the slit.

Right, she thought. A card from Oxford Street won't help them at all to find me. But they'll know I'm still alive so probably won't bother looking.

Ellen retraced her steps, intending to go down the stairs to the tube. Instead, when she reached the roundabout she looked round and saw the sign 'Regent Street' on the wide road leading south and decided to explore. This was another of London's famous sights that she recognised from the television and that she had visited occasionally with grandpa. On either side were sturdy stone buildings, with ornate pillars built into the walls, elaborate carvings and metal balconies. Outside Hamleys toy shop a soldier with a large red hat marched up and down, banging a drum. In other shops there were expensive clothes, discreetly and elegantly displayed. One building was topped by two green domes. Piccadilly Circus was familiar too. On this bright October day the steps surrounding the statue of Eros were packed with people, feeding the pigeons, consulting guide books, chattering. Ellen heard a shout behind her as she passed by: 'Cheer up, love, give us a smile.' She felt uncomfortable but made herself walk on without turning round. Two young men, apparently irritated by her ignoring them, continued, 'You're a right misery, you stuck up cow. Who do you think you are?' Ellen felt humiliated and angry but carried on walking, staring straight ahead.

The autumn sunlight lit the sky and Ellen, into her stride now, kept going. She walked down the Haymarket, into Pall Mall and across Trafalgar Square. She passed tube stations and buses but she couldn't stop. Her need to keep walking was urgent. When she reached the Strand she realised that she was hungry. How long was it since she had eaten? She couldn't remember. There'd been a banana on the train that she had put in her bag before she left Fineston but nothing since. A hamburger was what she needed. Where could she find a café? The Strand was busy with black taxis, one behind the other, hooting in frustration at some unseen jam ahead. Ellen scoured the shop fronts: a bank, a dress shop, a chemist and – yes – there was a café. A blue and green sign prominent above its glass front advertised 'hamburgers'.

As Ellen got nearer, she planned what she would eat. A giant hamburger, with cheese and onions, large fries and a milkshake. That would keep her going. As she approached she noticed that the pavement outside the bar was crowded. A knot of irritated people were pushing each other and walking into the road to get past. What was happening? As she approached she could see a line of ten or so women standing in front of one of the glass windows. In their hands were banners made of sheets and cardboard that they held up high in front of them. They were shouting:

'Ban the men who rape, not women.'

'Don't eat in here – sexist pigs.'

'Make cafés safe – ban men after 10 p.m.'

Ellen paused to look. The women were all young, in their twenties, and they wore casual clothes – jeans or dungarees – and comfortable shoes. They exuded energy and their faces were alight with confidence. Ellen sensed that they were angry too. She imagined what her uncle would say if he could see them, and smiled. She liked them. But right now she was hungry; she leant against the door, ready to pass through.

'Don't go in there,' said the woman standing closest to her, gently.

Ellen turned to look at her. She was slim with shoulder-length black hair, and she radiated vitality.

'But I'm hungry. Why not? What's happening?'

'We're demonstrating because they've banned women from going into this place on their own after ten at night. It's sexist. They assume that women on their own are prostitutes, that unless they've got a man with them they're not safe. They're just provoking men to attack them. It's outrageous. Why should we be policed like that? We want to be able to go where we want, whenever we want. If men can't stop themselves harassing women who are on their own, it's them who should be kept out. Not us.'

Ellen thought about this for a moment and remembered the men who'd shouted at her earlier – and that scary man at the station. She felt some of the demonstrators' anger and their surge of power at doing something about it.

'OK. But I'm hungry. Do you know where I can get something to eat?'

'Not sure. I don't know this part of London very well. You could try the South Bank. I'm Lily by the way.'

'Could you tell me how to get there please?'

Ellen felt the black-haired young woman looked thoughtfully at her, observing the rucksack she was carrying on her back. She felt tired and frightened and uncertain. Lily asked, 'Are you OK? Do you live in London? Have you got somewhere to go?'

'No… yes… I mean… I've come to see my grandpa, but he's not at home. I'm waiting… I'll go back later.'

Ellen was aware that Lily was still watching her closely.

'We're finishing here soon. Come and stand by me – or over there if you're embarrassed. We're going to eat soon. You can come with us.'

The congestion on the pavement had slackened and passers-by, after a quick glance, mostly stared at the pavement as they passed the women.

'Give us a smile, girls,' said a man with a ladder attached to his bicycle as he rolled past them. 'If it's men you need, I'll take you in there any time you want.'

The demonstrators ignored him and carried on pressing leaflets into the hands of anyone who was willing to take them. Ellen stood to the side, watching. Next to Lily was a small, comfortable woman with curly hair and a broad smile, and beyond her a tall, rather beautiful pale girl with sharp cheekbones and glistening eyes. Ellen thought that they both looked lively and interesting. At two o'clock, Lily announced, 'OK, that's it for today. Let's go and eat. This is Ellen. She's on her own in London and she's coming with us.'

Ellen saw an amused glance pass between the others before the small dark-haired woman said, smiling, 'OK Lily.' And then, 'Hi Ellen. I'm Marion –and this is Helen.'

Helen, the tall girl, smiled too.

'Let's go, we can walk over the river.'

Several of the others demurred. They had things to do and wouldn't be staying for lunch. Lily, Helen, Marion and Ellen set off together. At Embankment station they climbed the steps to Hungerford Bridge. A chilly breeze blew despite the autumn sun. Ellen stared at the three tiers of glass windows in the Festival Hall which lay in front of her. To her left stood the dome of St Paul's Cathedral, and to her right she could glimpse, through the metal railings of the railway track, the Houses of Parliament and Big Ben. This really was London. Halfway across the bridge the group passed an old man who was sitting on the ground. His head, covered by a red hat, lolled forward onto his chest. On his knee lay a child's blue plastic guitar and at his feet a begging bowl, almost empty. Lily stopped and felt in her pocket for some change. She bent down to put the coins into the bowl and looked closely at the man, but he didn't stir from his slumber.

'I hope he's OK,' she said. 'Best not wake him I suppose.'

On the other side of the river they went into the Festival Hall and queued up at the café to buy hot soup and coffee.

'Have you got any money, Ellen?' asked Lily quietly.

'Yes thanks.'

At a table by the window the women reflected on their demonstration. Helen started.

'Well, the guy from the *Standard* who took a picture was interested. I'm going to ring him for a phone interview later. I said I'd talk to him at about four. I've got to go and sign on first – don't want to lose my benefit! Unless anyone else wants to phone him?'

Marion replied immediately. 'No that's fine. You do it. I don't think we got anyone from the *South London Gazette*, did we? We sent them a press release. I'll follow that up with a phone call if you like.'

'Thanks, Marion,' said Lily as she put the clipboard with the signatures on the table and started to count. 'We did pretty well, another hundred or so. We'll do the Oxford Street branch next time and then, when we've got to a thousand, we'll present them to the café's management. We'll need to think about how to do that.'

Ellen sat quietly, trying to follow the conversation. She liked these women, their confidence, their care for each other. But she couldn't stay all day; she had to find her grandfather.

'I've got to go now, I need to find grandpa. It was good to meet you all.'

Ellen saw the same expression of concern on Lily's face that she had seen when she had given the old man on the bridge some money.

'Ellen, we all live in a squat in Brixton. It's a large house with plenty of room. If your grandfather's not there and you can't get into his flat come and find us. I don't want you to be wandering around London all night on your own.'

'But – I couldn't. I… I'm sure grandpa will be there.'

'Ellen – I'm a teacher. I can sense when young people are in trouble. We all believe in looking out for each other and this is half term, so I'm around. Promise me you'll come if you need us.'

She took out a notebook, tore out a piece of paper and wrote on it: 64 Ellsworth Crescent, Brixton.

'Put that somewhere safe and come if you need us. Turn right at the town hall when you get to the centre of Brixton. Ellsworth Crescent is on the left. Have you got an A-Z?'

'Yes – and thank you. I can get to the Elephant easily from here, can't I?'

Lily gave Ellen instructions about finding the right bus outside Waterloo station and then patted her arm.

'Take care, Ellen.'

It was half past four. Grandpa was certain to be back by now. Ellen found the bus and when she got off retraced her steps of the morning to 24 Watley Buildings and rang the bell. Still no reply. It occurred to Ellen that a neighbour may know where he was so she rang the bell of the other door on the landing. Nothing. OK, she would wait. She put her rucksack against the wall and leant on it. Waves of tiredness together with a now familiar feeling of detachment, as if none of this were really happening, began to flow over her and she allowed her eyes to close. Soon she was asleep. A voice woke her.

'Hey, what are you doing here?'

Ellen heard the sound but couldn't make sense of it. Her eyes opened and she saw a young man standing over her in the cramped hallway. He was in his twenties, maybe, with long dusty brown hair. He had a canvas work bag over his shoulder and was wearing overalls and heavy boots.

'What are you doing here?' he said again.

'I'm waiting for my grandpa. I've come to see him – and stay with him for a while.'

'But – didn't you know?'

Ellen tensed, as a sharp premonition stabbed her. Something bad had happened. 'Know what? What's wrong with grandpa?'

'He's in hospital. St Thomas's. His stomach pains got really bad. Didn't you know? Didn't anyone tell you?'

'No. Stomach pains? I knew he had a bad tummy, but what does it mean?'

Ellen was frightened. She couldn't lose grandpa.

'I have to see him. Is he alright? How do I get to St Thomas's?'

'I'm on an evening shift, so I've got to leave, but I can show you the bus stop. My name is Michael by the way. I live at number 22 downstairs. It was my mum who called the ambulance when he was took bad.'

'I'm Ellen. Can we go now, straightaway? I have to see grandpa.'

'Come on then.' Michael picked up Ellen's rucksack. 'You look tired. I'll carry this for you for a bit. Get the key to the flat from your grandpa at the hospital then you can come back here.'

Michael and Ellen clattered down the concrete steps together. Nine o'clock and it was dark now. A few figures scurried into the pub at the end of the street. In front of them a dog ran beside its owner, stopping now and then to sniff the ground. It was cold and Ellen pulled her scarf around her neck. Panic gripped her. Her head seemed to be floating in the sky above her. It reminded her of the day her mother had died. She knew this was real but felt as if she were quite separate from her body.

Michael asked her questions as they walked. Would she be able to find her way back? Did she have enough money? Ellen answered without really thinking; she knew she had to reassure him if she were going to be left to visit grandpa by herself. She didn't want anyone to do anything that would interfere with her plan. As they walked, they passed through a quiet council estate, blocks of three-storey flats with balconies that looked onto the main road. A woman in an apron carried rubbish to a communal bin. Through the door she had left open, Ellen could see a flickering television screen. Everyone else's life, it seemed, was calm and ordinary and uneventful. Michael stopped.

'This is where you get your bus,' he said. 'Any of them will take you to Westminster Bridge – just tell the conductor you're going to the hospital and he'll tell you where to get off. Have you got money? Look – here's a bus – jump on this one.'

Ellen climbed aboard and settled into a seat by the window downstairs. When the conductor came to collect her fare she said, 'I'm going to St Thomas's hospital. Can you tell me where to get off please?'

'Course, love.'

Trees lined the wide road and behind them were tall Georgian houses with long front gardens. They looked like houses Ellen had read about in books. She couldn't imagine anyone actually living there and having a normal sort of life. Outside one, a policeman stood, very still, on duty – protecting someone, presumably. But who?

'Your stop, love.'

Ellen saw the river as she jumped off the bus. The lights from the large, cream-coloured hospital building were reflected in the water. Opposite the hospital, on the other side of the river, Big Ben and the Houses of Parliament looked unreal. A picture she'd seen in a hundred books and photographs and films. Everything seemed like a fantasy tonight.

There were steps leading down from the bus stop on the bridge to the hospital's concrete walkway. Inside the entrance Ellen stopped and looked around. It was half past eight and most people were leaving the hospital; it must be the end of visiting time. At a long table directly opposite the doors sat a woman with tight curls and a purple cardigan. She was looking at her watch. Ellen walked up to her.

'Excuse me, please, I wonder if you can help me. I'm trying to find out which ward my grandpa is in.'

'Visiting time is just finishing, you know. You'll have to come back tomorrow. You won't be allowed on the ward just now.'

'Please find out where he is for me. I've come all the way from Yorkshire to see him. I need to find out where he is. I didn't know he was in hospital 'til I got to London. Please help me.'

The woman in purple shrugged and picked up the phone.

'What's his name? And when is his birthday?'

'George Maddox. 10th February – not sure of the date, but he's 65, so it must have been…' Ellen did a quick calculation in her head. 'About 1905, or 6.'

'Excuse me, front desk here. I'm trying to trace a patient.'

Ellen didn't listen to the rest of the call. Her heart was thumping fast. She had to see him.

'OK, thank you. Well, dear – it seems he is here.' The receptionist's tone had softened a little. 'He's on Kingsland Ward – but you can't see him now.'

'Thank you.'

Ellen had no intention of leaving the hospital without seeing her grandfather, but she turned and walked obediently out of the exit through which she had entered. There must be another way in. Instead of climbing back up to the bridge she turned right as she left the building. A path through a car park led up to a main road and as Ellen followed it she saw, to her right, the rest of the hospital. A sign said 'CASUALTY'. That would be a way in. A concrete walkway led pedestrians around the parking space for ambulances and to a swing door. Inside, the Casualty waiting room was full. A mother sat with a baby lying limply asleep in her arms. A group of men sitting with legs stretched out in front of them had let their heads loll onto their chests. It looked like a long wait.

Ellen walked as confidently as she could across the room towards a door that led – she hoped – back into the hospital. On the other side, she found herself in an empty corridor, with a drinks machine set against one wall. Beyond that she could see uniformed staff interspersed with the occasional late visitor, bustling up and down a wider passageway. Ellen joined them. She just needed to see a plan of the hospital. If she asked anyone, she'd draw attention to herself. After a few hundred yards, the passageway opened into a vaulted hall with dark brown woodwork, oil paintings and a grand piano. Ellen paused for a moment and felt the peace of the room, then she continued towards the lifts at the other side. At last. There on the list of destinations was Kingsland Ward. Level three.

Beside the lift a sign pointed to the stairs. It would be easier to escape notice there. Ellen pushed the swing doors and started up the deserted steps. At level three she emerged and saw the sign 'Kingsland Ward'. Cautiously, she pushed the door. Immediately a nurse with a white apron who was holding a clipboard stopped her.

'Visiting times are over, I'm afraid. I can't let you in. Who have you come to see?'

'My grandfather – George Maddox. I have to see him. I've come all the way from Yorkshire. I have to.'

The nurse's shrewd blue eyes scanned Ellen. Ellen was uncomfortably aware that her hair was unbrushed and that she probably looked rather tired.

'My mum died. He hasn't got anyone. I have to see him.'

'Ah – he told me about you. That was terrible what happened. I know he's been worried about you. We're planning his operation for Monday. You can come and see him tomorrow. Visiting hours start at two. You can come and see him then.'

'What's going to happen? What's wrong with him? Someone said it was his stomach.'

'Yes, we think he's got a burst ulcer. You know he'd had problems with his stomach, don't you? But we've been doing all the tests we need to do and getting him ready for surgery. He was going to tell you after the operation – he didn't want to worry you.'

'His ulcer burst?'

'We think so, but, as I say, we're doing the tests and we're confident that we can do something. Have you got somewhere to stay tonight?'

Ellen thought quickly. Her plan had been to collect the key to her grandfather's flat but she could hardly go through his things while he was asleep. If she let the nurse know that she had nowhere to go she might call a social worker or someone and she didn't want that. There had been enough telling her what to do in her life. Her fingers found the slip of paper that Lily had put into her hand that afternoon. 'Come any time,' she had said.

'Yes,' said Ellen. 'I've got some friends in Brixton. I can get the bus.'

'OK. Try not to worry – and we'll see you tomorrow.'

Ellen remembered that Lily had told her that there were bus stops outside Waterloo station. She found her way back there. On the top deck of a number 159 she sat and watched the gleam of the lights from oncoming cars passing to and fro in front of her. Lily's address circled in her head and she took out the A–Z to check its location. It looked easy enough to find.

'Brixton Town Hall' shouted the conductor and Ellen swayed along the gangway and down the curving steps, holding tight to the rail before jumping off the bus. Now she just had to find Ellsworth Crescent. 'Walk past the town hall,' Lily had said, so Ellen crossed the road and turned by a town hall that looked solid and reassuring like the one in Fineston. She checked her A–Z. Ellsworth Crescent, third on the left. A young man with a cap pulled down over his eyes and a scarf round his head stopped.

'You lost, love? Where do you want to get to?'

Ellen started to say, 'Ellsworth Crescent…' Then, remembering what had happened at the station she wished she hadn't spoken. This young man smiled though.

'Second left – and I should hurry. I wouldn't hang out round here after dark.'

'Thanks.'

The Crescent was lined with large Victorian four-storey houses. To Ellen they looked enormous, like the houses she had read about in story books but never been inside. Steps led down to a semi-basement on each one. From one open window reggae music played loudly. At the other end of the street a group of kids, about Ellen's age, were giggling and smoking together. Ellen checked the door numbers: 58, 60 – ah, here it was: number 64. She climbed the steps, took a deep breath and picked up the heavy brass knocker in the middle of the front door and banged it. Inside, there were sounds of loud talk and laughter. A smell of something cooking, stew perhaps, wafted into the street.

'Who is it?' asked a voice from the other side of the door.

'I'm Ellen. I was at the demonstration today. Lily gave me your address and she said I should come round if I were in trouble.' There was no response. Ellen spoke again into the silence. 'My grandpa's in hospital, I've got nowhere to go.'

'Hang on a minute. Lily, it's someone for you.'

Still the door remained firmly shut. Ellen noted the peeling paintwork, the worn steps, the crumbling mortar. She looked nervously back to the road. What could she do if she weren't let in here tonight? Her feelings of panic and loss were so familiar now she couldn't remember any other emotional state. It was a dark blankness, beyond fear, and it seemed to be who she was now. A beam of light appeared on the step and the door opened a crack. It was Lily.

'Ellen, are you OK? Come in.'

FOURTEEN

Inside, the hallway floor and high walls were bare. It looked like a house that had been stripped for decoration but the painting had never happened. Coats were slung over a rickety table. The cooking smell came from a room at the far end of the house but Lily led Ellen through a door on the left. This room was similarly bare, the only furniture an old sofa and a few mismatched wooden chairs. Ellen thought Lily must have seen her puzzlement in her face as she immediately started to talk about the house.

'We're squatting this house. It had been left empty for years, even though there are thousands of homeless people in London. We took it over and are doing it up, gradually. Don't look shocked, Ellen – it's not a criminal offence, as long as you don't break in. Letting people starve on the streets, without shelter, is much worse! Now, tell me what's happened.'

It didn't take long for Ellen to tell her story. 'I have to be back at the hospital tomorrow at two,' she explained.

'OK. Come and have something to eat and meet the others then we can make you a bed up in the empty room.'

The kitchen stood at the back of the house. A wooden table was laid with places for six, with mismatched cutlery and plastic tumblers of different colours. Beyond the table the room narrowed and it was here that a black pot simmered on an ancient gas cooker. Marion, one of the women that Ellen had met at the demonstration, was there, kneeling down to take a bowl from a set of shelves that had been made out of bricks and planks of wood. Behind her, stirring a pot on the stove, was young man who introduced himself as Patrick. He was tall and skinny with shoulder-length ginger hair, sharp bones and keen, intelligent eyes. Lily addressed her two friends.

'This is Ellen – she's come to stay. Her grandfather's in hospital and she can't get into his flat. So she'll be here for supper tonight. I'll lay another place at the table.'

Ellen saw Patrick's eyebrows lift slightly as he exchanged a look with Marion. He seemed about to say something, but then decided not to. Instead he smiled at Ellen.

'Hi Ellen. I'm sorry to hear about your grandfather. And yes, there's plenty for all of us. It's nearly ready. Do you want to go and call the others, Lily?'

At that moment, two more people entered the kitchen. A young man was short and stocky, with floppy brown hair and a wide grin. Behind him came a young woman with short blonde hair and a kindly face who looked, Ellen thought, rather stressed and tired. Unlike the others, who wore a variety of jeans and dungarees, the woman was dressed in a smart navy blue suit. A few minutes later Helen, who Ellen remembered from the demonstration, entered the kitchen.

'This is Ellen,' announced Lily again. 'She's coming to stay for a bit while her grandpa is in hospital. We met at the demo today.'

Ellen felt everyone's eyes on her as she was introduced for the second time. It was uncomfortable being the focus of everyone's attention. She saw the same questioning, perhaps slightly amused, look that she had seen on Patrick's face exchanged between the newcomers to the kitchen. Like him, they said nothing and instead smiled at Ellen.

'Hello! I'm James and this is Carol. Welcome!' said the stocky young man.

Noisily, and with much shuffling and joshing, the members of the group each found a place to sit. 'Here it comes,' said Patrick as he took the lid off the black pot he had carried carefully over to the table. He put a spoon into the pot so that everyone could start helping themselves. Then, turning to Carol, he said, 'How did it go today?'

'Terrible. We had to take that baby I told you about into care. It was horrible. The baby cried and cried and so did her mother. I'm going to try and get her into rehab in the women's project in Exeter Road. If she can get off the drugs she might be able to get her baby back. But they were full last week. I'm going to keep pestering them.'

'Poor you. It's tough being a social worker! But mainly, poor them,' said Lily. 'I had some good news today. I was talking to someone from the union about the demo on Saturday and they'd heard – at last – that they're finally going to close the secondary modern down the road. It means all the schools round here will be proper comprehensives.'

Patrick grinned. 'Hope that means they're going to get round to shutting down places like my posh school! Sending kids away from home to live with strangers and get beaten – I think it's child abuse. I remember one housemaster, he used to make the poor victim put on gym shorts and lean over a chair then he'd run up at him and beat him with a cricket bat. He'd invite some prefects in to watch – and to hold him down.'

There were some gasps round the table. Then Jamie spoke. 'Getting caned isn't just another privilege of you public school boys, you know. It happened lots at Greenfield secondary modern too. And we didn't get any exams or any leg ups in the world when we left, like your lot did. I bet loads of people on your course went to public school, didn't they?'

Patrick shrugged. 'Probably – I haven't got to know them that well.'

Marion put down her knife and fork and pushed a strand of her long black hair behind an ear. 'I know it's right, but I don't suppose I could have got to college if I hadn't been to a grammar school. No one else in my family did.'

'Bet you would have,' said Carol. 'I've met your mum, remember. She's really bright and you've told us she used to read to you a lot when you were little. That's what makes a difference – having parents who support you, especially when you're under five. We should be campaigning for better education for small children if we want to make a difference.'

'Maybe,' replied Marion. 'But the people I teach – who've grown up and never learnt to read – aren't stupid. They've just missed out on schooling. We should make sure people can go on being educated however old they are. And another thing…' Ellen noticed Marion's voice getting louder now. 'I think schools should be mixed. The worst thing at my school was being with all girls. It was so uptight. And we were all expected to be teachers or nurses.'

'Yeah,' said Helen, 'but the trouble with having boys around is you never get a word in. The boys shout out most and the teachers always seem to ask them first. They didn't seem to care about me – even though I'd passed my eleven-plus. I just opted out. Might have been different if my parents had made a fuss but they were scared of the teachers. They'd never been near a grammar school before.'

'The thing about comprehensives,' said Lily, 'is that teachers should care about everyone, whatever their gender or race or whether they're poor or not.'

So far, Ellen had been sitting silently in a corner, watching this group of friends and saying nothing. She felt too young and out of place. It was all so strange and unreal – and they were all so vehement and confident. Rather to her own surprise, words came.

'They're doing that where I live. Making the schools comprehensive.'

Everyone turned to look at her expectantly, waiting for her to continue.

'I wrote a letter to the paper – my aunt and uncle were cross – that's why I'm here. I had to get away.'

'Tell us what happened, Ellen,' said Carol gently.

Six sympathetic and open faces turned towards Ellen. Instinctively, she felt that they were on her side and, unbidden, the words started to flow.

'Well, my mum died. She'd been ill and she killed herself so I was taken to a foster home and then, after the funeral, I had to go and live with my aunt and uncle. They're horrible. They're really bossy and they make me do stuff around the house but Uncle Walter and Marcus – that's my cousin – don't do anything. They just sit and watch telly while Aunt Christabel and me cook and clear up. It makes me really angry but I can't say anything.'

Ellen was aware that everyone had stopped eating. They were listening to her intently, so she carried on speaking. 'And they're snobs too. Once I went round to my friend's house – her dad's a miner – and my aunt was really rude to her mum. I hate it there. I don't ever want to go back.'

'I'm so sorry, Ellen. I can't imagine how terrible you must be feeling. What about school, can anyone there help?' Lily's face was all concentrated concern.

'I'm in trouble at school. I wrote a letter to the local paper saying that I thought my school – it's one of those direct grant schools – should be made into a comprehensive like the others and everyone was very angry. My aunt and uncle made me write a letter of apology and I did but then I ran out of school. I don't want to go back.'

Lily continued her questioning. 'Where do your aunt and uncle think you are now? Won't they be looking for you?'

'I sent a postcard saying I was OK – didn't tell them where I was.

I didn't want them to know. But thinking about it now, I reckon they'll guess I went to see grandpa.'

'And now your grandpa is in hospital. Ellen, is there anyone at home who can help? You can stay here but your aunt and uncle will have gone to the police. And someone's going to turn up at your grandpa's soon to get you back.' Ellen noticed James was beginning to think practically about what should be done.

'My best friend's Jennifer. But I don't want to get her involved. I know my aunt, she'd make trouble for her. It's best if she doesn't know where I am then no one can put pressure on her. Or there's Stuart. He's a friend who helped me when I ran out of school. I know his phone number.'

'Why not ring him? Tell him you're safe and that you're staying here. He can get a message to your aunt and uncle. And Ellen – I know you hate them, but they will be worried about you, you know. And you don't want to get yourself into worse trouble than you're already in.'

'OK.' Ellen felt reluctant but could see the sense in this; it would be good to talk to Stuart too.

'After we've eaten, I'll come to the phone box with you.'

Ellen felt Carol watching her closely. She was aware of Carol's suit and the official air it gave her. It made Ellen feel nervous. When she spoke, though, Carol sounded sympathetic.

'Ellen – your mum – I can't Imagine how terrible that must feel. But people make their own decisions about their life, you know. Her happiness wasn't your responsibility. You mustn't blame yourself.'

Ellen could feel the tears begin to prick her eyes but she wanted to go on talking.

'I wasn't a very good daughter though. I went to school and left her that morning. I knew she wasn't right.'

'Ellen – I can see from just knowing you this little while that you're a sensitive, caring person. When people are ill and want to kill themselves, they find a way. There is nothing you could have done. Whatever happened in your mother's life to make her so unhappy happened before you were born.'

Tears began to roll down Ellen's face. It was the second time she had cried in someone else's presence since her mother had died. Lily got up from her seat and, squeezing past James and Patrick, walked round the table and put her arm round her.

'It's OK, Ellen – you cry. Do you want to come next door for a bit?'

Ellen sniffed. 'No, I'll be alright.' She didn't want to leave this group of young people, sitting round the table together, in the gentle light of a table lamp. No one had told her to stop feeling, to be brave, to dry her eyes and 'get on with it'. Even though they were older than her, grown up, they seemed to accept her just as she was, and the feeling that gave her was comforting and peaceful.

Spoons were dipped into the stew and the rice. Salad was passed around the table. Everyone was hungry, including, she now realised, Ellen herself. They ate quietly for a while and then Patrick said 'Right. Shall we talk about the demo?'

'We've got most of the placards made; we just need to write some slogans on them now. And there's the anti-racist banner we made for last time. We can use that again.' Marion was brisk now, a light of determination and excitement flaring in her eyes. 'And Patrick – you're the art student – maybe you could think of a way of jazzing them up a bit?'

Ellen noticed Patrick smile and nod an amused agreement. She thought he seemed friendly and easy-going.

Then Lily turned to her. 'There's a big march, Ellen, by the British First Party – we call them the BF – planned for next Saturday. They're racists – they want to *send black people home*' and they spread vicious lies about people from other countries '*taking our jobs* and *holding our children back in school*'. Lily used emphasis to underline her disdain. 'We've organised a protest. There's loads of us. As well as the Anti-Racist Alliance, there are women's groups, trade unions, community groups. We are going to try and stop the racists from marching.'

'OK. Well, I can do some placards this evening. And we need to get more leaflets out. Can someone go to the community centre tomorrow and get some more printed? Then we can give them out at the bus stops in Brixton.' Patrick's tone was brisk.

'I can,' offered Helen.

By the end of the meal, they had agreed a plan of action. Ellen listened closely, enjoying the energy created by the discussion. For a while she forgot about her mother and running away from school, and even stopped thinking about her grandpa, asleep in his bed in St Thomas' Hospital. When she remembered him she had lost self-consciousness sufficiently to say to the whole table, 'I need to visit my grandpa tomorrow. He's having his operation on Monday. I'm really worried about him.'

'Of course you are. Do you want someone to come with you, Ellen?' Helen had been the quietest of the group so far. 'It can sometimes be hard to hear what the doctors are saying when you're worried.'

'Oh, yes please, if you're not too busy…'

'I'll take some time out from placard writing!'

'Never your favourite thing, eh Helen?' said James and then, turning to Ellen, continued, 'Meanwhile, Ellen, let's go and make that phone call.'

Obediently Ellen left the table and picked up her coat from the banisters at the bottom of the stairs. She hunted through the front pocket of her rucksack and found Stuart's address and phone number, which she'd packed without really thinking why, just before she had left Fineston.

The street outside was alive in the darkness. A motor bike roared past. Three young men were listening to music in a parked car.

Police sirens wailed as patrol cars flew up Brixton Road. A tired-looking young woman pushed a buggy with a sleeping child; two full shopping bags were hanging over the handles. At the end of the street, the phone box was empty.

'Off you go,' said James. 'Be brave. Have you got enough change?'

Ellen hunted through her purse and found enough ten pence pieces to pay for the call. Inside the box smelt of urine. Small cards advertising escort and other, rather more explicit, services were stuck to the walls. She picked up the receiver and dialled the number, coins ready to insert in the slot when the call was answered. One ring, two ring, three rings... Ellen started to feel relieved. There was no one home so she wasn't going to have to speak to anyone after all. And no one would be able to blame her. She had tried.

'Hello, Fineston 4324. Can I help?' A woman's voice, brisk, business-like. Perhaps a little tired – it was getting late now, after all. She should have thought of that.

'May I speak to Stuart please?'

'It's rather late. I'll see if he's still awake. Who can I say is speaking?'

'It's Ellen.'

'Oh! I'll get him right away. Hold on.'

Ellen realised that Stuart must have told his mother about her. She hadn't thought about that either. Insofar as she had considered it at all, she had imagined that no one other than her aunt and uncle – and Jennifer and Stuart perhaps – would have given a second thought to her disappearance. Maybe that wasn't true.

'Ellen – is that really you? I'm so glad to hear from you.' Stuart's voice sounded relieved and warm. 'Where are you? Are you OK? '

'I'm fine. I came down to London to see grandpa but he's in hospital – I couldn't get into his flat. I'm really worried about him. But I'm staying with some people I met in Brixton. They're squatting. They're really nice.'

'Squatting! In Brixton! Ellen, that doesn't sound safe at all. Who are they?'

'One's a teacher, one's a social worker, not sure yet what the others do. But they do lots of political stuff. They're organising a march against the British First next Saturday – you know, against racism and things. And one of them is going to come to the hospital with me tomorrow. I'm really worried about grandpa. He's got to have an operation. Stuart – can you tell my aunt and uncle that I'm OK? I don't want them coming down here.'

'Of course. Could I come, do you think? I'd like to go on that demo too. And I want to know that you're OK. Is there anything I can do? Have you got money?'

'I've got a bit left. Grandpa gave me some, when he went back to London after the funeral. I'm all right for now.'

'Ellen, I've been really worried.'

'I'm sorry. I'd love to see you… and if you come, do you think Jennifer might come too? It is half term up there next week isn't it? Though I know they've haven't got very much money.'

'I can find out. Ring me tomorrow, after the hospital. I'll be at home all day – got loads of homework. I want to get it done so I can enjoy half term next week. And make sure you've got the address of where you're staying.'

A peeping noise on the phone warned that Ellen's money was running out and the call would be cut off. She put in the last of her coins and said, 'And Stuart – if you see Jennifer could you tell her that I'm all right? They haven't got a phone, but I know she'll be worried.'

'Of course. I'll find her.'

There was time only for a quick goodbye from each of them and the phone went dead. But Ellen felt better. Stuart might be coming and that made her feel more light-hearted than she had for a long time. On the way back, James chatted to her about his day. He worked at a hostel for homeless men.

'My mum did that, helped out at a homeless hostel. She used to cook for them,' said Ellen.

'Did she? I do that sometimes too,' replied James. 'It can be hard work – you never know how many people will come in and they're always so hungry.'

A picture came into Ellen's mind of her mother at the hostel, busy, solicitous of the clients, capable. How could that woman have done what she did?

– – –

Back at the house, Ellen found that the table was still strewn with dirty dishes that the housemates had pushed aside to make space for their coffee cups.

'Hi Ellen.' Lily looked up from the paper she was reading. 'Was that all right?'

'Yes thanks – it was fine. Stuart – and maybe another friend – want to come down for the demonstration you were talking about next Saturday. Could they stay here too?'

'I should think so. The more people we have on our side the better.'

Helen moved her chair back from the table as she said, 'I think I'll go and get ready for bed now. I'm tired.'

Lily and Marion looked at each other with slightly raised eyebrows. It was Lily who spoke.

'Er, what about the clearing up? Who do you think is going to do that?'

Helen looked taken aback. 'It's not my turn – I did it the other day.'

Marion leapt in. 'The dishes need clearing up EVERY day, not just now and again. Patrick cooked so he shouldn't have to do it tonight. But the rest of us need to help.'

Lily supported her. 'Yes, it's not fair. It's always the same people who end up clearing away the mess. And I'm one of them. I'm fed up with it. I think we should start the cooking and clearing up rota again.'

Ellen noticed Helen tighten her lips and stiffen her shoulders, but say nothing. She watched as Helen picked up her plate and glass and carried them over to the sink. She moved the cooking dishes that Patrick had left soaking there, filled the sink with water and detergent and began to scrub a pan. Lily and Carol glanced at each other but Ellen wasn't quite sure what the look meant. Feeling that she should help, Ellen stood up and put her own plate next to the sink. Lily and Carol followed her and then, shortly afterwards, James did the same. He picked up a cloth and wiped the table down, sweeping crumbs into his hand and then putting them in the bin. Still there was silence but there was something in the looks on the faces around her that told her that there was history behind this exchange. It reminded her of her own resentment at her aunt's house at the expectation that she would do more housework than the boys. When the table was clean, Lily turned to Ellen.

'Come on, Ellen, I'll show you where you're going to sleep tonight. It's not the Ritz, but I think you'll be comfortable enough. And you must be really exhausted.'

Lily led Ellen up the stairs to the very top of the house, pointing out the bathroom and the other bedrooms on the way.

'The boys sleep in the basement, so we women have the top two floors to ourselves. A friend, Stella, had the room you're in until recently. She went off to Africa to do VSO and she's left her mattress here, so you should be comfortable enough.'

The attic room was tiny but had windows overlooking the roof tops. Ellen could see row after row of chimney pots in the streets parallel to this one and, beyond, a net of tower blocks, their lights twinkling in the darkness. It felt safe. The room was empty apart from a single mattress covered by a sleeping bag and a tartan travelling rug, like the one her mother had kept in the airing cupboard. It reminded Ellen of the times she and her mother had gone to the park in summer and had a picnic under the trees. When she was very small, she remembered, she used to lie down on the grass with her arms stretched above her head and roll down the hill to the lake. The memory made her want to cry.

Ellen lay on the bed. She felt as if she had fallen into a deep well, a well that was both inside her and outside. The deeper she seemed to sink into it the lighter, though never pale, the water became: silent, cool, thick, resistant. At the surface of the well all was dark, and clanging with noise and movement, a rumble, a jumble of sound and people panicking and pushing. Lights flashing and jarring. Ellen wanted to be under the water in the cool peace. Eventually she fell asleep.

FIFTEEN

As soon as Ellen woke in the morning she felt a familiar feeling of dread and apprehension. A red wound gaping inside her. What was it today? Then she remembered. Grandpa's operation was soon, on Monday. She had to see him today. Immediately, she leapt out of bed, got dressed and began to creep tentatively down the stairs. She felt shy and awkward in this strange house. Who would be here? How had this happened, that she'd spent the night at the house of people she didn't know in Brixton? As she reached the first landing she heard voices coming from the kitchen and realised that they were talking about her. The first voice sounded like James.

'Lily, we ought to tell someone – the police, social services – that she's here. We can't just take in a runaway teenager.'

'What will happen if we do? They'll either make her go back north to her aunt, which she'll hate, or they'll try and find her a foster home. It might be miles away and she won't be here for her grandfather's operation. Don't you think she's had enough to cope with? Anyway, she's told us she's in her last year at school, so she'll be sixteen soon. Social services will lose interest then.'

Ellen thought it was Marion who spoke next. 'We do have a room free. We're supposed to be socialists, aren't we? And she seems a nice kid!'

Carol joined in the conversation. 'And she has told her friend she's here and he'll certainly tell her aunt. Everyone will know she'll be going to the hospital to visit her grandfather. The hospital social work team will probably contact her there. I think we should leave it to them.'

Ellen didn't want the conversation to go any further than this. She wasn't going back to Fineston, not when grandpa needed her. She set off down the last staircase, making her footsteps as heavy as she could so the others would hear her. It seemed to work. When she entered the room, she found everyone sitting round the kitchen table, reading the newspapers.

'Hi Ellen, did you sleep well? We're going off to Brixton soon to give out some leaflets about the demo tomorrow. Do you want to come? They won't let you in the hospital until this afternoon.'

'OK.'

– – –

An hour later they were all wrapped up in scarves and woolly hats, standing on the main road, by the Saturday market stalls, in the centre of Brixton. Each of them had a bundle of leaflets giving details of the planned march. 'MARCH AGAINST THE RACISTS: DON'T LET THEM PASS' was printed in red and below, in black, the details of the time and place. The pavement was bustling. Crowds of people poured off a succession of red buses that halted by the market entrance. Shoppers with large baskets carried home yams, mangoes and sweet potatoes. Children tightly clutched their parents' hands. Kids on bikes weaved along the outside edge of the pavement, ducking on and off the road.

'You stand with me,' suggested James and the two of them, positioned by the market entrance, held out leaflets to passers-by. Mostly, they were received with interest and a 'Thanks love'.

Occasionally someone walked past with deliberately averted eyes, turning a shoulder to Ellen and looking cross. But Ellen quickly became inured to this and patiently waited to hand out her leaflet to the next person who passed. It seemed like a good thing to do. Her mother would, she thought, have approved. A year or so ago, Ellen remembered, mum had had a vicious argument with an old friend who had complained that 'these Asians are moving into our street and house prices are going to fall'.

'They've got as much right as anyone to live here,' her mother had said angrily. Ellen remembered and felt proud.

Everyone was hungry by the time all the leaflets had been given out.

'Let's go to Frank's Café,' said James. 'I could do with some chips now. And I reckon we've deserved a fry-up. We've done well this morning.' He led the way, past the market entrance towards a side street off the main road.

Ellen was walking behind James and Patrick, listening to Marianne talk about a woman in her literacy class whose inability to read properly had left her embarrassed and awkward ever since. 'She used to pretend she had poor eyesight and had lost her glasses whenever she was given anything to read in public.' As they turned off the main road a glass bottle landed at Ellen's feet and shattered into jagged pieces.

'Look out – get back,' shouted Lily as she moved quickly in front of Ellen. On the other side of the road two tall white men with shavedheads were strolling slowly down the narrow pavement and laughing. One was opening a beer bottle with his teeth. Ellen could see that the other man was wearing a Union Jack t-shirt under his leather jacket. She found his expression odd – a kind of sneering grin that frightened her. There was a glare of excitement in his eyes.

Walking towards the men were two black teenagers, a boy and a girl who were talking earnestly together. Ellen could see they hadn't seen the men coming towards them. As they got closer one of the men shouted, 'Here – move.' But the teenagers didn't move. They were too wrapped up in their conversation and carried on walking until the girl bumped into the leather-jacketed man.

'Oi – I said MOVE,' he shouted as he reached out and pushed the girl away by her shoulder. 'Go back to the jungle, you wog.'

As Ellen felt a surge of fear and rage she saw Patrick rush up to the men and put himself between the girl and them. 'Leave her alone,' he said.

James, Carol and Lily were by Patrick's side now. Together they formed a shield between the teenagers and the men.

'Who's gonna make me?'

'We are,' said Carol calmly. 'You need to stop threatening people. The police station is round the corner and the cops can be here in two minutes.' She turned round and said to Helen, who was standing behind her, 'Helen – go to the police station now and ask them to send an officer. Quickly.'

'Be careful!' shouted Lily. 'They've got knives!'

And Ellen saw, for a moment, a flash of steel in the hands of one of the thugs. Later, recalling the moment, she said it was if her mind closed down and her body took over. She started to scream, 'Stop it, stop it, stop it.'

Both men looked round, startled, and at that moment a policeman appeared, running round the corner from the main road. The two men looked at each other and, without a word, turned and ran back up the side street. Pushing through the crowd that was gathering the policeman followed, running now. The men were soon out of sight and Ellen was aware of Marianne's arm around her and a soothing voice.

'It's OK, Ellen. They've gone now.'

As Ellen's fear and anger subsided she became aware again of the housemates around her. Lily was talking to the young girl who had been pushed out of the way.

'Are you sure you're OK?'

The girl nodded as her friend put a protective arm around her and said, 'We're alright, thanks. I'll take her home.'

Patrick looked round at the others and let out a long breath of relief. 'I think we've earned that fry-up, don't you?'

'Certainly have,' said Lily. 'And Carol – you were brilliant! You manged to stay so calm.'

'Comes in useful being a social worker sometimes. I'm used to dealing with angry people!'

— — —

Helen suggested that she and Ellen went and found a cup of coffee at the hospital. It was going to be visiting time soon. At 2.00 p.m. exactly, Ellen left Helen behind in the cafeteria, climbed the stairs, pushed the swing door of Kingsland Ward and walked through. Two nurses in crisp white uniforms were sitting at a desk on the right of a wide corridor with a faded red linoleum floor. Beyond them were two rows of high metal beds, each with a white cover. On the high pillows of each bed Ellen could see a face. The faces looked curiously similar. Each seemed pale and distant, with eyes that were barely focused. How could she find grandpa? It seemed rude to walk up and down staring at people. She went back to the desk. 'Excuse me, could you tell me which bed Mr Maddox is in, please?'

'He's halfway down on the left hand side, dear.'

'Thanks.'

Ellen set off slowly down the middle of the ward. The faces she had imagined to be blank a few moments earlier now all seemed to be looking at her suspiciously. Right, this was halfway. Could that be him? A head of curly grey hair peeped out above the covers. Blue eyes, staring at the ceiling.

'Grandpa?'

'Eh, what?'

'Grandpa. It's me. Ellen.'

The head shook from side to side, as if its owner were trying to return from some distant thought. Then the familiar blue eyes settled on her face.

'Ellen! What are you doing here?'

'I've come to see you, Grandpa. What's the matter with you? I've been so worried. I came to London and then there was no one in your flat and your neighbour told me you'd been taken to hospital. What's wrong with you?'

Grandpa eased himself up onto his elbows so that he could see more clearly. Ellen reached over and adjusted his pillow to give him support.

'Thanks, love.' Grandpa looked her full in the face for the first time and smiled.

'I'm having an operation on Monday but you're not to worry. I'm very lucky really. Got this terrible pain in my stomach and Mavis downstairs, she called the hospital and they sent an ambulance for me.'

Ellen gasped. She felt her chest tighten. All her other worries disappeared and she was concentrating only on grandpa.

'They're very good here and the doctor says I'm ready for the op and they can patch up the hole and I should be fine afterwards.'

'Why didn't you tell me, Grandpa?'

'I didn't want to worry you, not after everything that's happened. I was going to tell you after the operation, when I was better.'

'I'm going to stay here, Grandpa, and look after you.'

Grandpa smiled and patted Ellen's hand. 'There are lots of questions I need to ask you, young lady, but they can wait. Where are you staying? Do you need the key to my flat?'

'It's OK. I'm staying with some friends in Brixton. They're really nice.'

'Friends? What friends? Who are they? What do they do? And does your aunt know?'

'It's fine, Grandpa. Lily's a teacher and another girl in the house is a social worker. And, yes, Aunt Christabel knows.'

This would be true by now, thought Ellen. She knew that she mustn't worry her grandfather, so she said nothing about what had happened in Fineston and how she had run away. There would be time for all that. Now, she just wanted to make sure grandpa had everything he needed and wasn't frightened.

'Can I get you anything from the shop? Would you like some grapes? Or some juice?'

'No thanks, love. I'm not allowed anything like that. But if you like you could read to me. I've got one of my detective books over in the cabinet by the bed.'

Of the many things Ellen had always loved about going to stay with grandpa were the stories he used to make up about a battered old teddy bear that had lived for nearly a hundred years. The teddy bear had a Yorkshire accent and a nasal, rather mournful voice. Passed down from one generation to the next it had been loved by lots of children – and had lots of adventures. Ellen remembered some of them now as she sat by grandpa's bed.

Through the glass windows she could see Big Ben and the Houses of Parliament, reflected lights already twinkling in the river as the afternoon darkened. The sight seemed familiar to her, and comforting. Memories of walks along the river with grandpa floated into her mind. She remembered how they used to climb round the curved stairs at the back of the red bus and sit, if they could, on the front seat. At Waterloo, they'd walk along the footpath under the railway tunnel to the concrete splendour of the Royal Festival Hall. Sometimes they would turn left and follow the river path until they reached Westminster Bridge and the stone bulk of County Hall. Everything had always felt safe when Ellen was with grandpa. Now he lay, looking much smaller than usual, vulnerable in his hospital bed. The faraway expression in his eyes frightened her. If anything happened to him she would be completely alone. She picked up the book and started to read. At eight thirty a nurse walked down the ward, reminding people that visiting time was over. Ellen couldn't bear to leave.

'I'll be here tomorrow,' she said, leaning over to kiss him.

Grandpa squeezed her hand. 'I'm going to be fine, you know. I'll see you tomorrow.'

– – –

Ellen stumbled out of the ward. It was odd to see so many people going about their mundane daily tasks as if nothing out of the ordinary were happening. A dark-haired young man she passed on the stairs was telling the young woman with him about his plans for the evening. An administrative assistant was carrying a tall pile of files. Doctors, with their stethoscopes casually strung around their necks, chatted amiably to each other. Ellen continued down the stairs. Where was the cafeteria? Would Helen still be there? Ellen walked along the wide corridor leading from the hospital's main entrance to the cafeteria and saw Helen sitting at a table by the window, overlooking the river. Several newspapers were spread out in front of her.

'Looks like there's a lot of publicity for the march next weekend,' she said. 'How was your grandfather?'

'OK, but he looked old and sort of shrunk. I'm really scared, Helen. He's going to be alright, isn't he?'

'I'm sure he is. They're very good here, you know.'

Ellen felt as if she had been dismissed. Part of her wanted to share her anxiety about her grandfather, to talk about how she was feeling. She had hoped that Helen might understand, but her mind seemed to be on other things.

'Come on, let's get the bus home and you can help make some banners this evening for next Saturday.'

On the journey home Helen talked more about the coming demonstration. It looked as if the British First march was going to go ahead. Their right to free speech and to protest would be upheld by the police, even though the BF was a racist organisation. It was vital to get thousands of people there to try and stop them. Ellen remembered that her grandfather had been in a trade union when he had worked for the council as an electrician.

Once when she and her mother had visited him, he had been planning a demonstration with some of his fellow union members. His flat, Ellen now realised, though she hadn't noticed it at the time, was tiny. There was a living room, with a window onto the street, two small bedrooms and, beyond them, a tiny space opening off the hallway that contained a dining table. At the back of the flat, overlooking a concrete roof area a narrow kitchen and shower room had been converted from a store room. These flats had been built without bathrooms. An old swimming baths in a nearby street had changing rooms round the side of the pool and a number of bathrooms that you could pay to use. Many families had gone there once a week, or, if they were hard up, less often, for their regular wash and scrub. When Ellen and her mother had gone to stay grandpa had given up his bedroom for them and slept in the smaller one himself.

On this occasion, Ellen remembered, there had been six or seven men in the living room. They were angry.

'What they've done to Mick. It's just not right.'

'Sacked for no reason.'

Ellen hadn't really understood what the men were talking about but she remembered the feeling in the crowded room well enough to think, now, that if she got involved in this demonstration grandpa would be proud of her.

Her mind came back briefly to Helen's chatter about the march, but she still couldn't focus properly. Instead a conversation between two young men sitting across the aisle from them drifted across her attention.

'Are you inviting Polly?

'No, I don't really like her.'

'What about Sarah?'

'No, I don't like her either.'

'You do like Sarah.'

'Nah… I don't like anybody. I can't stand so many people – they just stress me out.'

Ellen glanced at the plump bespectacled boy who had just spoken and felt a wave of sympathy and compassion for him.

– – –

Back at the house, everyone was home. Lily was cooking paprika chicken and rice for supper. Patrick was sitting on the battered sofa in the living room strumming on his guitar and the others were laughing as they sang along. The song, 'On Ilkla Moor Bar T'at', was familiar to Ellen. Her grandfather had sung it to her when she was young and he had taken her walking on the moors. It used to make her laugh then. Now, she felt very alone as she listened and watched this group of people, whom she hardly knew, amused by their friend's playing. She remembered that she had promised to ring Stuart.

'I'm going to the phone box,' she said.

'Will you be OK on your own? I'll come with you if you like,' offered James.

'I think I'll be OK.'

'Here – better take the spare key. You can hang on to it for now.' James went into the hall and fished around inside a tin box filled with pencils that stood on the rickety table in the hall until he found the key. 'Take care of it – it's our only spare.'

As before, the street was buzzing with energy. Music came from the top floor of the house opposite. Kids stood on the corner. Ellen liked it much better than the stiff curtains, the protected gardens and the silence of her aunt's road. In the phone box she dialled the number and listened to the phone ringing back in Fineston; it was answered immediately and she heard Stuart's voice.

'Hello, Fineston 4324.'

'It's me, Ellen.'

'Ellen! How good to hear from you. How was your grandpa?'

'He's having his operation on Monday. He looked really old. I'm frightened.'

'I'm sure they'll look after him, Ellen. And it's good that you can be there when he has the operation'?'

'Yes – I'll be there.'

'Ellen, I've talked to mum and dad and they've said I can come and see you next weekend, and go on the demo. They feel guilty I think that they don't do anything political these days, they're so busy at the law centre. But they support the demo and were quite pleased, I think, that I wanted to go. Any chance I could stay with you?'

'I did ask and they said yes. I'm sure it will be fine. It will be so nice to see you.'

'And, Ellen, I told mum and dad about our conversation and they've rung your aunt and uncle. They've been terribly worried about you. I think they do care what happens to you, you know. They've been to the police, but when they told them about the postcard, they said they didn't think you were a priority for the cops. A policeman came round here to talk to me and I told them I'd spoken to you and that you were safe and that you wanted to see your grandpa. I don't know what they might do now.'

'Oh no,' Ellen gasped. She wanted to stay hidden. She didn't want to go back to all that – though she knew, deep down, that she couldn't hide forever.

'Ellen, I think you should ring them. Wait until I'm down next weekend maybe. But do it. It will make things easier in the long run. You can't run away forever and there's your education to sort out.'

'I know. But I can't think about it just now. Tell them I'm OK and I'll ring next weekend. They'll be so angry with me – again. I'm not sure I can bear it.'

– – –

Ellen was waiting at the ward door just before two the next day, Sunday. The nurse she'd met the day before was on duty at the desk again. She smiled when she saw Ellen and beckoned her over.

'You're OK, love – you can slip in and see him now. He's had a good night.'

'Thank you.'

Ellen remembered where the bed was and went straight to it. Grandpa was sitting up, propped by several cushions, reading his book.

'Hello, love.'

'Hello, Grandpa. How are you feeling?'

'Well, it's like a hotel in here. All these nurses bring you things when you need them. And look out the window – you'd pay a lot for a view like that!'

Ellen followed her grandfather's gaze and saw the tranquil river lapping gently against the stone walls of the parliament building. It seemed unreal and very vivid, as if the scene were lit by spotlights on a stage. They sat and gazed for a moment. Then grandpa spoke.

'Ellen – you're not to worry. I'm going to be OK. And when this is over, we'll sort out what's going to happen to you.'

Ellen felt a tear rise in her eyes and forced it back. She felt grandpa watching her closely, but couldn't speak. There was so much to talk about and plan but it seemed too distant now. It was all too hard. All that mattered was what was going to happen to grandpa. The silence lingered for a while and then grandpa smiled at her.

'Tell you what. Read to me again. You're a really good reader and my eyes get tired after a bit. Here – start with this story. I've just finished the last one.'

At five o'clock it was time to go. Ellen bent down and kissed her grandfather on the cheek. He reached up and squeezed her hand.

'Night Grandpa.'

'Night love – and thanks for coming.'

'See you tomorrow.'

'Yeah – see you tomorrow.'

Back at the house, all was quiet and peaceful. Lily, whose half term was now over, was sitting at the kitchen table planning her lessons for the next day. Not wanting to disturb her, Ellen went through to the sitting room where the boys were playing their guitars together. Marion and Helen were reading the newspapers. They all looked up as Ellen came in.

'Hi Ellen – how was your grandpa?'

'Good. I'm going there first thing tomorrow, so I can be with him when he goes for his op.'

Marion smiled at her. 'He's very lucky to have such a wonderful granddaughter, Ellen,' she said.

Ellen didn't know what to do or say. She felt uncomfortable. Everyone in the room seemed relaxed and involved in what they were doing. Could she just sit here for a while? Would they think her odd, an intruder? She wasn't sure, but she didn't want to climb the stairs alone to her room at the top of the house and find her thoughts, her memories of the past, her fears for her grandfather crowd in on her. As she hesitated James looked up and smiled.

'Hey, Ellen, come and listen to us. You know we like an audience. We're show-offs!'

Ellen pulled up one of the bare wooden chairs, sat down and

listened to a haunting blues riff. When they paused Patrick asked, 'Do you play anything Ellen?'

'Piano, a bit. But not guitar.'

'Do you want to have a go? Go on, it's easy. I'll show you.'

Ellen felt reluctant, but she was even more nervous of saying no than of picking up the guitar, so she sat on the wooden chair James had pulled up for her and took the shiny red instrument. It was small but very heavy and solid, not like the one her music teacher sometimes used to lead singing lessons. The curve in the body of this guitar fitted neatly onto her knee though, and felt comfortable. James adjusted her left hand on the instrument's neck so that she could reach the strings easily.

'OK. Each string is tuned to a note – like each note you play on the piano – but you make different notes by holding the strings down on the guitar neck. Here – play the top string – that's an E.' Ellen plucked the top string with her thumb.

'Sorry,' said James. 'I called it the top string but that's because it's a higher sound. It's the one on the bottom of the strings – nearest to the floor.'

Ellen plucked again, more firmly. The sound was a bit fuller this time.

'Good. Now you can turn that into a G by putting your finger on the third fret here – see?' James guided Ellen's left hand down the guitar neck until she could hold the string down with her finger. She plucked the string again and the note sounded different this time. 'OK. Now you can play a chord while Patrick sings. Strum those four strings. That's it.'

Patrick started to sing again and Ellen, following the beat of James's nodding head, strummed the chord. It felt good.

'OK, now play the G note and then the chord – then the D string and the chord. Just keep going like that.'

Patrick kept on singing. It reminded Ellen of listening to Bob

Dylan with Stuart and she felt a shooting pang of loneliness as she remembered how warm and comforting it had been to be sitting with him, talking about what had happened to her.

The singing stopped and Ellen heard James start talking again. She could hear the words but she couldn't make sense of them.

'Chord patterns are harmonised scales. Start with C E G – C scales are all white notes so if you go up the scale harmonising a C scale, C will go to D, E to F and G to A. F major will go to G7 which will make a dominant 7. The key point is that chords are sets of scales put together.'

Ellen had no idea what he was talking about but she felt comfortable listening to him. She wasn't used to being given so much attention and his voice sounded friendly and enthusiastic. Marion's voice interrupted James's flow.

'All right, you two. Time for the rest of us to join in, I think. Let's sing 'All around my cap.'

Marion and Helen stood up from their seats and came to stand by the others, next to the window. Patrick started to pick out the chords and Marion, who had a strong, clear voice, started to sing. Ellen listened as the others joined in and then, having picked up the chorus, 'All around my cap I will wear the green ribbon', she sang too, but very quietly, so no-one else could hear.

In her attic room that night, Ellen remembered how warm and safe it had felt to part of the group singing together downstairs. She felt a little less lonely.

SIXTEEN

Ellen got up very early on Monday so that she could be at the hospital and see grandpa before he went down for his operation. It was dark and cold as she waited for the bus on Brixton Road. Beside her at the bus stop stood a man in overalls and a woolly hat, with a tool box in his hand, and a woman with a shawl wrapped around her shoulders, her hands thrust deep in her pockets. They all shivered. The bus was empty and rattled quickly along the road up to Waterloo. In the hospital bright lights glared as, Ellen imagined, they had all night. A nurse and a porter, eyes lowered, were walking along the corridor to the lifts. Ellen followed them. The lift was empty. She pressed the button for floor three, walked down the corridor and pushed through the doors into Kingsland Ward where the reception desk was brightly lit too. A nurse looked up from her notebook.

'Ah, you're here to see Mr Maddox, aren't you? Go through, he's awake.'

Grandpa was lying back in his bed, eyes open, staring at the ceiling.

'Hello, love. You shouldn't have got up so early, you know.'

'I wanted to see you before, you know, before you went down for your operation. I'm going to wait here until you're back.'

Grandpa smiled. 'You're a good lass. But you're not to worry. The doctors here are really good. I'm looking forward to my cup of tea afterwards!'

There was a look on grandpa's face, though, that scared Ellen. His blue eyes looked paler than usual and more translucent. She felt they were staring at something far away, beyond her. They sat quietly for a few minutes until a large, white-coated doctor with curly brown hair came and stood by the bed.

'Hello, Mr Maddox. I'm your anaesthetist. I just want to make a few checks before your operation.'

Ellen moved away.

'It's OK, you can stay if you like. The porters will be here soon. You can go down in the lift with him.'

Ellen sat silently on the edge of her chair watching as the doctor checked Grandpa's pulse. Two orderlies arrived. Brisk and cheerful they took the brake off grandpa's bed and began to manoeuvre it out into the centre of the ward.

'Are you coming, love?' one of them said to Ellen.

'Yes please.' She followed as the bed was pushed the length of the ward, out of the doors to the lift. As they passed the reception desk the nurse on duty passed Ellen a card and said, 'Ring us at about twelve o'clock. Here's the number. Have you got money for the phone box?'

'Yes, I think so.'

There was a moment's pause before the lift arrived and they all got in. It stopped at floor five and the porter looked gently at Ellen.

'This is where you leave us, love.'

Ellen squeezed grandpa's hand. 'I'll see you later, Grandpa,' she said. And she watched as the bed disappeared through a plastic screen into a forbidden area of the hospital. A feeling of loss and bewilderment overwhelmed her. Now what? What should she do?

The cafeteria on the ground floor was busy. Breakfast was laid out on the long stainless steel counters and the smell of bacon pervaded the space. Ellen found a brown plastic tray and chose a slice of toast and a cup of coffee. Then she remembered her mother saying 'You must have your vitamin C in the morning' and she picked up a glass of orange juice too. She wasn't sure she was going to be able to eat anything. The river beyond the plate glass window of the cafeteria was silver grey in the pale sunlight and Ellen sat and stared as the waves bashed into the bank, exploded and then retreated. Up and back, up and back; they went on forever. Ellen felt her stomach rise and fall with the movement of the water, as if the fear that gripped her had been given a reality in the world outside her mind.

When had she felt frightened like this before? A memory flooded back. It was soon after they had moved into their council house in Fossett Crescent, so she must have been about four. Ellen knew that she had had an empty, dark feeling inside. She knew her dad wasn't in the house with them, but she didn't know why. There was a large mahogany wardrobe decorated with a swirly pattern of lighter wood. It shone in the single beam of sunlight that entered her parents' bedroom. There was a large bed too, covered in a green candlewick bedspread, and a dressing table with three mirrors hinged together on top of it. A glass tray held a hair brush and the small mirror that her mother used to see the back of her head when she put her hair up with long pins. The pins often fell on the floor and Ellen would find them and bend them into toy figures.

She didn't dare do that today though. Her mother was standing sideways on to her, trying to fasten the zip at the back of her dress and muttering to herself as she couldn't quite reach. Her hair was already done and she wore scarlet lipstick that made her lips look startlingly large. Her mouth was frowning and Ellen knew that she had done something to upset her mother. She had no idea what it was. But she was frightened. She knew they had to go shopping and that her mother didn't want to go. She knew she was going to be a nuisance. She wouldn't be able to walk quickly enough and she was too small to carry anything. There might be something else but she didn't know what it was. She had to go though. And she would try to be good and not upset her mother. If she did she would be lost and alone.

As she would be alone if grandpa died. If he didn't come round after his operation. If they couldn't repair the damage in his stomach and he didn't recover. Ellen felt her ribs moving slowly out and in and she could feel a sharpness as her breath moved through her lungs. Colours around her were searingly bright: the scrambled egg and the tomatoes on the serving trays, the dark red tiled floor, the yellow patch where the sunlight shone onto the wall. Her fellow diners, though, seemed far away, pale and insignificant.

Ellen sat for a long time. She listened to the chimes of Big Ben: one, two, three, four... and, finally, ten. She could see the clock over the river and, without thinking, got up from her seat and took her tray with her dirty plate and cup on it over to the trolley in the centre of the room. She remembered her mother saying, 'Scrape ALL the crumbs off the plate, Ellen', and she put her foot on the pedal of the waste bin and removed as much of the mess on her plate as she could. Then she walked out of the hospital.

The air was cold but the winter sun still shone. She walked towards Westminster Bridge and climbed the steps from the Embankment up onto the pavement. In front of her were the now familiar Houses of Parliament, proud and stern against the pale blue sky. Each delicate spire suggested a memory or a dream. The large, confident tower over the House of Lords was a counterpoint to the spire above Big Ben which rose, taller than she remembered it, to a distant point in the sky. Set into the side of the building were long lines of windows, with curved tops, smaller panes within the large frame. What was going on behind them? Were there people just like her, ordinary people, in there? As a child she had had a picture book called *Sights of London* and on the front cover had been exactly this picture. London had seemed a magical, faraway place. Her mother had spoken wistfully of it sometimes; 'I should have gone back there,' she would say, 'not stayed here in this horrid little town, with nothing to do. I could have made something of myself there.' Ellen wondered if it would have made a difference. Would her mother have found a new self if, when she became a widow and a single parent, she'd escaped from the black stone of Fineston and gone back to the London of her childhood?

Ellen set off, walking slowly across the bridge. Red buses passed her. Barges with covered loads drifted calmly along the river. Ellen headed towards Westminster, past the hot dog stall and an American couple who were taking pictures of each other. At the other side of the bridge, a policeman stood very still at the entrance to the Palace of Westminster car park, his hands clasped behind his back. He looked like a character in one of the story books that she had read when she was small. Ellen carried on walking. She crossed Parliament Square and set off towards St James's Park, her feet crunching through dying autumn leaves. At the far side of the park stood the pale bulk of Buckingham Palace. More toy figures here – the guards standing stock still with their bearskin hats, and swords held across their bodies. Ellen wandered on, down the other side of the park and over the bridge, stopping for a moment to watch the ducks serenely skimming the pond. The café was open and she joined a short queue of mothers with toddlers in pushchairs and bought a cup of tea.

The clock struck again. One, two, three and, finally, twelve. It was time to contact the hospital. Worried now that she would be late, Ellen left her tea and ran back to Parliament Square. A red telephone box stood at the entrance to Victoria Street. That was the one. Ellen took out the piece of paper with the number that the nurse had given her and went into the phone box. She lifted the receiver and dialled the number. It seemed to ring for ages then, as the panic was rising in the chest, there was an answer. 'St Thomas' Hospital, can I help?' Ellen heard the pips and put her money into the slot.

'Hello. I'm ringing about Mr Maddox. He had an operation this morning. I want to know how he is.'

'One moment, please, I'll put you through.' A wait. Ages and ages.

Then, 'Intensive care, how can I help?'

'I'm Mr Maddox's granddaughter. I want to know how he is.'

'Good. He's out of the operating theatre and recovering well. You can come and see him in a couple of hours. Give us until three o'clock. Come to the intensive care ward – they can direct you to it at reception.'

Ellen fell back against the side of the phone box, relief making her weak. Grandpa was still alive. She could go and see him. The winter sun over Westminster Bridge continued to shine. Ellen walked back slowly towards the hospital and leant for a while over the green balustrade halfway along the bridge. A small girl was laughing as she waved a balloon on a string.

— — —

Steely neon strips threw a bright, harsh light on the ward as Ellen entered cautiously. They cancelled out the sun beyond the windows and the ward seemed like a brightly lit underground cavern. Down each side of the room there was a line of high beds, each with an occupant attached to a series of tubes and machines. How would she know which one was grandpa? A nurse passed.

'Excuse me, could you tell me where my grandpa, Mr Maddox, is please?'

The nurse smiled. 'He's in bed number 14 on the right. He'll be very sleepy, love, and might not be able to say much.'

'How is he? How did the operation go?'

'He's recovering well. It all went smoothly. The doctor will be round later and you can talk to him then.'

Ellen carried on down the ward and stopped by bed 14. Like the other patients, grandpa was fixed to a machine and bags of liquid. His head was turned away and his eyes closed. He looked very small and very fragile. Ellen moved closer.

'Grandpa. It's me.'

There was no response. Ellen reached out for the hand that wasn't attached to any tubes and tried again.

'It's me, Grandpa. Are you OK?'

This time, his eyes fluttered open and a tiny smile flickered across his lips.

'Ellen! Hello love.'

'Are you OK?'

'I am – especially now you're here.'

And then his eyes closed and he drifted back to sleep. Ellen sat there for a while. A nurse passed. 'Is he OK?' Ellen asked.

'He's fine. He just needs to sleep. I should sit with him for a bit and then slip away.'

Ellen watched her grandfather breathing peacefully. It was just good to see him, alive and restful. Time passed by. Ellen had no idea how long she had been there. There was a flurry at the end of the room and a doctor with wiry red hair and a white coat that seemed too small for his big frame pushed through the doors at the end of the ward. With him were some younger doctors, three men and a woman. They walked slightly behind him and looked nervous. A nurse hurried to Ellen's side.

'The doctor's here, you'd better go.'

'But I want to know how grandpa is. Can't I ask him?'

'Later, not now. You mustn't get in the way while he's doing his rounds.'

Reluctantly, Ellen stood up and edged down the ward. As the group of doctors passed her she found herself speaking.

'Excuse me. I'm Mr Maddox's granddaughter. Please can you tell me how he is?'

Ellen thought she saw a flash of irritation pass across the older doctor's face. Then he focused on Ellen. She felt him soften; she wondered if her anxiety showed in her pale face. He paused.

'The operation went well. I'm pleased to say that we were able to repair the damage. He will need a lot of rest. We'll need to keep him in for a few days and then, when he gets home, he'll have to stay in bed. And definitely no stairs!'

Ellen started to cry.

'Is someone with you?' Then, looking round, 'Nurse – can you look after this young woman please?' A nurse hurried forward and ushered Ellen out of the doctor's way and soon afterwards she was back in what she was beginning to think of as her Brixton home.

— — —

When Ellen arrived at the hospital the following day, grandpa had been moved to a new ward. There was still a lot of equipment in there and patients were attached to tubes and monitors, as they had been the day before, but the atmosphere was more relaxed. Visitors around the beds seemed cheerful and relieved. This was where people recovered. Ellen moved to the desk to ask which bed her grandfather was in when a young nurse tapped her on the arm.

'Are you Ellen? Mr Wentworth's granddaughter?'

Ellen's heart leapt. Did this mean something had happened? Something bad?

'Don't worry, dear, your grandfather's doing fine. It's just that our hospital social worker would like to have a word with you.'

'A social worker!' Ellen could hear the note of panic in her own voice. 'Why?' In her head she thought, they've found me. They're going to make me go back. She looked back at the ward entrance. Could she run away? But if she did she wouldn't be able to see grandpa. She stood silent and uncertain for a moment, panic swirling inside her head.

'Ellen,' said another voice beside her. This time it was that of a young woman with long, wavy, light brown hair.

'Don't be alarmed. I'm Marie. I'm a social worker and I want to help you.'

'I need to see grandpa. I can't talk now.' Ellen wanted to run, to get away from this person who, she was sure, was going to make her go back to her aunt's.

'Ellen, I need to talk to you. The police have been in contact with me. They're looking for you. Don't be frightened. I know your grandfather is ill and that you want to see him. I'm not going to stop you doing that. But I must speak to you. Tell you what. Go and say hello to your grandpa and then we'll talk. I'll wait here by the desk.'

Ellen looked around. The desk was by the door. There was no way she could get past it without Marie seeing her. She was caught. The only thing to do now was to see grandpa and then make it clear to Marie that she wasn't going back to her aunt's, ever.

When she arrived at his bedside grandpa smiled at her.

'Hello, love.'

'Hello, how are you feeling?'

'Well, the nurses here give me stuff to take the pain away, so I'm happy just lying here. Though they keep coming to look at me and poke and prod me and stick needles into me! Don't know why they can't leave an old man in peace!'

'I'm sure they know what they're doing, Grandpa – and you're to do as you're told.'

'When my head's a bit clearer, we need to talk about you and why you're here just now.'

'Grandpa – I'm here to look after you. And I'm going to stay and…'

Grandpa raised a hand, as if to interrupt her, but Ellen continued.

'I've decided, Grandpa. I'm sixteen soon and then I don't have to live with my aunt any more. There's a social worker here I'm going to talk to, so I'm not all on my own. And you're not to worry. I'm going to look after you. Now, would you like me to read some more of your book to you?'

Grandpa smiled and Ellen took the book out of the bedside cabinet and started to read.

— — —

Grandpa fell asleep before the story ended. Ellen sat for a moment or two watching him breathing evenly, a gentle snore gradually deepening into a rather louder one. He looked very peaceful. Beyond his bed Ellen could see the grey river flowing past the hospital and she felt herself sinking into a calm that reflected the gentle wash of the waves. A few minutes later, she was aroused by a touch on her arm. It was Marie.

'Ellen, this might be a good time for us to talk. Come over here, there's a quiet space by the desk.'

Marie led the way to a tiny alcove behind the ward desk that had just enough room in it for two chairs. The two sat opposite each other and Ellen was able to look closely at this new social worker without feeling that she was making her uncomfortable. She saw a slightly furrowed forehead, brown concerned eyes and a hand covered with rings that kept sweeping her long hair back from her face. Marie was wearing trousers and a t-shirt covered by a cream shirt. Ellen thought how young she seemed. And, maybe, a bit nervous.

'Ellen, I want to help. I know what a terrible time you've had. But when you ran away everyone was worried.'

Inside Ellen was thinking, 'I bet they were relieved,' but she said nothing.

'Your aunt and uncle were frantic when you didn't come home from school. They rang the school, of course, and when they found out that you hadn't been there all day they went round to your friend Jennifer's house.'

This did surprise Ellen. But she went on listening quietly.

'Then, of course, when they didn't know where you were they had to go to the police, and they contacted your social worker. It was your friend Stuart who let your aunt know where you were.'

'I know, I rang him up. He said he was going to tell people.'

'Then the police contacted the police here and they went round to your grandfather's flat and found out what had happened to him. We all guessed we'd find you here.'

Ellen was beginning to feel as if she was being told off – again. Did she always have to be in the wrong? Would anyone understand how she felt? Marie waited a moment then said gently, 'Ellen, you must have felt terrible to do what you did. I can only try and imagine how you feel. But why were you so desperate to get away from your aunt's house?'

'They didn't want me there. They didn't care about me – they just took me in because they thought they had to. And they treated me like a servant – made me do loads of jobs while Marcus just sat around. And I wrote this letter to the paper, about my school going comprehensive, and it got me into trouble. But I was just saying what I thought – what my mum would have thought too. And grandpa. I wanted to be with grandpa.'

'I can understand that, Ellen. This has been a really difficult time for you. I think you've been very brave. But now we need to work out what happens next.'

'I'm not going back.' This time, Ellen didn't hesitate. There was no silence. She was determined about this. She wasn't going to be made to do something she didn't want to do.

'I'm not going back and you can't make me. If you try I'll just run away again. I'll be sixteen soon and I can do what I want then. I don't have to stay at school. And I'm going to look after grandpa. I can stay here with him.'

'Ellen – it might be possible, but you're not sixteen yet.' Marie paused and checked her notes. 'You're not sixteen until next June. That's nearly a year. And after what's happened to you, we all want to make sure you're safe and that good decisions are made about your future. You've got your education to think of.'

'June! Where did you get that from? I'm sixteen on 30th October.' As Ellen said this she realised her birthday was in a few days' time. She had completely forgotten. But she knew that being sixteen made a difference. How could the social worker have got the date wrong? Her resolved deepened.

'I'm not going back.' Ellen felt strong and clear when she said this; the feeling was comforting. Marie looked at her.

'I understand what you want, Ellen. I'll need to discuss it with your social worker in Fineston and with my manager here. Then we'll have to have a case conference to decide what to do.'

Ellen could feel her face setting into a resentful, frustrated glare. It was a look that had often prompted her mother to say, 'and you can take that look off your face'. But Marie ignored it and carried on.

'I know it's difficult, Ellen, but we have to be sure that good decisions are made for you. Look, let me report back to the police and your social worker in Fineston that I've seen you and that you're OK and we'll take it from there. There is another thing, though. These people you're staying with, I'll need to check that they're suitable. Let me have the address and I'll arrange to come and visit you there.'

Ellen thought hard. She didn't want to get her new friends into trouble and even though they'd explained to her that squatting was perfectly legal she wasn't sure that was how officials at the hospital would see it. On the other hand, if she didn't tell them the address, she might be forced to go back to Fineston, and leave grandpa. So she took a breath and said, 'It's in Brixton. 64 Ellsworth Crescent. But I'll need to let them know that you're coming.'

'OK. I'll find you at visiting time tomorrow and we can talk then.'

SEVENTEEN

Supper was early that evening. When Ellen returned from the hospital she found James tossing his hair out of his eyes back as he fried sausages in a large black pan. As she walked in he turned and smiled at her.

'Hi Ellen. How was your grandpa?'

'OK. They've moved him out of intensive care into another ward, not the normal one. As a sort of halfway step. He's still got lots of wires and things. But he was more awake today.'

'That's great, Ellen. Would you mind setting the table? We're almost ready here.'

Ellen pulled open the badly fitting drawer in the pine dresser that stood on one side of the room. It rattled as she did it. Then she took out the knives and forks and laid them carefully on the table. She didn't mind doing jobs here. In fact, she liked it. It felt fair because the chores were shared and she was pleased to do something to show her gratitude to these people who had taken her in.

'OK, can I do anything else?'

'Um, yes, OK. You can mash the potatoes. Thanks. Masher's in the other drawer in the dresser. And I think there's some butter in the fridge.'

The fridge was huge, with a heavy rounded door and big handle. It looked ancient and made a lot of noise. James saw her looking at it.

'That's a bit of an antique. We found it in a second-hand shop. But it seems to work.'

Ellen took the potatoes from the cooker and used the lid to keep them in the pan while the water drained away into the sink. Then she added a knob of butter and started to crush the potatoes. James set out six plates and began to divide the sausages between them. Neither of them spoke, but the silence wasn't uncomfortable. Ellen felt as if nothing were expected of her. For a moment, she thought how unusual that feeling was. Then James said, 'Your grandpa's very lucky to have you, you know. Without you, he'd be all alone just now.'

Ellen didn't know what to say. But inside she thought, He's right. But I'm lucky to have him too. And I'm going to look after him.

A clatter of the door and the others entered the room. Lily, Marion and Carol came first, followed by Patrick, who was carrying a newspaper under his arm.

'Hi Ellen, hi there. How's your grandpa?'

Ellen repeated the news she'd given James earlier. The words were coming more easily now and she liked the confidence she felt in being able to say what she was really thinking and feeling, even though these people were older than her and she didn't really know them.

'He looks quite frail. But the nurses are sure he's going to be OK and I'm going to look after him, make sure he is.'

Ellen felt the others, who were all sitting round the table now, watching her closely. She imagined they must be thinking that sometime, probably soon, they were going to have to talk with her about her plans for the future. This seemed as good a time as any to tell them about Marie.

'Something happened today, at the hospital. I need to tell you about it.'

The faces around the table were all focused on Ellen.

'A social worker came to see me. My friend Stuart – you know, who I rang the other night – told my aunt and uncle where I was. I told her I wasn't going back to Fineston. She said I might be able to stay with grandpa but in the meantime she made me give her your address. I'm sorry… I don't want to get you into trouble… I didn't know what to do and I was scared of getting sent straight back.'

Ellen was scared her confession would be met with anger. Instead, Lily laughed.

'Gosh, perhaps we're going to be visited by a social worker! Don't worry, Ellen, we all know how to talk to officialdom! And remember, what we're doing isn't illegal. We've got a licence from the council.'

Relief swept over Ellen. They weren't angry with her after all.

'In any case, if they're anything like as busy as we are in my office, they probably won't get around to it!' said Carol, laughing.

Lily smiled. 'Ellen, three of us are going to the Women's Centre tonight for our usual meeting. Do you want to come? It's a chance to talk about stuff that's happening to us, and get some support. You don't have to say anything if you don't want to! I think you might like it.'

'OK.' Ellen was intrigued. She liked Lily and the others and, when supper was cleared away, walked happily down the road with them into the centre of Brixton. They crossed the main road by the stone grandeur of the town hall and turned into a narrow side street. Reggae music was playing loudly from several open windows and people called to each other across the street. On the right hand side Lily stopped at one of the terraced buildings with a large shop window in its front. It didn't look as if there was anything for sale there though.

'Some friends of ours are squatting here,' explained Carol. 'We use the place for meetings.'

Lily knocked and the door was opened by a young woman of about twenty with long black hair and bright eyes.

'Hi everyone. Come in. I've just put the kettle on.'

Ellen followed the others along the narrow hall that led to a flight of stairs. Wallpaper with a pattern of leaves and squares that had once, Ellen imagined, been cream was coming away from the wall in places and there were several large brown stains evident. A noticeboard with a wooden frame that was falling apart was tacked to the wall. The notices on it, advertising the demonstration at the weekend, were familiar. Next to them, a piece of paper torn from an exercise book had a list of chores: cooking, shopping, cleaning upstairs, cleaning downstairs, each with a name next to it. That seemed to Ellen to be a good and fair way to get way things done.

'This way, Ellen,' said Lily.

The room the women entered had once been the shop front. Its wide glass window was covered by sheets tacked to the wall, and it was empty of everything apart from a circle of cushions, each a different size and colour. One wall was painted purple and had a poster of a group of women holding a banner that said 'WRITE WOMEN BACK INTO HISTORY' painted on it in red letters. A poster of Emily Davison, one of the suffragettes that Ellen had read about at school, was stuck to another wall. The women stood around and waited for others to join them. The person who had opened the door came in with a tray of mugs of tea and was introduced as Aileen. She smiled warmly at Ellen.

'Hi, it's good to see you here. Lily's told me about you. You're very welcome.'

Aileen had left the front door open and several other women arrived for the meeting. At eight o'clock, Lily said, 'Right, shall we start? Sit down everyone.'

There were just enough cushions for the nine women. Ellen looked around. Most of them were young, in their twenties Ellen guessed, though one girl, with strikingly long red hair, looked not much older than herself. They were all wearing casual clothes, jeans or dungarees, and they seemed comfortable, confident and at ease with one another. No one seemed to be thinking about the impression they were making. Ellen observed in silence and felt herself relaxing.

'OK.' Lily looked round at everyone. 'Shall we do a round of how we are and what's happened to us since last time?'

There was silence for a moment then Carol said, 'OK. I'll start if you like. I was at a meeting today at the town hall to talk about how we work with schools – we always seem to be at loggerheads with teachers. They blame us social workers for not doing anything for the kids and we blame them for not being understanding enough. Richard, the deputy director, was running the meeting and he just started slagging off schools again and said we'd have to send out another letter telling them what they had to do. But I know – from Lily partly – how hard teachers work to look after the kids. So I said I thought we should meet with some teachers and talk about how we could work together because we all cared about the children. Richard completely ignored me. It was as if I hadn't spoken. Then he went on talking to some of the other social workers – all men – who were there. I was furious.'

Another moment of silence greeted Carol's contribution, then Marion said, 'I'll go next. I was walking to the bus stop today, on my way to college, minding my own business and a bloke who was painting one of the shops whistled at me and then shouted out, "Get 'em off, darling". I shouted back, "Fuck off". And he got really angry. He climbed down his ladder and stared at me and shouted, "Don't you speak to me like that."' There was a ripple of incredulous laughter in the room. Marion continued, 'I know it seems funny now, but I was furious and a bit scared. I thought he might come after me. But why is it OK for men to insult us and not OK for us to talk back?'

'I saw something horrible the other day.' It was Aileen's turn now.

'I was on the bus coming home from work and a man was dragging a woman by the arm down the street. She was screaming to him to stop but everyone just watched and didn't do anything. So I got off the bus at Buxton Place and went to the police station. I had to wait ages in a queue before I spoke to anyone but they said I was right to tell them. Don't expect they did anything though – they'd probably gone by the time they got anyone there.'

Next to speak was the young woman with long red hair who Ellen now learnt was called Liz.

'Well, I've had a pretty good week. I was really brave at college. We had a seminar with the head of English. I don't think he does much teaching usually, at least not of first year A-level students! He's really scary. You feel he's looking down on you and that you can't possibly have anything to say. Well, we were talking about Blake's 'Ah Sun-flower' – do you know it?'

Ellen nodded. She did. They had read the poem in her English class at school and it stayed in her memory.

'Well,' continued Liz. 'I wanted to say something about that image, of the weary sunflower climbing towards the sun, but I was scared. I looked round the room and everyone seemed to be really confident. I thought I'd probably just keep quiet. Then I thought of all of you and I suddenly found myself talking. I said something about the sunflower pining for the sun being like a search for perfection – or death. I can't remember exactly what I said. But the thing was, nobody laughed at me. I saw Ed – he's one of the other students – look surprised, but he smiled so it didn't put me off. I went on for ages. And afterwards it felt great!'

Everyone smiled at Liz and there were murmurs of 'That's great' and 'Well done'.

No one spoke for a minute. Ellen remembered the last time she had waited in silence. That time she had been refusing to answer her uncle's questions and she'd had to use all her courage not to give in and speak. This quiet was different: thoughtful and peaceful but focused. It felt respectful of all the women sitting on their cushions beneath the bare light bulb. It was Lily who spoke first. She glanced up at Ellen and said, 'Ellen, do you want to say anything? You don't have to.'

'I'm not sure. Well, OK, I think I want to say how I like it here. I'm glad I ran away. And now my grandpa's ill – he's just had an operation – I don't want to go back. I want to stay here and look after him.'

Ellen stopped and wondered what she'd said. It had all just come out. She sensed an alert questioning beneath the silence. Everyone was focused on her. Lily sat up on her cushion and looked around the room.

'Ellen, would you like to talk about what happened and what you should do next with us? Would that be OK with everyone?'

Ellen was silent. She saw Lily look around the room, gauging reactions. The women nodded or murmured assent: 'Of course, if Ellen would like us to' and 'If that would help Ellen'. Everyone was looking at her. Ellen sensed a concern and comfort in the room and after a moment she began to speak.

'Well, my grandpa's in hospital. He's had an operation for a burst ulcer. He lives on his own here and hasn't got anyone to look after him. I really want to stay. I could live at his flat with him and not go back to Fineston. Since my mum died, I've had to live with my aunt and uncle and I hate them.'

'When did your mum die, Ellen?' Helen leant forward on her cushion and asked the question in a gentle, low voice.

'In September.'

'This year?'

'Yes.'

'So it's only just happened. I'm so sorry, Ellen', continued Helen. 'Was she ill?'

'Yes… no… sort of. She was depressed and she killed herself.'

Ellen was getting used to the reaction this news provoked in her listeners. The room went quiet again. The women all seemed to be waiting for her to speak but she couldn't. Her memory of what had happened felt far away, locked in a small box in a cold and distant place. She wasn't at all sure that she wanted to retrieve it, or if she could. And if she were able to she was sure she couldn't find the words to explain it to these people she hardly knew. She wanted to say something though. The women were listening and giving her time; she felt that she couldn't just ignore them, so she said, 'I don't think I can say any more about that just now. It's too hard to think about. In a way, it's as if it happened to someone else. I'm just left trying to make my life work. I just have to get on, but I don't know what to do. I want to help grandpa.'

Everyone was listening intently. No one spoke until, tentatively, Liz said, 'I think, I mean, I wonder if… Does it help to think you can go on talking to your mother in your head? I still talk to my granny. She died last year. We were really close.'

Ellen felt herself stiffen as an unexpected flare of anger overtook her as she heard this. Inside she was thinking, 'How could you imagine I'd want to talk to her, after what she did? Can you imagine how angry that makes me?' At the same time she thought she would sound like a horrible, uncaring daughter if she said that out loud. Her anger surprised and frightened her and she couldn't speak for a few moments. She knew that if she were going to continue talking, she'd have to change the subject.

'I saw this social worker today. She was at the hospital and came to the ward to see me. My friend Stuart told my aunt and uncle I was with my grandpa and the police found out that grandpa was in hospital and they told her. She was OK. I've got to meet her again tomorrow. But I think that as I'll be sixteen soon, I won't have to stay at my aunt's if I don't want to. I could live at grandpa's, look after him after his operation and then stay.'

Ellen felt Lily watching her closely, then she spoke.

'I can see why you want to do that, Ellen. But you mustn't give up your education. The rest of your life – the choices you have, your independence - they all depend upon you getting those exams and going to university. Don't let it go. If you're going to stay in London, you need to find a new school. Why not come and visit mine? I could ask tomorrow if you can have an interview and a look round. I think you might like a comprehensive school.'

Ellen felt one of the knots in her stomach release and a tingle of excitement. A comprehensive school? Not ever go back to the High School and have to face the disdain of her headmistress, the patronising and embarrassed looks from the other girls – or her own failure to keep up with the work. She could start again. She smiled at Lily.

'I'd like that a lot. Thank you.'

— — —

That evening, in her bedroom, Ellen thought over what had happened at the meeting. She remembered the flare of anger she had felt and realised how many questions she'd been pushing away, not wanting to think of them, let alone try and find answers. She remembered the unopened brown envelope, with its official city stamp. Maybe now she should open it. She walked over to the corner of the room and felt in one of the pockets of the rucksack she had brought with her. The letter was still there. Ellen looked at the address: *Mr and Mrs Ash.* She supposed she shouldn't really open it but she didn't really care whether what she was doing was wrong. Slowly, she began to tear at the closed flap, sitting down on the bed as she did so. The glue was coming away at one edge and it was only seconds before Ellen had removed the bundle of papers it contained.

At the top of the first page was an elaborate coat of arms with two lion-like creatures, looking like illustrations in one of her nursery rhyme books, holding a large crown. Below them was written 'DIEU

ET MON DROIT'. Ellen was in one of the French sets at school and thought this meant 'God and My Right', but she couldn't imagine why it was written here. She felt the pack of papers in her hand – there were seven or eight pages, some typed, the others handwritten. Her eye ran over the first line of the top page:

Report of post-mortem on the body of Bess Wentworth, deceased, made at the City Mortuary, Fineston, September 1971.

Two sub-headings followed: *External Examination* and *Internal Examination.* Ellen's chest tightened as she read on. Part of her urged her not to read the report but her eyes were pulled towards the page. Against her will they picked out phrases she didn't really understand: *'constriction band of brown dried skin', 'superficial abrasions', 'lungs are very congested and oedematous', 'a few small scattered petechial asphyxial type haemorrhages'.*

Then, point seven, *'Cause of death: Cardiac inhibition and asphyxia'.* The handwritten paragraph that followed was harder to read. Ellen strained to make out the words; a few she couldn't decipher:

cardiac… and asphyxia due to hanging herself by the neck with cord attached to the bannister of the stairs in her house… Killed herself whilst the balance of her mind was disturbed.

So it had happened as she had imagined it. This was real.

There were further pages in the pack, mostly covered by a sprawling, spidery hand-writing that Ellen couldn't read. One page was signed 'Dr J Austell' and Ellen picked it up to study it more carefully. As she struggled to make sense of the indistinct letters some words stood out: *'threatened to kill herself before'…* *'having shock treatment at Aston Green mental hospital'.*

Ellen felt fear like a bar of cold steel travel through her body. This had – almost – happened before? The shock treatment her mother had had when her brother was born had been repeated? Had it happened last year, when her mother had been taken to Aston Green and her grandpa had come to look after her? Before that, when her mother had been with Ellen, looking after her, making meals, reading stories – she had been thinking of killing herself? Could this be true? As she sat there, the report still in her hand, she thought about other occasions during her childhood when her grandfather had come to stay. Once, just before school broke up for the Christmas holidays, Ellen had returned home to find her mother sitting stiffly in her usual chair by the sitting room window. She was still wearing her coat and there was a faraway look in her eyes.

Ellen spoke tentatively, 'Mum...?' But her mother didn't reply. Grandpa hurried into the room.

'Don't bother your mother just now, Ellen, she's not feeling very well.'

It was an instruction that Ellen had followed, without thinking, all her life.

EIGHTEEN

Grandpa was sitting up in bed when Ellen arrived for visiting time the next day, Wednesday. He was still wearing his hospital gown and had tubes attached to monitors by his bedside, but he was smiling.

'Hello, love.'

'Hello, Grandpa. How are you feeling today?'

'Much better. And I've been out of bed. The nurses are very strict here – they make you walk around however you're feeling. That poor bloke opposite could barely stand but they made him march up and down. Worse than being in the army!'

Ellen smiled. This was more like her grandpa.

'I've brought you a paper.' Ellen handed over a copy of the local paper, the *South London Gazette*. 'I bought this for you – I know you like to read it sometimes.'

'Thanks, love.' Grandpa glanced at the front page. 'It's funny to think the world's been carrying on out there while I've been in here. Look – it says here that the BF are planning a march on Saturday. Bastards. I wish I could be there, stop them marching.'

'I'm going to go, Grandpa. The people I live with are organising a protest. I've already given out some leaflets in Brixton.'

Grandpa looked at her with surprise and interest. 'Are you indeed? I didn't know you'd got into politics. But the more the better. Racist pigs. Take care though; if there's a confrontation with the police it might get nasty. You look after yourself. But now, tell me a bit about you. Did you say you were meeting the social worker yesterday?'

'Yes, I did. And I told her that I wasn't going back and that I wanted to stay here and look after you. I've got to see her again today.'

'Ellen – you know I'd love to have you. I've said that to the social worker. But you have to put your life and your education first. I couldn't stand in the way of you getting your exams and going to university. You've got your own life to lead.'

'But my friend Lily, who I'm living with just now – she's a teacher – she says I can probably go to her school. It's a comprehensive. I think I'd really like that.'

'A comprehensive, eh? Well, I approve of that! Let's wait and see what this social worker says.'

'OK – but have you seen the doctor again, Grandpa? What did he say?'

'I have and he's pleased. He thinks I'm doing very well for an old 'un! I'll have to have some more treatment but he thinks I'm going to be all right. So you'll be stuck with me for a while longer, love!'

Ellen smiled. At that moment the world didn't exist outside this hospital room and everything there seemed larger and brighter than usual, as if light were flooding into the space. She had been so frightened. Now, as the relief radiated from her heart and lit her whole body she felt as if she could deal with whatever happened at the meeting. It was a surprise, though, when at the end of visiting time Marie touched her shoulder and led her along the corridor. They stopped at a door on the right that was partly open. Through the gap Ellen could see the end of a large table surrounded by plastic chairs.

'We're going to have the meeting about your future, Ellen. Don't be frightened. And it's important that you say what you want. I'll be there to support you.'

Marie pushed the door open and Ellen could see, sitting at the end of the table, by the window, her aunt and Andrea the social worker who'd first taken her to foster care in Fineston. Ellen started. She hadn't expected this. Her first feeling was one of fear. She was going to be in BIG trouble now. Her aunt was looking down at a paper on the table in front of her. Marie gestured to Ellen to sit down on one of the seats along the side of the table. As she did so, Ellen glanced at her aunt and realised that she looked nervous. No one spoke as Marie settled herself in a chair and pulled out a file and a pad of paper before starting the meeting.

'OK, thanks for coming, everyone. We've all met each other now. Ellen – I've told your aunt and Andrea a little bit about our conversation yesterday. Now we need to decide what happens next.'

Ellen felt a spurt of anger. Why had Marie told her aunt about what she'd assumed was a private conversation? Then she remembered: of course, it wasn't private. This was social services. They could do what they liked with her. She didn't have a say over her own life. How could her mother have left her to be pushed around like this, with no home of her own? Her rage filled her, red, seething smoke seeping from her heart to every limb in her body. What she really wanted to do was throw the chairs about the room, upturn the table, smash the windows – but a warning voice in her head reminded her that that would make things worse. Her goal was to get free of Fineston and go and live with grandpa, so she had to behave. She knew what it was like to control her emotions, to keep her moods to herself. At home, with her mother, it had been dangerous not to. So she kept her eyes on Marie and tried to give the impression of listening carefully.

'I'm going to give everyone an opportunity to say what they think should happen next. I'd like us all to listen carefully to each other and then, when everyone's had their say, we'll begin to make a plan. Andrea, would you like to start. Tell us what the position of Fineston Social Services department is?'

Andrea pushed her glasses up her nose. Ellen thought how young she seemed. Both the social workers did – how could these young women, who were not so much older than she was, have such power?

'Well, we want the best for Ellen obviously, but what has happened to her has been very distressing. We need to know that she is going to be safe. I think I'd like to hear from Mrs Ash and Ellen.'

Aunt Christabel was still looking down at the pad of paper in front of her. There was a long silence. Eventually, she spoke. As she did, she stared at the other end of the room, avoiding the eyes of everyone round the table. Ellen expected her to be angry. Instead, she sounded frightened and confused.

'I don't know why this happened. We – Walter and I – tried to make a good home for Ellen. She's my brother's daughter and our responsibility. What happened was dreadful. We wanted things to be as normal as possible for her. We made sure she got back to school and that there was a routine at home, but...' Aunt Christabel, still staring into the distance, paused. 'Ellen wasn't easy. She truanted from school, she wrote that letter to the paper, she wouldn't talk... Maybe I'm just used to boys... We did our best.'

As Ellen looked at her, Aunt Christabel seemed to lose all her power. Why had she been frightened of her? The recognition that her aunt seemed to feel nervous and unsure of herself gave Ellen confidence. She knew now what she wanted to say.

'What Aunt Christabel says is true – they did try and give me a home, but I felt as if they were trying to make me be like them and I'm not. I wrote that letter because I believe in comprehensive schools. And I think boys should do housework as well as girls. If I went back there, I still don't think we'd get on. And it's my job to look after grandpa. He's loved me more than anyone and he needs my help now. It's not that I'm not grateful. I am. But I can't go back to Fineston. If you make me I'll run away again. Anyway, I'm almost sixteen, so I'm old enough to make my own decisions.'

Marie and Andrea glanced at each other. Marie spoke first.

'Thanks Ellen. That was really clear, and I'm glad you acknowledged what your aunt did for you. I don't think there's any objection in principle to your coming to live with your grandfather – you'll soon be old enough to look after him. And, given that we think the operation has been successful, it shouldn't be too heavy a burden, or interfere with your schooling. But we'll need to check out his flat. What do you think, Andrea?'

For the first time, Ellen noticed her surroundings. Beyond the window the sky was grey, the late afternoon sun hidden by drifting clouds. On one wall of the narrow room that had space only for the table and chairs were some posters advertising a staff social event. It seemed odd that ordinary lives were lived in this hospital, that people came here, did a day's work, went home and cooked supper, said goodnight to their children and got up the next day and did it again. For the patients and their relatives, this was a place where momentous, life-changing things happened. Every visit was infused with emotion: hope, fear, relief. She waited for Andrea to speak.

'Well, I'll need to confirm the decision with my team manager and we will need to check your financial situation – what benefits you're entitled to and so on.'

Aunt Christabel raised her hand a little and moved forward in her seat as if she wanted to say something. Ellen found her diffidence curious and touching.

'Her uncle and I are prepared to pay Ellen a small allowance until she leaves school, to help with her education.'

'Thank you. We can discuss that later, Mrs Ash.' Andrea smiled, acknowledging Aunt Christabel's contribution and then continued.

'But it seems fine to me for Ellen to stay with her grandfather. Provided we are confident that Mr Maddox's flat is suitable I don't see any reason why Ellen shouldn't live with him. It will be important to check out schools too, so that she can carry on with her education.'

Ellen's relief flowed through her. She looked up at Aunt Christabel and for a moment their eyes met. Ellen felt able to speak.

'Aunt Christabel, I am grateful for what you did for me. But I want to live my own life now.'

Her aunt looked down again. Ellen could see the muscles round her mouth moving but she stayed silent for a few long moments. Then, 'Well, maybe it's for the best. But, Ellen, I want you to know that if you need anything... your uncle and I... we would like to do what we can. I'm going to stay in London for a few days and you might welcome some help when your grandfather comes home. Here – take my phone number – I'm staying with a friend. Call me if you need me and, in any case, I'll pop by your grandfather's as soon as you both get home to see if there's anything I can do.'

Ellen reached out and took the piece of paper that her aunt had given her. She sensed the effort her aunt was making and, for the first time, she felt able to smile, just a little.

'Thank you,' she said.

'Thank you, Mrs Ash, that would be very helpful,' said Marie.

Soon after that the meeting ended. There were some practical arrangements to be made. Marie promised Ellen that she would find her when she visited her grandfather the next day and let her know what had been arranged for his discharge.

— — —

Ellen went straight back to Brixton when the meeting ended. The housemates were all there, sitting, as they usually did at this time of day, in the kitchen. James was cooking again; tonight he had made chicken stew for everyone.

I'm going to miss them all a lot, thought Ellen. This had been the only place she had felt at home since her mother died. James carried the stew pot to the table and set it down with a flourish of the cloth he was using to protect his hands from the heat.

'Ta da. Ladies and gentlemen, a fine chicken casserole for your delectation, brought to you by one of the country's most talented chefs.' Everyone grinned.

'Thanks, James. Can we have some bread to eat with it, please?' When everyone had helped themselves, Lily turned to Ellen.

'How was your grandfather today?'

'OK thanks. He's coming out in a few days and, guess what, the social worker says I can live with him. Well, probably. They've got to check out that the flat is suitable and things, but I think it's going to be all right.'

'That's great, Ellen. So now we need to sort out your schooling. I had a word with the head of fifth form today. She'd be happy to see you – there are some spaces at the school and, frankly, they'd be really glad to get a student like you who's going to do well. I told her it was urgent – lots of decisions being made – and she said it would be fine for you to come into school tomorrow, have a look round and meet her. What do you think?'

Ellen's heart fluttered. This was really going to happen. She was going to move to London and have a new life. It was scary, but she was ready. She looked around the table at her friends and felt she wanted to say something. Talking had begun to feel more powerful than silence.

'Everyone… I… I want to say something.'

There was an immediate hush as all eyes turned towards Ellen.

'I want to say thank you for looking after me here. I don't know what I'd have done without you. I suppose I'd have had to go back to Fineston and left grandpa alone in the hospital. I wouldn't have been able to help him and I wouldn't have got away from my aunt and uncle. So thank you, everyone. It's been great living here with you all and I want to do my bit for the demonstration on Saturday. I told grandpa about it – he used to be really involved with his union – and he said he wished he were well enough to go. So I'll be going for him too.'

It was probably the longest speech she'd made since she'd arrived. It was met with smiles. Lily spoke first.

'Ellen – it's been a real pleasure. And we've all admired you, your courage and loyalty to your grandfather.'

'Hear, hear,' said Patrick, 'and I'm glad you're going to be living in London. There's lots of campaigning against the racists to do yet!'

Ellen grinned. 'Yes – I want to do that. And I just wanted to check that it's still OK if a friend comes to stay here, so he can come on the march on Saturday?'

'Of course, the more the merrier. If he wants to bring a mate or two, that's fine. We've got spare mattresses and we can use the cushions off the sofa for beds. It will be great to have some young people there.'

'Thanks. I'll go out to the phone box after supper and let him know.'

Lily and Ellen left for school together the following morning. Ellen was nervous but determined; she didn't want to sit around waiting. This was her new life and she was going to make it happen. She hadn't any formal clothes with her but she had brought a pair of navy blue trousers as well as the jeans she mostly wore, so she had put those on with a grey jumper. Lily had lent her a jacket to wear, saying, 'You'll feel less nervous if you look smart. Not,' she added with a smile, 'that you need to be nervous!'

Maybe not, thought Ellen, but still…

The road to the centre of Brixton was busy as people made their way to work and school. Lily and Ellen took a bus south. There was lots of space as most people were heading the other way, into town, so Ellen stared out of the window at large Georgian houses, divided into flats, and a housing estate with cars parked haphazardly by front doors and children already setting out for school. They passed a park as they moved down the hill and Ellen saw, just beyond it, a two-storey sprawling building, with a concrete car park in front. Lily said, 'We're here', and the two of them got off the bus and crossed the road.

As they got closer, Ellen saw the sign at the gate of the low building: 'Fernhill Comprehensive School, Headteacher Ms Christine Wilkinson, MA'. So this was it. It was still early, but students were already arriving. Ellen was amazed to see that they weren't wearing uniforms but their normal out of school clothes. Most were carrying bags or rucksacks but they were all different. Ellen remembered how strict the rule was at her school about the kind of satchel you were allowed to carry. It was definitely odd to see youngsters arriving without anything on their heads! Being seen in town without a High School beret in Fineston was a grave offence that would earn a severe telling off at her school. It was odd too to see boys as well as girls there, but they were all very relaxed.

'They're here early for breakfast club,' said Lily. 'I think, it would be good if you could sit in with a class for a few lessons and then meet the head of year. What do you think? I could introduce you to someone who'd look after you in 5L'

That sounded scary, but Ellen, still determined to be brave, said, 'OK – that's fine.'

The door to the main entrance hall of the school was propped open and, as Ellen and Lily walked through, a girl with shoulder-length light brown hair turned and said,

'Hello, Miss.'

'Hello, Julie. I wonder if you could do me a favour? This is Ellen, she's come to visit the school this morning – she's probably moving down to London. Could you take her round with you? I thought it would be good if she could sit in on some lessons, find out what it's like here.'

'You mean what it's *really* like, Miss?' said Julie, grinning.

Lily smiled back. 'Of course, warts and all – she needs to get a proper picture. I'll come and pick her up later.'

'OK. Come and get some toast with me, Ellen. We're part of some experiment here, seeing if poor kids do better at school if they get breakfast, or something.'

Ellen followed Julie through double doors at the opposite side of the entrance hall and out into a paved yard dotted with further low buildings. Beyond she could see a playground with some wooden seats scattered around it. They walked diagonally across the courtyard to a dining hall that was already filling up. At one end of the room a wide metal serving hatch displayed toast, packets of cereal and jugs of orange juice. Unlike the students, the women behind the counter were wearing uniforms. Ellen and Julie joined the queue and Ellen noticed how relaxed everyone seemed. Too nervous to eat at first, Ellen began to bite slowly into a piece of toast as she listened to Julie talking to her friends about the homework they'd had the night before. No one paid her much attention but she didn't mind. She thought they weren't being unfriendly, just busy. The first session of the day was tutor time. Ellen was amazed to find herself in a room with thirty children of all ages.

'We call it vertical grouping,' explained Julie. 'It's so we older ones can look after the younger ones and we stay in the same group all the way through school. It's good when you start here – a bit like having a family.'

The class tutor, Miss Davis, was a young woman, confident and cheerful, who reminded Ellen of Lily. She walked round to the front of the desk and sat on it, opening her register as she did it.

'Ok, good morning everyone. Let's see who's here.'

At that moment a ruler sped across the class and landed on the floor near the teacher's feet. The class went silent. All eyes turned to a small boy with a pale face and untidy brown hair, who shrank down into his desk as the teacher continued to watch the class. Ellen could see that the clothes he was wearing were too big and rather shabby. Passed on from an elder brother or two, she guessed. His shoes were dirty plimsolls.

'Who was responsible for that?' asked Miss Davis quietly.

There was silence. Students glanced at each other and Ellen could see a boy in the front row covering his mouth to hide a laugh.

Miss Davis continued to wait. Then a tall, older boy spoke. He sounded concerned.

'It was Erin, Miss, but he's upset today. I'll sit with him if you like.'

'Thank you, Leroy, I appreciate that. Erin, stay behind after tutor group, I want to talk to you.'

Ellen was amazed. She couldn't imagine what would have happened at her school if one of the girls had thrown a ruler in class. Or rather she could. It would have been a referral straight to the headmistress and worried discussions with parents. Of course, such a thing had never happened there so far as she knew. This teacher didn't seem angry, rather she seemed concerned and anxious to help the boy who was now cowering at his desk with his head on his hands. Leroy went to sit beside him and Ellen heard him say, 'Don't worry, mate. Miss'll sort it out.'

Miss Davis calmly carried on reading names from the register and the pupils answered politely.

'Yes, Miss,'

'Here, Miss.'

Again, Ellen thought about Fineston High where everyone had to stand up and say 'good morning' together to the teacher before answering to their name. When the register was complete, Miss

Davis said, 'OK everyone, we've got ten minutes of tutor time left. There are no notices today, so take out your reading books and read quietly. Sonia and Chris and Julie, could you listen to Helen, Sarah and Martin reading today, please?'

As the children in the class read, Miss Davis went over to Erin, touched him gently on the shoulder and indicated that he should follow her. The teacher put out two chairs at the front of the classroom, where the two could speak and not be overheard. Ellen watched them closely. Miss Davis was looking intently at Erin as she spoke. The child was silent for a while and then, looking up for the first time, began to speak. He looked relieved rather than frightened. A louder buzzer sounded and Miss Davis stood up.

'OK everyone. Time for first lesson. Have a good day – work hard.'

A few pupils said 'Thank you, Miss' in return as they gathered their books together and filed out of the classroom. Erin was almost the last to leave, and as he approached the door Miss Davis smiled at him.

'See you tomorrow, Erin.'

'Yes Miss.'

First lesson for Julie was English. Ellen walked with her along a packed corridor and then up a flight of stairs to the first floor. On the walls of the stairwell 'Keep Right' notices in red were dotted between cabinets displaying animal costumes that had been made for a recent school performance. On one board pupils' work was nearly mounted on coloured card. The theme was 'memories' and Ellen paused for a moment to glance at the poems pasted there. She was glad she hadn't had to write about what she remembered.

Ellen and Lucy joined the queue that had formed outside the English classroom. A young man in a beige corduroy jacket whose dark hair brushed the collar of his mauve shirt hurried towards them.

'Good morning everyone.'

He opened the classroom door and stood by the entrance, gesturing to pupils at the front of the queue to enter. As they filed into the room he greeted every pupil by name. When it was Ellen and Julie's turn he smiled.

'Ah, you must be Ellen. I heard you were joining us today. All the way from Yorkshire I hear! Welcome.'

'Thank you for having me, Sir,' replied Ellen, thinking she should be polite, but feeling foolish when she saw two girls smirk after she had spoken.

When everyone was through the door and in their seats he moved to the front of the classroom and said, 'Right, everyone. Good to see you all. We're going to have a great lesson today. You've all been practising writing dialogue and we're going to extend that by having some arguments!'

Ellen thought about the silent filing into class at Fineston High School, the pupils waiting for their teacher to arrive and, when she did, the standing up in unison and the formal exchange of greetings.

'Good morning, girls.'

'Good morning, Miss Harte.'

This felt very different. The teacher, Mr Edwards, began the lesson enthusiastically.

'OK everyone, before we do our dialogue writing today, we're going to see what it sounds and feels like to have an argument. Now, who can tell me a common topic for an argument. What do you argue with your friends or your parents about?'

Mr Edwards picked up a piece of chalk and stood expectantly by the board. He waited for a few moments to give everyone time to think. A boy put up his hand.

'Yes Winston?'

'Staying out late at night… me and my mum fight about that.'

'Yes, that's a good one,' said Mr Edwards, writing it on the board. 'Any more?'

'Clothes, sir. I argue with my sister about her taking my clothes without asking.'

'People borrowing stuff – records 'n' that – and not giving them back.'

When the board was full of ideas, Mr Edwards asked everyone in the class to turn to a neighbour, decide which argument they wanted to have, work out who was going to be who and then act it out.

'Ten minutes to plan, to think about the scenario and what the issues are and pretend to be the people involved. Remember, though, this is a small classroom and although you're fighting you're going to have to keep your voices down. Any questions?'

Mr Edwards paused for a moment, and when there were no further questions, he continued. 'OK – start planning now. I'll tell you when five minutes is up and you'll have a further five minutes to act out the scene.'

The classroom buzzed while Ellen, not sure what to do, edged to the side of the room. She saw two girls turn and watch her for a moment, then one of them whispered to the other and they both laughed. She heard a few words, 'A'm off ter 'av a bath now', spoken in a heavy, flat-vowelled northern accent. Ellen froze, aware that they were mimicking her.

If I come here, she thought, there's going to be a lot of that when I start. Will it be worse or better than the High School?

Meanwhile, Mr Edwards circulated, listening in to what one or two pairs of students were doing, and then moved to the back of the room. Two young men were beginning to shout loudly at each other.

'OK boys, keep it down, please,'

'But sir, he…' The shorter of the two boys looked angry. 'He said I was…'

'No, I didn't,' retorted the taller boy and, as he spoke, he lunged forward but Mr Edwards intervened.

'Right, you two, separate. Jason, go and stand at the front by the door. Lewis, stay here. I'll see you both after class.'

'But sir…'

'I'll see you after class. Jason, move.'

Jason threw a harsh, angry look at Lewis and then moved towards him, as if he might hit him. Mr Edwards put a hand on his arm and repeated the instruction.

'Go and stand at the front, Jason. I'll see you after class.'

Reluctantly, and with a dark backward glance at Lewis that seemed to say, 'I'll get you later', Jason moved as his teacher had asked him. Mr Edwards took out a notebook, scribbled something on a piece of paper and gave it to one of the girls at the other side of the room.

'Could you take that to Mr Jones, please?'

The rest of the class scarcely seemed to notice what had happened. Was this sort of incident common here? wondered Ellen. It was certainly different from Fineston! And, she realised, she was frightened by it. What would it be like in a school where fights might break out in lessons? Calm, for now, was restored, however. Mr Edwards spoke to the whole class.

'OK – that's ten minutes. Let's see some of them. Any volunteers to go first?'

There was silence for a moment and then a slim, black girl with long elegant limbs raised her hand and spoke in a soft voice.

'We will, sir,'

'Excellent, Donna. Thank you. Do you mind going to the front of the class?'

Donna and her friend Joanne walked confidently from their seats. Donna raised her eyebrows at her partner and the two of them acted out a scene between a mother and daughter. The mother was angry because she had discovered that her daughter had been to a party and been caught drinking beer. The fight was lively and confident. Ellen felt it had the ring of authentic experience! She wondered what her mother would have said if she had been found with alcohol – or, for that matter, what her aunt and uncle would have done. The thought made her smile. She was away from all that now.

Ellen was very absorbed and a little disappointed when, a few moments into Donna and Joanne's argument, a short blonde woman wearing a grey suit put her head round the door.

'I'm so sorry to interrupt, Mr Edwards. I can see you're having a good lesson here, but I've come to take Ellen out.'

Ellen smiled at Julie and a few of the other students smiled back. They must have been wondering what was going to happen to this new girl now – as indeed Ellen herself was. As the two of them left the classroom and set off down the corridor the woman turned to Ellen and held out her hand.

'Good to meet you, Ellen. I'm Miss Lawrence, and I look after the fifth years here. Lily – Miss Grey – has told me a bit about you. Come in here and we can have a talk.'

Ellen seemed to have spent a lot of time recently in small rooms talking to adults. She didn't want to go over it all again, but she sat down on the chair by a small table that Miss Lawrence offered her in what looked like a book store. A poetry collection that caught her eye was the one the class had read in her first year at secondary school. She felt a sharp thrust of nostalgia at this reminder of her younger self, of the person she used to be – before. She glanced out of the window and could see the empty playground in the distance. If she came here, she'd have to walk out into the playground alone, not knowing anyone. How easy would it be to make friends in a new school, in the fifth year when everyone else had known each other for years? Especially when she was different, a northerner. Miss Lawrence started to speak.

'Ellen, thank you for coming to see us today. I know what a terrible time you've had and I want to say how sorry I am.'

She paused for a moment and Ellen could feel her watching her face closely. Sympathy always made Ellen want to cry.

'If you decide to come here we'd be delighted to have you. We'll give you all the support we can. I expect you'll be nervous about making friends but we'll find one or two pupils to look after you. And this is a friendly school. It will be very different from the school you've been to. It's very relaxed in lots of ways. As you've seen, we have no uniform; we just expect our pupils to dress sensibly. And we do expect people to work! We want you to get those GCEs. What are your plans for your future, Ellen?'

'Well, I want to go to university, not sure what I want to do after that.'

'OK. Well, that's a good goal. You'll find several other pupils who are going to university too. You'll get lots of support from me as your head of year. And, Ellen, I want you to know that we care about our pupils here, about all aspects of their lives. What you've been through is very difficult. If you feel low or that you want to talk at any time there will be someone here you can ask. You mustn't ever feel that you're all alone and that you're carrying the burden of that memory by yourself.'

For the second time that morning Ellen felt the tears coming. Miss Lawrence leaned over and touched her arm.

'It's been good to meet you, Ellen. As I said, if you do decide you want to come here, we'd be delighted to have you. I know that you're part way through your GCEs and are expected to do well. This has been a huge disruption but we'll make sure that we make a plan to help you catch up. You can do some of the exams next year, if necessary. When you've decided, let us know. I'll contact your school in Fineston and get the details of all the courses you're doing and we can work it out from there. I know you're a clever girl.'

'Thank you.' Ellen felt she ought to say more but she couldn't think what so she smiled instead. Miss Lawrence smiled back and led her out of the room.

– – –

At the hospital that afternoon, Ellen found that grandpa had been moved again. This ward seemed much more relaxed. There were fewer machines and wires strapped to patients and some of the men were sitting by their beds or walking slowly around. Grandpa himself was sitting up in bed when she arrived, a few minutes after visiting time had started.

'Hello, love. You've just missed me walking up and down. Bit shaky on the old pins but the nurses here are tyrants. If they say walk, you walk! How are you?'

'OK – but the important thing is how you are, Grandpa.'

'I'm feeling much better today, much more myself. They say I can go home on Monday. And yesterday I had a visit from a social worker so, young lady, you'd better tell me what you've been plotting while your old grandpa was strapped to his hospital bed!'

'Well, I told her – them, 'cos Aunt Christabel was there too – that I want to stay here, to come and live with you and go to a new school. I went today. It's a comprehensive and I really liked it. It was a bit scary, but good.'

As she said this, Ellen realised that it was true. Although she had been scared, she had really liked the school. It couldn't be more frightening than facing those snobby girls at the High School who looked down on her because she was poor and a scholarship girl. And Miss Lawrence had been very kind. She knew it would be hard at first, but not so hard as trying to get on at Fineston High School when the head teacher disapproved of her so much and so many of the other girls saw her as an object of curiosity or pity. Here no one would know what had happened. She could start again.

– – –

That evening, the house in Brixton was full and busy. On the floor of the long living room Ellen could see, spread out on a white sheet, three long strips of hardboard surrounded by cans of red paint, rags, paint brushes of different sizes and smaller pieces of cardboard.

'Go on, you're the artist.' Carol was looking at Patrick and laughing. 'Let's see what you can do!'

'OK – but are we sure what we want to say?'

The others called out suggestions:

'Racists out'

'Stop racism'

'United against racism'

'One race, the human race'

'Everyone is welcome here'

'British First Party go home'

'Stop the march'

'OK, OK – which ones for the long boards?' asked Patrick and then, turning his head as Ellen walked in, said 'Hi Ellen. What do you think? What should we put on our banners for the demo on Saturday?'

Ellen thought for a moment. She knew the demonstration was planned to protest against the march organised by people who wanted to stop anyone who wasn't white coming to live in England. She knew what it was like not to feel welcome, as if she were different and didn't belong.

'I like "Everyone is welcome here",' she said.

'Pick up a paint brush then – there's a board and some paint. Get going. Do you want to plan it on some paper first so you get the letters even? I'll help if you like.'

Patrick beckoned to Ellen to crouch down next to him and together they used a thick pencil to draft the letters onto the board, spacing them carefully. Then Ellen picked up a brush and dipped it into a can of red paint. She painted very carefully and it took ages, but while she was doing it she forgot everything that had happened and that might or might not be about to happen. The others were working on two long boards and some smaller placards. For a while there was silence in the room and Ellen was aware of chatter in the street outside as the evening darkened. She had no idea what to expect on Saturday, but for now she felt as if she was where she wanted to be.

NINETEEN

Half term in Yorkshire was a week later than it had been in London so Stuart was able to leave Fineston early. His train arrived at King's Cross at eleven on Friday morning. Ellen stood at the barrier, scouring the mass of tired travellers who hurried along the platform and crowded the exit barrier. She waited for five minutes and began to get alarmed when she couldn't see him. A tall, fair-haired boy pushed past her and she started, about to shout Stuart's name, but it wasn't him. A few seconds later a girl with long black hair threw her arms around the stranger. Ellen watched their closeness, their pleasure at seeing each other, and felt even more alone.

'Hello.' The voice behind her made her jump.

'Stuart! I thought you'd missed the train.'

Ellen smiled but inside she thought she was going to cry.

'Are you OK? It's really good to see you.'

'Let's get back to the house.'

The underground train was still crowded, even though rush hour was technically over, so the friends didn't get much chance to talk. It wasn't until they emerged from the Elephant and Castle tube station and were sitting upstairs on the back seat of the bus that would take them to Brixton that Stuart said, 'So, tell me how you are. We've all been so worried about you.'

'Well, the main thing is I don't have to go back. I'm going to live with grandpa and look after him'

Stuart looked keenly at Ellen, but said nothing. For the rest of the journey they talked about what had been happening in Fineston. When they arrived back at the house it was empty. Ellen led her friend past the placards that were propped against the wall on one side of the narrow hall. Stuart stopped to read them.

'I see we're all set for tomorrow.'

In the kitchen dishes from the morning's breakfast were piled in the sink. The dining table was clear of plates but covered in crumbs and smears of marmalade.

'Here, sit down. I'll clear up and then put some coffee on. Then I'll show you where you're sleeping.' Ellen squeezed detergent into the sink before filling it with hot water. Feeling unusually shy with her friend, as if the last week had caused a huge crater between them, she busied herself putting the kettle on to boil, washing the dishes and drying a mug for each of them. When she joined him at the table, Stuart smiled and reached out to touch her arm.

'It's really good to see you, Ellen. I've got a letter for you, from Jennifer, by the way. She said to give you lots of love. She would have come but they couldn't find the train fare.'

Ellen smiled; she so missed her friend and this letter would be something to savour later. The kettle boiled and Ellen poured hot water on the coffee in two mugs.

'Here.'

'Thanks.'

There was silence for a moment. It wasn't uncomfortable though, as if they had run out of things to say to each other. Rather the opposite: there was too much to say. Ellen felt Stuart's eyes on her and she half-looked at him and smiled. She felt his sympathy pour over her, the air between them seemed warmed by it and alive. Stuart reached out and touched her hand. Ellen left it there for a few seconds and then, feeling suddenly awkward, she pulled it away and stood up.

'I have to go and see grandpa. Do you want to come? You could see the river and the Houses of Parliament and stuff.'

'Yes, I'll come.'

Half an hour later they were back on the bus. They hopped off at Westminster Bridge, together with a mother and her two young children. Stuart pulled a face at one of them and the child grinned then hid his face in his mother's skirt. Then Stuart turned to Ellen.

'Look, I'll go and get a coffee. Come and find me when you're done. I might walk along the river a bit too. How long will you be?'

'About an hour. I'll see you in the café – I'll show you where it is.'

— — —

The hospital was familiar to Ellen now. She led Stuart across concrete paving and through the glass doors of the entrance and showed him where to wait for her. Then she left him and went to find grandpa. When Ellen got to his bedside, he was looking excited.

'I can go home, love,' he said. 'On Monday. They're very pleased with my progress. I got up for lunch – sausages and mash – and ate it in the day room. Full of old people and they're all ill! I don't know what I'm doing here. I'm only a lad yet!'

Ellen smiled. This was the grandpa she remembered. As she took her seat by his bed she felt a touch on her arm. It was Marie, the social worker.

'Hello Ellen. I've just come to tell you that I've been in touch with Fineston Social Services and your aunt and uncle and it's all agreed. You can live with your grandfather instead of going back there. I'll come and find you in an hour, when you've seen your grandfather, to discuss the arrangements.'

'Oh.' Ellen found she couldn't say anything. She didn't have to go back. She didn't have to live in that house where she wasn't wanted. She could stay here with grandpa. Her chest felt light, as if she could breathe freely for the first time for ages.

'Thank you. I – I've got a friend here, from Fineston. He'll be waiting for me in the café when I've seen grandpa. Could you come there?'

'Yes, I'll come and look for you. See you later.' And Marie, clutching her files close to her, walked quickly from the ward.

Ellen turned to grandpa.

'Did you know? Did they tell you that I'm going to look after you now?'

'Yes.' Grandpa smiled. 'But not so much of the looking after me, young lady. I'm going to be as right as rain when I get home. And I might do a bit of looking after you!'

The same feeling of comfort came over Ellen that she had known as a child.

— — —

A memory of a time she had been in London with her mother years before floated into her mind. When they had arrived at grandpa's flat he had made tea and toast with honey, and after Ellen had finished eating, he had said, 'Here, I've got something for you.' He had gone to the back of the flat and brought a wooden scooter into the dining room. 'I made it for you,' he said.

Ellen had looked at the scooter, made of polished dark wood with red wheels, with a piece of rubber stuck to the body for her to put her foot on. It was exactly what she wanted. Her friend Jane had a metal scooter, with Mickey Mouse designs painted on it. This was better.

'Oh, thank you, Grandpa – can I go and ride it?'

'Tomorrow, in the park.'

Ellen smiled now at the memory. Grandpa wouldn't be making any more scooters for her and she would be making the toast from now on, at least for a while. But this was where she wanted to be.

- - -

In the café, when visiting time was over, she found Stuart sitting staring out of the window at Big Ben.

'I know, it's lovely, isn't it?' said Ellen as she joined him at his table. 'It doesn't seem quite real at first.'

'How was your grandfather?'

'He's doing well and, guess what, they've said I can definitely come and live with him and don't have to go back to my aunt's. The social worker just told me… she's coming to meet me here soon to talk about arrangements.'

Ellen felt Stuart looking at her, but said nothing. Beyond the glass, an unbroken line of people, leaning forward slightly against the breeze, hurried across Westminster Bridge.

'Hello.' Marie's voice caused them to turn. 'You must be Ellen's friend.'

'Yes – I'm Stuart. Hello.'

'Hello Stuart. Could you give Ellen and me a minute or two please?'

'It's fine,' interrupted Ellen. 'I don't mind him being here. He's my friend.'

Marie hesitated then said, 'OK. I wanted to let you know what's been arranged, Ellen, about you moving to London. As you know, your grandfather is being discharged on Monday morning and your aunt is going to stay in London for a few days to help you look after him and bring the things you'll need.'

Ellen gasped. Despite the moments of sympathy she had felt for her aunt at the meeting with the social workers, she still wasn't sure that she wanted her around. She'd be perfectly all right on her own. Marie looked at her.

'I know you've found it difficult with your aunt, Ellen, but she does care about what happens to you. It was a dreadful shock when you ran away and she wants to make it right. And your grandfather will need some care at home. So, you should come in to the hospital on Monday and go home with grandpa. Your aunt will come and find you at the flat in the afternoon. I've spoken with the head at Fernhill, the school you went to visit, and they are going to put you on the roll, so you can start there as soon as possible. I'll be in touch about details.'

Ellen felt as if all this were happening to someone else. She paid scant attention to the arrangements and knew she would have to ask Stuart to go over it with her later. Underneath the blankness she sensed some feelings but wasn't sure what they were: relief, fear, excitement, loss. She was going to become someone completely different, living in a new place, going to a different school, having new friends. Who would this new person be?

The house was still empty when Stuart and Ellen arrived back there.

'You know, Ellen, I'm going to miss you back home. I'm so fed up of that school and all the pressure. It's been great having someone to talk to.'

'Your mum and dad? Can't you tell them?'

'Not really. They met at Oxford and they're kind of determined that I should go too, but I don't want to. I'm not clever like that. And it's odd. They're both lefties and think everyone should have equal chances and are against elite education and all that, but when it comes to me, they seem to want me to be just like them... I kind of envy you in a way. I know that sounds stupid after what's happened to you. You can be anyone you want now.'

Maybe I can, thought Ellen. But the thought was scary. There was so much to sort out, so many new things to get used to and, someday, she was going to have to think more about her mother and what had happened. Not yet though… not yet… She turned and looked at Stuart.

'My school was a bit like that too – had very clear ideas about what you were supposed to do. Mainly you were supposed to go to university and then, probably, be a teacher before you got married and had children. If you weren't clever enough you could go to teacher training college and if you couldn't do that you could go to secretarial college. They never talked about anything else we might be. Only about how to be a *'young lady'*.

Ellen's scornful emphasis made Stuart laugh.

'Well, they failed with you, didn't they? Running away, living in a squat, going to a comprehensive school. All sounds much more fun to me!'

'You can come back, you know, to Fineston. Stay with us. Or Jennifer. You don't have to cut yourself off from that life altogether. And I… I'd really like to go on seeing you.'

'Thanks, I don't want to lose you – either of you.'

A key turned in the lock and the door slammed behind James, who had arrived home with a large bag of mince and a packet of spaghetti.

'Can I help?' asked Stuart, after he had been introduced. 'I'm used to cooking for myself!'

'Sure, thanks.'

As Ellen sat at the kitchen table and chopped onions, the other members of the household returned. Lily told everyone how a child who had just started school had run out of class and climbed onto the roof. She and a deputy head had waited patiently in the playground below and talked him down, doing their best not to frighten him.

'Weren't you scared?' asked James.

'Yes – but we knew the head would have contacted the police, so we'd have backup. And we knew from his junior school that the kid was having problems. His dad went to prison recently for drug offences and his mum is an addict. He used to run out of school a lot. So we were expecting something to happen. Luckily, he climbed down the way he'd climbed up.'

'What will happen to him?' asked Ellen, trying to fit this picture of school life – the school she was planning to go to – with her own experience in Fineston.

'We'll contact the social worker and see what's going on. And we'll probably put him into our support unit at school for a while.'

'Support unit?' asked Ellen

'We have a teacher who runs a small group for the kids who are having problems. They stay there until they're ready to go back to normal classes.'

— — —

After the supper dishes had been cleared away, James lined up the placards ready to take to the following morning's demonstration and found a Lilo for Stuart in the basement. It was late, but Ellen couldn't wait any longer to open Jennifer's letter. In bed, she settled under the covers and tore the envelope.

Dear Ellen,

How are you? I'm sending this with Stuart because, of course, I don't have an address for you. Can you send one? I have been so worried about you. And (Mrs Brown wouldn't like that – starting a sentence with and!) I'm missing you lots. The first we knew about you going was when your aunt turned up at our house that Friday night. She'd driven herself in that big car and looked really upset. It was about nine o'clock so they must have been to the police station and everything first. I think she really hoped you'd be here and when you weren't she didn't know what to do. It wasn't a bit like last time – you remember how snooty she was with my mum? She sat on the sofa and mum made her a cup of tea and she kept saying, 'I don't know what my brother would have said' and 'What do you think I should do now?' So it was really good when you rang Stuart. He came round on Saturday and told us that he'd spoken to you and that you were OK. His mum got in touch with your aunt as soon as you rang so everyone was really relieved. But worried about you. Who are these people that you're living with?

It's been funny at school. None of the teachers have said anything. I could tell that Janice and that lot were talking about you because whenever they saw me they'd suddenly shut up and start talking about something else.

There's loads of work now. We get at least three hours homework every night and everyone keeps going on about GCEs and how we must do our best and not let the school down. I went to the rugby club dance though, with Sheila. There was a really good band playing – you remember Jimmy from Queen Mary's? We met him at the youth club that night. Well, he's started a band with his friends and they were really good. The two Dereks were there too – you know, the one with red hair and his friend. We danced with them a couple of times and the red-haired one kept asking Sheila out. He was a bit drunk and wouldn't take 'No' for an answer.

I'm wondering what you're planning to do Ellen. Are you going to stay in London? If so, I might be able to come and see you soon. Mum has got a leafleting job next month and if I do some I might earn enough for the train fare. Write to me!

Love
Jennifer

Ellen read the letter twice. She missed her friend so much and reading about her made her ache. It was all very well Stuart talking about a new life and possibilities and she was trying to be brave but at home in Fineston everything was just going on as before. If she were still there, if this hadn't happened, she could have been carrying on with her life too. She would have complained about school and homework, of course, like everyone does, but she would have made it to university and created a life for herself. Now, who knew what was going to happen. That familiar red flare of anger that licked around her heart grew stronger and stronger until she found herself saying aloud, 'How could Mum have done this to me? How could she?' The flame of rage intensified and burnt through her body.

'I hate her, I hate her,' she said over and over to herself. 'How could she do this?'

TWENTY

Depressing drizzle clouded the Saturday morning of the demonstration. The residents of 64 Ellsworth Crescent travelled together to Camhill Fields, in a neighbouring borough. This was where the march to protest about the British First Party would begin. Ellen had learnt to call the British First the BF, and she knew that the aim of the counter-demonstration was to stop the BF from marching. Negotiating the walk to the bus wasn't easy. Brixton was busy that morning and James, who was carrying the rolled-up banner on his shoulder, had to manoeuvre carefully so that he didn't hit people with it as he walked along. Everyone else in the group was holding a placard or two and a pile of leaflets. On the bus they headed for the back seat on the lower deck and laid the banner across their knees. Ellen sat next to Stuart and listened to the chatter, feeling too shy and ignorant to join in. Phrases drifted past her.

'I hope there's a good union turn out.'

'You did contact the *South London Gazette*, didn't you?'

'Did you remember to bring some water? We're going to be out for a long time.'

Ellen was aware of Stuart sitting beside her, his leg pressed against hers, their arms touching as they clutched the banner that was lying across their laps. She felt too shy and nervous to speak, but he turned his head to Patrick, James and Lily who were sitting on the back seat and asked, 'Will there be legal observers? You know what the police can be like. My mum did it at a miners' demo recently and stopped a couple of people being arrested.'

'Yeah – some people from a solicitors' in Brixton are coming. Hope they remember to bring arm bands.'

Stuart turned back and he and Ellen sat in silence for the rest of the journey.

— — —

Ellen wasn't sure what to expect but she was nevertheless surprised, when they arrived at the small park where some of the demonstrators were gathering, that it seemed as if not many people had come. As she watched, though, more and more of the anti-racist demonstrators began to flow through the park gates and stand their damp banners on the grass. Stuart and Patrick unfurled their own banner and stood at each side, holding it upright.

At eleven the demonstrators formed into a line and the march began to move along the largely deserted streets of the south London suburb. Ellen knew that the plan was to follow the route of the BF demonstration and, if possible, stop the racists from marching. Shopkeepers, advised beforehand by the police, had mostly closed up for the day. Windows were boarded up. They headed off towards the planned route but hadn't gone far before they found that the police had blocked the road to stop the demonstrators from moving forward.

'What do we do?' asked Lily.

'Quick, there's a back route. Turn off here.'

James, who knew the area best, led the way up a side street; they all ran as fast they could, following James as he navigated a maze of streets. Twenty minutes later they were standing at the top of Jegton Rise, looking down a steep hill onto a broad main street. This was where the BF planned to march and where, Ellen knew, the demonstrators were determined to stop them. Ellen gasped as she reached for Stuart's arm, and the two of them stood holding onto each other as they watched the scene below. There were several thousand people already gathered on the road, completely blocking it from the top of the hill, past the railway station entrance, all the way to the bottom. There was confused anticipation in the air. No one seemed to know what was going to happen, neither police nor demonstrators. Ellen felt both scared and excited. This was unlike anything she had experienced before and she stared around her, for those moments all else forgotten.

Beyond the station, at the bottom of Jegton Rise, she saw that a group of protestors had erected a barricade of upturned dustbins, wooden planks and metal scraps across the road and now they stood, with cameras and banners, swaying and surging on top of it. Knots of police formed and re-formed within the crowd, moving to block side roads and, inexplicably, to unblock them again. Officers moved in to clear demonstrators from sections of the road and then allowed them to be overrun again. They formed circles and seemed to want to separate the crowd into sections, but there were too many people and they failed. The constant movement caused irritation and frustration. There were scuffles here and there, and Ellen watched as a protestor wearing a red bobble hat struggled with a policeman who was trying to fold the young man's arms behind his back. A second policeman joined the first and between them they lifted and pushed the man through the crowd to a van parked nearby. A cry came up from the crowd: 'Pigs, pigs, pigs'.

At the bottom of the hill, close to a patch of open ground, out of Ellen's sight, but where James had told her the BF were gathering, tempers were rising. She could hear the demonstrators chanting 'Racists out, racists out'.

Suddenly there was a roar and the air was filled with shouts. 'There they are. There. They're here.' Ellen stood on tiptoe and leant on Stuart to stop herself falling as she strained to see what was happening. Flanked by police the BF demonstrators emerged from a side street at the bottom of the hill. At the same time, a group of police horses, four lines deep, galloped into the crowd, scattering people to right and left. The makeshift barricade the protestors had erected was crushed. Demonstrators who had been standing on top of it tumbled to the ground. Ellen gasped. The brutal, provocative obstinacy of the movement took her breath away and she shouted out to Stuart.

'They're riding straight through them.'

The crowd, enraged, pushed back and surrounded the horses, cutting them off, momentarily, from the wedge of hundreds of policemen who followed on foot. Suddenly, a line of Union Jacks appeared. The BF marchers, flanked by lines of policemen who were linking arms, had begun to march. Overhead an eerie, surreal blood-red smoke from lighted smoke bombs mingled with the grey dust of a thousand flying missiles: bricks, wood, bottles. The air was dense with flying objects. Running, scurrying, panting, the BF marchers scrambled along the road. Many of their heads, injured by thrown bricks, ran red with blood. Some, defiant, grinned cruelly, their banners held aloft. Others cowered, hands over their heads, cringing from the attack. Ellen had never seen violence before. She felt tearful and a little sick, but also sensed a power and confidence growing within her. If someone had passed her a brick and told her to throw it at the racists she thought she might have done it. Instead she screamed, along with her comrades who were all shouting now, 'Nazis, Nazis, fascist scum'. Overhead the flames of burning Union Jacks, dropped by the BF as they defended themselves, and captured and set alight by the demonstrators, showed above the dust.

Still the BF marched on, protected by the police who were, apparently, determined that the march should not be prevented. After they had passed out of sight James again led the group through the backstreets to the shopping centre where the BF were heading. A few moments later a coach screamed to halt in front of them and dozens of police scrambled out and erected a hasty road block in the narrow street. James turned and found another way through and Ellen and the others followed him. As they reached the centre, they saw a group of demonstrators who had arrived there before them marching down the middle of the road. Their clenched fists were held aloft, punching the rhythm of their words in the air as they shouted, 'The workers, united, will never be defeated' in fierce, combative unison. Behind them a row of protestors pounded out the same beat with sticks on dustbin lids.

They waited for the BF supporters to come into sight but this time, instead of marching them down the middle of the road, the police diverted them onto a narrow path into the backstreets. A brick wall protected the marchers from the crowd's taunts and they sang 'Rule Britannia' defiantly as they scurried and scrambled, urged on by the police and often in single file as the slowest of them hurried to keep up. Occasionally, a BF member attempted to climb the wall and return to the main road but the police pushed them back until it was clear that the lines weren't holding. This was when Ellen found herself pinned to the wall by a string of sprightly, side-stepping police horses. One of them stumbled, nostrils flaring, and as it veered to the side Stuart clutched Ellen to him, fearing she might be crushed by the falling animal.

They didn't see the BF again. The crowds at the clock tower in the shopping centre had occupied the road, erecting barriers from abandoned road blocks and debris. A protestor, intoxicated by the crowds, shouted through his loud hailer urging them to 'occupy, occupy'. Ellen and Stuart stood on a street corner, pressed against the wall, watching as two police vans squealed round the bend. Immediately, angry protestors began throwing stones and pieces of wood, breaking windows and scratching paint. Out jumped fifty or so policemen, while the vans were still moving. They formed a line and, arms held high, started running towards the crowd.

'Get on, move away, keep going', they shouted, shoving protestors in the back and occasionally grabbing people's shoulders and hurling them forward. Ellen and Stuart moved as quickly as they could through the crowd, dodging and diving but holding onto each other's hands. Behind them, the police, some of whom had equipped themselves with dustbin lids as shields, were dodging missiles.

Ellen and Stuart kept walking. They didn't know where they were now, but allowed themselves to be swept along by the crowd which was heading in one direction. Passing a car park by a bingo hall they saw a police van, all its windows broken, its paint pitted and scored. Paving stones and bricks from garden walls littered the streets. Outside one house a crowd of young, excited householders passed bottles of lemonade round the thirsty policemen.

There were too many people on the road to allow buses to pass so Ellen and Stuart trudged along with the crowd which seemed to be heading north, like them. Gradually, the road cleared and, at last, a bus with 'Brixton' listed as one of its destinations passed them slowly. The pair ran as fast as they could and reached the next stop in time to jump onto the back of the bus as it began to accelerate away. Laughing, they held onto each other as they climbed the stairs to the top deck and found a seat together near the front.

— — —

It was nearly eight o'clock by the time Ellen and Stuart reached Brixton. The others were already home. Lily came into the hall as she heard the door slam.

'Ah, at last. We were beginning to get worried about you. Thought you might be in a cell in Brixton police station after scrapping with the police!'

'Tell you what,' said Patrick as they went into the living room, 'let's go for a drink. We deserve it.' Then he paused. 'Oh sorry, we can't, you're not sixteen, are you, Ellen?'

Ellen grinned. 'Well, as a matter of fact I am. Just. It's my birthday today…'

'What!' said Stuart. 'And you never said. Let's get to that pub straight away and buy you a celebratory orange juice and we can celebrate not getting arrested today too! Though, come to think about it, that would have made my parents sit up and take notice!'

Ellen had never been in a pub before and the first thing that struck her about the King's Head was the noise. Excited voices all shouting loudly to be heard. The dark wooden bar with the glasses and bottles lined up behind it was partly hidden by a press of men – it did seem to be all men – trying to catch the attention of the two young women behind the bar.

'What will everyone have?' asked Patrick.

'A pint please,' said James, 'but we'll have a kitty. Money on the table everyone. Not you obviously, Ellen. You're the birthday girl!'

It seemed ages before Patrick was back with the tray of glasses.

'That's Saturday night for you,' he said. As he sat down Lily appeared behind him. Ellen had noticed she had disappeared at the same time as Patrick had gone to the bar and assumed she had gone to help him. But after Patrick had handed round the drinks, Lily reached into a plastic bag she was holding and took out a cake.

'Ta da. Happy birthday, Ellen. Hang on, I've got candles here. Let's light them.'

Lily stuck several candles straight into the cake as Ellen, a wave of gratitude and warmth sweeping through her, looked more closely at the chocolate cake, covered in gooey icing and decorated with a 'Happy Birthday' sticker. It was the best cake she'd ever seen.

'Right,' said Lily, as the last candle was lit, 'here goes', and she began to sing, 'Happy birthday to you, happy birthday to you'. The others joined in and people at the adjoining tables smiled and joined in too, until the whole pub was singing. As the song ended, Lily lifted her glass and said, 'I want to say something. Ellen, it's been a pleasure having you with us. I know you're going to live with your grandpa and this will be your last weekend with us, but I wanted to say how brave we all think you've been and we all want you to keep in touch and go on being involved in our campaigns and, of course, I'll see you at school.'

'Hear, hear,' said everyone, raising their glasses. 'To Ellen, to Ellen, happy birthday!'

Ellen glowed for a moment until, unbidden and insistent, memories of earlier birthdays flocked into her mind: a home-made cake with candles that wouldn't stay alight in the breezy back garden at Fossett Crescent; giggling with friends as they took it in turns to try and eat a chocolate bar with a knife and fork while wearing thick gloves; squashing into a tiny wardrobe during 'hide and seek'; dancing to one of her mother's records. She tried to block the pictures from the screen behind her eyes and found them replaced with tears. And, behind the tears, one of the unexpected flashes of rage that were becoming familiar to her. How could her mother have done this to her? Left her alone in the world? She had never loved her after all.

— — —

Next morning, the demonstration was all over the newspapers. '*Race riot in South London*'; '*March under attack*'. The stories focused on the disruption, describing torn-up fences and emptied dustbins. The friends spread the papers out over the floor in the living room.

'There's hardly anything here about the BF and how racist they are,' said Lily. 'It's all about the damage and the rubbish that was left – oh, and bits about our "heroic police".'

'What do you expect?' asked Patrick. 'The press is always on the side of the establishment.'

'Yeah. My mum defended some miners who were on strike at their pit last year,' said Stuart.

'Oh yeah?' said James, interested in this. 'Of course, she's a lawyer, isn't she?'

'Yeah, she does some work for free for the NUM. The pit managers were trying to sack some men and they protested. It got really nasty. But they won – the colliery had to take them back. I don't know the details. But the papers all talked about the miners "holding the country to ransom" and stuff.'

Marion entered the room with a plate of warm croissants and some coffee.

'OK everyone, you deserve this after yesterday. And Ellen, if you like I'll come with you to your grandpa's flat today and help you get it sorted, ready for him coming home on Monday.'

'No,' said Stuart quickly.

Marion looked startled.

'Sorry, I didn't mean to be rude, but I don't have to get the train back north until six so I'll go with her.'

'OK.'

— — —

It was one o'clock when Stuart and Ellen got off the bus at the Elephant and Castle and walked past the red-brick swimming pool with its ornate clock tower and double wooden doors. The golden roman numerals on the clock face gleamed. Ellen felt a surge of excitement as the two of them climbed the stone steps of Watley Buildings to number 24. She put the key in the door and felt a chill as she stepped into a flat that had been empty while her grandfather had been in hospital. Stuart carried her small bag through to her bedroom and she put the milk they had bought in the tiny fridge, together with some butter and cheese. On the kitchen table she put some apples in a bowl and a loaf in the bread bin. Everywhere looked tidy and neat. She could see signs of grandpa – his shelf with history and politics books, his plaid dressing gown with a brown cord that hung behind his bedroom door, his cookery book still open next to the cooker, the photographs he had taken on the wall. She was going to be happy here.

It seemed an age since she had waited for Stuart at the station. It was nearly time to say goodbye – for now. As they sat together on the tube, Stuart slipped his arm round the back of her seat.

'It's going to be OK, Ellen. If there's anything you need, you know, I'll help and I know mum and dad will too. And I'll come and see you again soon.'

Ellen turned and grinned at him.

'Thanks – and thank you for being here this weekend.'

At the station they dawdled on the way to the barrier at platform two, unwilling to say goodbye. Then they noticed that there were only three minutes before the train was due to leave and Stuart started to run.

'Got to go. I'll write – and see you soon!' He turned to Ellen who was running beside him and stopped for a moment. He bent down and kissed her, gently, on the lips.

'See you soon, kiddo.'

'Yes, see you soon.'

TWENTY-ONE

Grandpa was sitting on the bed when Ellen arrived at the hospital on Monday morning. The ward was busy, with nurses bustling from bed to bed offering medicine and taking temperatures, but grandpa, sitting on his bed, looked very alone. He wore a worn tweed jacket, grey trousers with turn ups and heavy laced shoes. Beside him on the chair lay his brown overcoat, trilby hat and a zipped mock leather shoulder bag that contained the few things he had brought with him. He looked thinner and smaller than Ellen remembered, as if his clothes were too big. Ellen noticed the grey streaks in his curly black hair. Grandpa smiled when he saw her.

'Well, love, so this is it. Home again…'

The ward sister smiled as she walked over to them, carrying a clipboard.

'I think you're ready, Mr Maddox. I've had a word with the doctor and you can go now. The hospital bus will pick you up from the waiting room downstairs in half an hour or so. Here's your appointment card for your outpatient check-up. You can expect a visit from your GP and remember, if you're at all concerned or feel ill, just ring this number.'

She handed grandpa a card and then looked over at Ellen.

'Here, you have one too. I know you're going to be looking after your grandfather. Ring us here on the ward if you're at all concerned.'

'Thank you,' said grandpa, 'and thank you for letting me stay in your nice hotel. I have had a lovely time here.'

The sister laughed. 'Get on with you. You've been a model patient. Now get yourselves downstairs, you don't want to miss the bus!'

Grandpa walked slowly, as if he wasn't sure that his legs weren't going to wobble. Ellen held out her hand.

'Here, hold my arm. It's a bit of a way downstairs.'

It took a long time to walk down the corridor to the lift. On the ground floor, they found themselves in the dark wood-lined hall of the old wing. Benefactors of the hospital looked out through oil-painted eyes in portraits set in gilded frames. Ellen felt more and more nervous as she passed them. Was she really going to be trusted to look after grandpa on her own? He was leaning quite heavily on her arm now and she could tell how tired he was. They reached the waiting room and sat on benches by the side entrance to the hospital, watching people come and go. Ellen wondered how many of those entering or leaving were frightened, for themselves or their loved ones.

She was going to be responsible? All by herself? Then she remembered the kindly ward sister who had said she could ring any time, and Lily and the others who had offered to help too. And, for the first time, she felt grateful that Aunt Christabel was going to be nearby for the first few days. She could do this. This was her life now and she was going to make it her own. It was as if a heavy curtain had been pushed aside and a new world lay beyond it, glittering with colour and joy. She was going to step into it.

ACKNOWLEDGEMENTS

For many years I worked with young people who were experiencing all kinds of stress from neglect and abandonment to cruelty and abuse. I have been inspired by their resilience and want to thank them for sharing their stories with me. Several people have made useful comments on drafts of this novel and I would like to say how grateful I am to all of them. Special thanks go to Frances Anderson, Jean Barr, Jessica Chappell, Suzan Harrison, Caroline Lodge, Sandi Matheson and Anne Seeley. Writing this book has made me even more appreciative of the love and comfort of my family. I offer love and thanks to all of them. My husband, John, has encouraged and supported me from the beginning; without him, this book might never have been finished. My daughters, Katy and Mary, have made many insightful suggestions and been, as always, a source of love and inspiration.

PERMISSIONS